DAWN
of
SPIES

DAWN
of
SPIES

A
CRUSOE
ADVENTURE

ANDREW LANE

ⓐ ADAPTIVE BOOKS

AN IMPRINT OF ADAPTIVE STUDIOS | CULVER CITY, CA

Copyright © 2016 Adaptive Studios

Visit us on the web at www.adaptivestudios.com

Library of Congress Cataloging in Publication Number: 2015951941
ISBN 978-0-9960666-8-6
Ebook ISBN 978-0-9964887-3-0

Printed in the United States of America

Cover design by Laz Marquez
Interior design and typesetting by Neuwirth & Associates

Adaptive Books
Culver City, CA

10 9 8 7 6 5 4 3 2 1

To Sam, Jon, Tracey and Mark—
collectively known as "Dreamcatcher Horror Theatre" or
"Circle of Spears"—who deserve to have at least something
dedicated to them. Thanks for being friends.

DAWN
of
SPIES

PROLOGUE

—⟨∂/∂/∂⟩—

Two Years Since The Shipwreck

Crusoe was checking his lobster cages when he heard the voices.

He had woven the cages from tough strands of sea grass. They had an open hole in the top through which the lobsters could crawl, but he'd deliberately made them so that loose strands of the sharp sea grass projected backward around the hole, preventing the hard-shelled creatures from crawling out again. Crusoe's baskets covered the island, but those on the south side seemed to catch more lobsters. He didn't know why. Maybe the temperature of the water was better for them there.

They also tasted better. Presumably that was linked as well.

The south side of the island was a mazelike mass of folds and ripples in the ground that led all the way from the hills down to a golden beach. It looked like a giant had taken the rock and given it a good shake, like someone would a tablecloth. The folds and ripples were large enough that someone bigger than Crusoe could have hidden in them. Some had trickles of water and even small rivers running down them. Crusoe wasn't sure how they had come about, or why that area was different from the rest of the island. It just was.

The sun was hot on the woven grass sheet that he had tied around his head to protect himself from sunburn. As he waded calf-deep in the clear, warm water, bending down and checking the cages for any lobsters, his ears were filled with the crash of the surf and the crying of gulls overhead: sounds that he'd been familiar with for two whole years. When the voices started up, he thought they were just hallucinations, just his brain trying to turn the sound of the gulls into something that he still dreamed about at night. It was only gradually that he realized these were real voices. Someone else was on the island.

He turned, gazing inland desperately and hoping to see someone. A ship must have arrived. Maybe they knew about the shipwreck and had come looking for him. Even if they hadn't and were just there coincidentally, surely they would take him back to civilization?

Whoever it was, they were hidden from sight somewhere in the twisted fingers of rock that led down from the hills. He abandoned his lobster baskets and started to run as best he could through the water and back to the shore. There were outcrops of rock in the water as well—smooth and brown, like seals—and he had to head slightly sideways so that he could get around them. As he was passing one of these outcrops, the new arrivals came into sight, walking out of the rocks and onto the beach as if they owned the place.

He dived into the water before they could see him, feeling his guts twisting with fear and disappointment. He'd hoped to be rescued by English or at least European sailors, but these were dark-skinned men with colorful silk scarves tied around their heads, and golden jewelry piercing their ears and noses. They had swords and knives as well, not casually strapped to their waists but held in their hands as if they were expecting trouble at any moment.

Pirates.

Crusoe let his head rise up out of the water until his eyes looked out above the surface. He pulled the woven grass sheet off his head.

With luck, his hair would look like one of the rocks: smooth, rounded, and brown.

He could feel the sun shining directly on his scalp. If he had to stay there for long, he would start to burn, but he couldn't move. If the pirates caught him, they would either kill him or make him their slave. He knew the stories. He knew what they did to people like him.

There were five of them: four men and a girl. The girl was as dark-skinned as the rest of them, but they were treating her like a prisoner, pushing her in front of them and laughing.

Crusoe watched with a mixture of wonder and terror. The sailors he'd been with on the Rigel had often talked about pirates—how bloodthirsty they were, how they would ransack entire ships and kill everyone on board just to get a handful of jewelry or gold, how they would take crews as prisoners and eat them if they started to run out of food. Every sailor had a different story about pirates and their ways. Crusoe had listened to them, long into the night, so he knew to stay hidden and still. But . . . these were the first people he had seen in two years. These were human beings—real human beings. He had been alone for so long that seeing them was like . . . like seeing something mythical.

He didn't recognize the language they were speaking, as they laughed among themselves and pushed the girl. She fell over, and one of the men reached down and grabbed her by the arm, pulling her to her feet again. She looked scared—but angry, as well. She turned her head and spat at him as he pushed her again.

They were probably heading back to their ship. Crusoe wondered who the girl was. She couldn't have been living on the island—he'd investigated every single inch of it in the past two years. Was she one of the crew who had done something wrong in their eyes, or was she a captive taken from another ship?

And could he do anything to help her? Should he do anything to help her, or should he leave her to her fate and hope the pirates left after they had replenished their supplies? He was only fourteen—what could he do?

If their positions were reversed, he wondered with a fluttery feeling of panic in his chest, what would he want her to do?

The pirates headed east along the beach, toward where Crusoe thought they might have come ashore. There was a protected cove twenty minutes' walk away where the rocks on either side stopped the waves from getting too high.

Crusoe was in an agony of indecision. A part of him desperately wanted to stand up and wave, to make them aware that he was there, to talk to them, even though he knew what would happen. He had been alone for so long that he had forgotten just how lonely he was. Seeing these men, and the girl, brought it all crashing back on him, like a tidal wave during a storm. Tears of frustration spilled from his eyes and into the water, making him blink. Why, after all this time, did it have to be pirates? Why couldn't it have been the Royal Navy?

The pirates were heading away from Crusoe now. Gradually he moved toward the shore, still keeping himself as low as possible: floating and using his hands and feet against the sand to move himself around. Eventually he got to a point where the water was too shallow, and he had to stand up. He tried to make as little noise as possible and moved quickly toward the protection of the rocks.

When he got to safety, he turned and took one last look at the first human beings he had seen in two years. He knew he would have to avoid this part of the island for a while, until the pirates had gone. He couldn't risk them seeing him.

As he watched, the girl suddenly pulled away from the pirates and ran back, toward Crusoe. She was fast: her feet seemed to hardly touch the sand as she raced away from her captors. After a few seconds' confusion, the pirates chased after her.

Uncertainty paralyzed him. Should he help or not?

Was there really a choice?

CHAPTER ONE

Sailing up the Thames toward London was like sailing through a forest. From Gravesend onward, both banks of the river were lined with boats and ships, all of them with their sails furled and their masts pointed upward like bare tree trunks in some winter landscape. All that was missing was the snow. The sheer number of vessels made navigation difficult, and the *Stars' End* had to keep stopping to let them pass by, or cross from bank to bank.

Robinson Crusoe stood at the bow of the ship, one hand holding on to a rope and one foot on an upturned wooden bucket. His eyes squinted as he looked into the distance, even though the bright sun of the Caribbean was weeks in his past. He didn't remember the Thames as being this busy, although it had been over five years since he had taken the trip in the other direction.

His gaze moved to his hand clenched around the rope. It was tanned, and there were calluses on the palm and scars on the back from the hard work he'd been forced to do to survive. Compared to the white, soft hand that had held a similar rope on the journey out of London, it was like he was a different person.

Perhaps he was.

Something floating past the ship caught his eye, and he watched it as it moved. It was just a plank of wood, rotted at both ends—one of the many pieces of flotsam and jetsam that clogged the river. There was a lump in the middle that he focused on for a moment, wondering what it was, until it suddenly jumped into the water and paddled away. A rat. The London he remembered had been infested with them.

A sudden gust of wind made the sails snap above his head. The sound didn't make him jump the way he remembered it had on the journey out. He'd gotten used to it. He'd gotten used to a lot of things, but there was equally a lot that he had forgotten about. The smell of smoke from all the workshops and foundries along the riverbank, for instance; the stench of the factories where whale blubber was being rendered down into oil; and the constant sound of hammering and sawing that drifted across the water.

There were the people, too. People everywhere, on boats, ships, and docks: working, walking, or gazing into the distance like Crusoe. They were like the red ants that had infested some areas of the island, living in anthills taller than he was. The sheer number of people made him edgy; the island had been virtually deserted apart from him and Friday. Well, them and the occasional ship full of pirates that had landed on the far side of the island for rest, recreation, and supplies.

"Different from what you remember, boy?" a voice said from behind him. He recognized the upper-class drawl of the ship's captain—Jonathan Maybury-Henson—without having to turn around.

"The river seems a lot more crowded," he admitted, "and a lot of the buildings are new."

"There's been a lot of construction," Maybury-Henson said, joining Crusoe at the bow. He had changed into his best uniform for their arrival at the London docks. "The fire saw to that."

Crusoe searched his memory for a moment before he remembered the great fire that had devastated the city before he had been born. It wasn't that the fire hadn't been important; it was more that so much had happened to him since that he had relegated his former life to the back of his mind while he fought to learn the skills to survive.

"A great deal of work has been accomplished since you left England in order to replace the buildings that were burned," Maybury-Henson continued. "You'll hardly recognize the place." He glanced backward, toward the ship's stern. "Of course, your . . . companion won't have anything to compare it to, she being from the Caribbean and all."

Crusoe followed Maybury-Henson's gaze to where, about two-thirds of the way down the ship, Friday was halfway up a mast, her legs wrapped around a crossbar and her arms intertwined with the rigging, the wind blowing her curls back from her face. Her real name was Vijaya Dinajara, but she had decided that she preferred the name Friday a while after they had met, and the name had stuck.

"She'll manage," he said. "Friday's used to new situations, new places, and new people. She's a survivor."

"It's more a question of whether the good people of London can get used to her," Maybury-Henson murmured.

"What do you mean?"

"Let's say her skin is a lot darker than they usually expect, or like." He gazed at Crusoe's face critically for a long moment. "Then again, the way the sun has tanned your skin over the past five years, you're more than halfway there yourself, boy." He smiled. "Funny, isn't it, how you can leave a plank of wood and a person out in the sun, and the wood will bleach nearly white over time, while the person gets darker and darker."

"I'd never really thought about it," Crusoe said honestly. "Things are the way they are, I suppose."

"Still, she does speak good English," Maybury-Henson acknowledged. "Put her in a cloak with the hood up, and people won't know the difference."

Crusoe looked away angrily, into the distance ahead of them, uncomfortable at the way the captain was speaking. After a few minutes of awkward silence, Maybury-Henson left, shouting instructions to his first mate as he went.

The ship kept moving slowly upriver. The *Stars' End* was big, but there were some ships that were even larger—two- or three-deckers either sailing or in various stages of construction on the docks, looming above the *Stars' End* like overhanging wooden cliffs.

As they neared Plumstead, the docks and the workshops thinned out, replaced with stretches of boggy marshland dotted with the skeletons of rotting boats that had been caught in the mud. Near Deptford, they passed the entire upside-down hull of a large ship half sunk in the mud close to the river's edge. It had, Crusoe thought, most likely been caught in a storm, wrecked, and overturned.

Up around Rotherhithe, the press of ships became so great that the captain had to order sails to be taken down in order to slow the *Stars' End*. Eventually he had to order the ship to be stopped, and the anchor dropped. It looked to Crusoe as if the docks ahead of them were fully occupied, and there were so many ships waiting to get into the first space to become free that the ships waiting to leave couldn't find a way through.

Crusoe looked up to where Friday sat in the rigging. Her cheekbones and chin were so perfect that no sculptor or artist could ever have done them justice, and her skin was so dark that at night she became invisible, apart from the gleam of light from her eyes and her teeth. She was incredible.

The moment he saw her face, she turned her head from looking upriver and stared down at him inquiringly, as he had known she would. Somehow, during their time on the island, separated from anyone else, they had become so close that they didn't need words anymore. Each knew what the other was thinking, most of the time.

With one exception. There was one thing that Friday didn't know, and Crusoe couldn't find the words to explain to her.

⟨⟨⟨∘⟩⟩⟩

The Shipwreck

Crusoe was fast asleep when he fell.

For a moment he didn't know what had happened. He was in midair, falling through darkness, something flapping over his head.

Something had thrown him out of his hammock. That was what was flapping above his head—the long piece of canvas, hanging from hooks on the bulkhead, in which he'd slept since leaving London.

He hit the deck hard, knocking the breath from his lungs. He tried to get his hands beneath his body so he could push himself up, but the deck was slanted hard to one side. Before he could stabilize himself, he rolled sideways, crashing into the corner where the deck met the far bulkhead. That bulkhead was now halfway toward being the deck.

The Rigel was listing to one side. It was sinking.

As panic grabbed hold of his mind, he became aware of shouting and the sound of bells from outside the bunk area. He scrambled desperately along the caulked join between the bulkhead and the deck, heading for the door. He reached up and grabbed the door handle, but when he pulled it, the door burst open and water spilled into the room. It was warm, and he could taste the salt as it sloshed across his mouth. He pulled himself over the doorframe and out into the corridor.

Oil lamps swung from their hooks, casting a flickering light across everything. All he could hear were bells and shouting and the deafening creak of the ship's timbers. Crew members were scrambling in both directions, like ants in a disturbed nest. The water was up to their ankles. They didn't look at him, didn't try to help, and when he tried to grab one of them, the man knocked his hands away and kept moving, sloshing away through the incoming water. It was hard to tell, in the darkness and with the ship listing over, which direction the water was even coming from.

What had happened? When he'd gone to sleep, the sea had been calm, and there had been no clouds in the sky that might have warned of a storm.

He had to find his father. He also had to get out on deck, otherwise he might get trapped by the water, and drown.

He used his body to push his way through the crew when he had to, and his twelve-year-old size to slip between them when possible. After six weeks on the ship, he knew every route to the deck. He managed to get into a group of crewmen all heading in the same direction, and he let them carry him along, forcing their way past and through the groups of crew members heading in the opposite direction. Everyone seemed to have forgotten whatever training they'd had and were instinctively heading for the open air.

"Father!" he shouted, and again, "Father!" but there was no response.

The ship lurched and seemed to slip sideways. Some of the crew fell into the now knee-high water. Their companions just climbed over their bodies, pushing their faces down into the water in their desperation to get to safety. If there was any safety.

Gray light was filtering down through a set of glass bricks set into the deck. Crusoe knew that they were set into a hinged wooden panel—a way of getting extra air into the lower levels of the ship if necessary— but the crew seemed to have forgotten that in their panic. He pushed his way through to the bulkhead and looked quickly for knotholes and flaws in the wood that he could use as fingerholds for climbing. As he saw a way up, a crew member knocked into him, pushing him off balance. He forced his way back, and before it could happen again, he leaped for a metal hook that had been screwed into the wall, high up. His wet shoes slipped on the wood, but his left hand closed on the hook. He pulled himself up desperately, feeling the metal cutting into his fingers. His flailing feet caught someone's shoulder, and he suddenly found himself propelled upward. His skull hit the glass blocks, sending stars shooting through his head, but his right hand closed around the bolt. He pulled at it, but it didn't shift. He was braced crazily now, with his feet against the bulkhead, and his shoulder and tilted head against the top deck.

He tugged again at the bolt, and this time it shifted. He threw every last shred of strength that he could muster into pulling it free. He could hear the grating of the metal bolt even above the cacophony that was deafening him. He could feel it tearing at the skin of his fingers, but just when the pain became almost too much to bear, the bolt suddenly shifted, and the hatch sprang open. Before any of the crew beneath him could realize what he had done and pull him away so that they could escape, he used their heads as a springboard to propel himself through the hatch and out into the open air.

Chaos.

As FRIDAY WATCHED her friend from the isolation of her position up in the rigging, she saw Robin raise his arms in a shrug. She quickly glanced around, her gaze flicking from ship to ship until it reached the shore. She looked back at him and raised an eyebrow inquiringly. She knew that *he* would know what she was asking— were the ships close enough together that the two of them could jump or swing from one to another until they got to shore? Surely

it was better than having to wait the hours or days until the *Stars'*
End could inch its way to a dock.

Down on the deck, Robin looked around, trying to work it out.
Friday had a better vantage point than he did and could better see
how close the ships actually were to one another. She also saw that
Robin was reluctant to risk it. A gust of wind or an unexpected
wave could shift the ships around, doubling the size of a gap in
moments, and both ropes and decks could be slippery. One of them
might fall in. To have come this far and then drown—that would
be ironic, to say the least. No, they could wait a few hours.

Robin shook his head. He knew her thoughts exactly. In many
ways he was her opposite: calm where she was impulsive, thoughtful
where she would trust her instincts. He made plans where she reacted to events. They should have driven each other mad by their
differences, but instead they were better together than they were
apart. Each of them contributed something that the other lacked.
Friday would have died on the island many times over had Robin
not stopped her from doing something dangerous. Equally he
would have starved while planning how to catch a fish or re-
trieve a gull's egg from a cliff face if she hadn't just reached out and
grabbed for them.

She smiled, remembering that time when it had been just the
two of them against the elements. Now they had to survive in a
different kind of jungle.

She waited while the ships in the great river all jostled for some
kind of advantage. At least the sun was warm, and the rain, when
it fell, was refreshing. She was used to sunshine that was so strong
it could burn the skin, and rain that fell so hard and so fast it was
possible to drown in it.

A small rowboat arrived alongside the *Stars' End*, and Friday saw
a man climb aboard their ship and speak with Captain Maybury-
Henson. As the man was dressed in some kind of uniform, Friday

assumed him to be an official from whichever group of people ran the docks. Something changed hands between the man and the captain—money, probably—and he left. Shortly after that, the ships surrounding them started to drift apart, leaving a channel through which they could move.

One ship, whose captain was more angry or desperate than the others, tried to take advantage of the newly created channel, sailing in front of the *Stars' End*, but three smaller boats moved in front of him within moments. After a lot of shouting, he ordered his crew to move the ship, his face as dark as thunder. Whatever Captain Maybury-Henson had paid, it seemed to have bought a lot of influence.

"What do you think of London?" Robin's voice said from behind her, in the rigging. Friday didn't start in surprise—she had known that he was there before he spoke.

"It's busy," she said. "It may be the busiest place I've ever seen."

To their right, Friday noticed an area of wooden decking that ran along the edge of the riverbank. There were buildings behind it—warehouses by the look of them—but the decking seemed large enough to take quite a crowd. At the edge was a strange wooden structure built over a hole in the wooden planks. Dangling from ropes that were fastened to the wooden structure were three black, irregularly shaped objects. They hung just above the surface of the river.

"What are those things?" Friday asked, pointing.

"Bodies," Robin said with a trace of reluctance. He obviously didn't want her to think bad things about his city. "Traitors to the king. They've been hanged, and then tarred."

"Kings and pirates aren't so different, it seems," Friday observed. "My father would have done the same."

"He would have done the same to you," Robin replied.

That shut them both up for a while.

Friday stared ahead, to where a bridge crossed the Thames. The *Stars' End* appeared to be steering toward the bank just in front of it so that the ship could be moored. The bridge was massive—seventeen arches of stone straddling the river from one side to the other. There were houses and shops on it, and in the center was a tower.

The *Stars' End* docked at a quay just before the bridge. Ropes were thrown from ship to shore, and shore to ship, and tied off. The anchor was dropped. There was a lot of shouting and general hubbub, but the feeling in the crew was one of expectation. They had landed again, after a long voyage.

Before the gangplank was dropped, the first mate lined the sailors up along the deck. He went down the line handing out canvas bags filled with money—the pay that the sailors had earned on the trip. Knowing the way that sailors lived, she suspected that they would spend the money within two days and be back on the ship, ready for another voyage.

"You two!"

Friday and Robin both turned around. Captain Maybury-Henson was standing behind them, holding two small canvas bags. "I know you're not officially part of the crew," he said, "but you've made yourselves useful on the voyage back from Barbados, and I wouldn't want you to starve now that you've gotten home." He threw one of the bags to Friday and the other to Robin. "Here's some money to get you started. Good luck to you both." As they slipped the bags into their pockets, Maybury-Henson turned to go, then turned back. "Be careful," he said in a more serious tone of voice. "The city can be a dangerous place for newcomers. Gangs of ruffians wander around, and there is little or no law to protect the innocent. If you want to stay on board, you can." He patted his uniform jacket. "That's why, whenever I leave this ship over the next few days, I'll be carrying a loaded flintlock with me. Just a small one, but it scares the thieves away."

"We'll be careful," Robin promised.

Maybury-Henson went on as if he hadn't heard the boy. "Once I've unloaded my cargo and loaded up again, I'll be off, sailing to the West Indies maybe, or to America, depending on the nature of the cargo I manage to get. You two would make fine additions to the crew." He glanced around, looking to see if any of the current crew were still present. "To be honest, I'd get rid of any man jack here just to get the two of you to stay. You're hard workers, and you don't cause any aggravation."

Robin shook his head. "I've been waiting a long time to get back home," he said. "I've been dreaming about this for years. I'm not going to turn around and run away now."

"It's not running away, lad," Maybury-Henson insisted. "A life on the ocean is a fine life. It'll make a man of you." He glanced at Friday and obviously decided not to pursue that line of thought. "But what about you, girl?" he asked. "London may be the greatest city in the world, but it's not the most welcoming, not for newcomers."

"I'll stay with Robin," she said firmly. He stepped toward her protectively, and Friday was suddenly very conscious of her friend's shoulder pressing against her arm.

Maybury-Henson nodded. "Fair enough, I suppose. I'll be here for a few more days, if you change your mind." He turned and walked away.

"Come on," Robin said. "Let me show you London." He took Friday's arm and led her toward the gangplank.

CHAPTER TWO

The quayside was bustling with people heading in all directions and carrying a variety of things—boxes, chickens, bottles, handkerchiefs knotted around some kind of food . . . Friday's head kept flicking in different directions, trying to catch everything that was going on.

Crusoe was aware that people were staring at her, and he moved protectively closer to her. She didn't seem to notice.

Different smells struck him as he moved—the stench of human waste and unwashed flesh, the mouthwatering smell of roasting meat, the cloying aroma of rotting vegetables. Someone had once told him that a man could navigate the city by smell alone. It was so different from the island, where the odors had been mainly flowers and ocean.

"What are we going to do?" Friday asked. She seemed nervous— Crusoe suspected that she had never seen this many people in one place before. She had also never had so many people glancing at her, either surreptitiously or openly, remarking on the color of her skin.

"We've got money, thanks to the captain," he replied, "so we don't need to find work for ourselves for a while. I don't have any family that I know about in England. We should find somewhere to sleep tonight, then tomorrow we can start looking for some place that we like and settle down there for a while—make a life for ourselves." He paused, a thought suddenly surfacing in his mind. "That is," he said carefully, "if you want to stay here. I mean, I know you've come all this way to England with me, but you might want to strike out on your own now—explore the country, maybe go abroad. I know you haven't ever spent much time in one place. You might get bored, just living in one town or village."

She smiled at him. "I'm willing to give it a try," she said. "Just for the variety. And maybe I'd get bored and want to go exploring after a while, but I hope you might want to go with me. Show me your world the way I showed you mine. I'd like to see more of this England of yours. It is very different from where I was born, and very different from where I met you."

Someone passing by brushed close to Crusoe, pushing him sideways. He felt a sudden desire to push back but suppressed it. No reason to get into a fight, he thought.

He felt a sudden coldness on his leg. He reached down curiously. His fingers felt a gap in the material that hadn't been there before—a straight cut, as if someone had sliced his breeches with a knife without cutting the skin. He reached inside to where his pocket should have been hanging, but it was gone—cut away, along with the bag of coins that the captain had given him.

Crusoe whirled around, trying to work out who had taken his money. Nobody was looking at him. Nobody was acting strangely. "Hey!" he yelled. Most of the people near him turned their heads, wondering why he was shouting, but one person in particular—a man with long but thinning black hair, dressed in rough clothes—was walking away rapidly and didn't react.

He was clutching something. Whatever the object was, it was hidden by the awkward way he was holding his right hand.

"Hey—you there!" Crusoe shouted, outraged. He didn't expect the man to turn—that was the test. If he turned, then he was probably innocent. If he didn't, then he was deliberately ignoring the shouts.

The man sped up. He didn't turn around or react to Crusoe's words. Instead it was the people nearby who glanced around, then looked away when they realized he wasn't shouting at them.

Friday slipped away from Crusoe's side, moving through the crowd, paralleling the path of the thief but moving faster. Crusoe made a direct line for him, pushing his way through the mass of people and using his superior height to keep track of the man's thinning black hair. "You!" he shouted. "Stop!"

The man kept moving. He sped up slightly, glancing over his shoulder to see where Crusoe was. Crusoe, for his part, was busy calculating Friday's likely rate of travel as she moved through the crowd like a fish. If he was right, then she was moving ahead of the man now.

Crusoe sped up again and grabbed at the man's shoulder. The man whirled around, backing away from Crusoe. His right hand was holding a small canvas sack—the one he'd sliced out of Crusoe's pocket—but his left hand was holding a sharp knife that he was waving in front of him.

"Leave it, son," he said. He was missing a few teeth, and Crusoe could smell the stench of his breath from several feet away. "You don't want to risk your life for a few pennies, now do you?"

"They're the only pennies I've got," Crusoe said, "and besides— they're not yours. You've done nothing to earn them."

"Finders keepers, they say," the man sneered. "I found them in your pocket, so they're mine. Now, you look like a good lad, so I'll tell you what's going to happen if you don't stop following me and shouting. In that eventuality, I'll cut your face open so your mouth runs all the way from one ear to the other. Children will scream when they see you coming. Women will pass out in the street if you even so much as glance at them. Any time you try to eat or drink something, it'll spill out of your mouth. You really don't want to risk that, do you? You can get pennies again—work for them like a fool, or take them from someone smaller and slower than you. You can't get another mouth, though. Think about it."

Crusoe put his hands up. He tried to smile. "You've got a point," he said. "Easy come, easy go."

"Good lad. Very sensible." The thief lowered his knife but still kept it ready in case Crusoe moved to attack him. He turned to move away rapidly through the crowd.

And fell over Friday, who was crouching down just beyond him.

His forehead struck the ground with a heavy thud, and his head jerked backward as his body followed through. The knife flew out of his hand and skittered across the ground. Friday grabbed it and brought it around in a sweeping arc until it was pricking his temple. Crusoe rushed over and knelt down on the man's arms, stopping him from getting up.

"My pennies," he said, "not yours."

He reached out to the man's right hand, which was flat against the cobblestones. He pulled it up, but the canvas bag wasn't there anymore. The thief probably let go of it when he fell. Crusoe glanced around wildly, trying to see where it had gone, but there was no sign of it. Someone must have picked it up and taken it. He scanned faces, looking for signs of guilt, but nobody was looking in his direction. Desperately he rolled the thief over, looking to see if the bag had gotten caught underneath him, but there was nothing there.

He stood abruptly, still glancing around. The thief took the opportunity to scrabble away on all fours. Friday kicked him as he passed her, sending him sprawling to the ground again.

"Someone out there has my money," Crusoe said bleakly. "I think it's gone. I think he might have thrown it to some accomplice in the crowd. That, or he just let go of it, and somebody else has it now."

"Don't worry," Friday said. "I've still got mine." Her hand went to the pocket of her breeches . . .

. . . which had been neatly sliced out, leaving a long slit through which he could see her dark skin.

Friday's hand followed his gaze. She felt the cut in the leather, and the absence of the money she'd been paid by the captain. Her face took on a tight, angry expression. "Ah," she said, "yes—some accomplice in the crowd. You were right."

"I wish I wasn't." He slammed his hand angrily into his leg. "For a few moments there, we were all right—we had enough money to survive. Now we have nothing."

"We have ourselves," Friday pointed out, resting a hand on his arm. "We have each other. That is enough."

"Is it?"

"We will survive, just as we did on the island."

"I'm beginning to think," Crusoe said bitterly, "that this place is more dangerous than the island. At least there the food was available, if we worked to get it. Here, I'm not so sure. We could spend a week working, me on the quayside, shifting cargo, and you in a tavern or a coffeehouse somewhere, serving drinks, and still have the money stolen from us before we get to buy any food or beds for the night."

"Then we look after our money more carefully," Friday said, her voice level. "We have learned a lesson here. As I recall, lessons on the island usually came with teeth and claws, or with poisonous juices."

"You make a good point." Crusoe glanced at her face and smiled. "You always manage to calm me down when I risk losing my temper and doing something stupid."

"If that's my role in life, then I am happy with it."

"Perhaps we ought to reconsider Captain Maybury-Henson's advice and re-sign on board the ship."

She shook her head. "Let's not run away just yet." She glanced up at him, wide-eyed, and seemed to want to say something else, but Crusoe suddenly became aware that they were being watched. He turned his head slightly, glancing sideways without being obvious about it. Off to one side, two men and a woman were staring at him and Friday. One man was tall and thin, the other short and portly. They were reasonably well dressed—the woman in a bonnet and dress, and the men in wigs, hats, breeches, and well-tailored jackets. They were talking together in low voices and frowning.

"Let's move off," he said to Friday quietly. He reached out to take her arm to guide her away, but this seemed to provoke the three watchers.

"You are obviously a newcomer to this town, unfamiliar with our customs," one of the men—the taller one—called.

Crusoe tried to ignore him and move away, but Friday was refusing to budge.

"I say," the man called. "You—boy! I said: you are obviously new to London."

"Just passing through," Crusoe said calmly.

"Then you should know that we are not accustomed to treating our servants as friends. Their place is two steps behind us at all times. We do not engage them in conversation, and we certainly do not touch them, or let them touch us, if we can possibly help it. This is a civilized town, and we wish to keep it that way."

The shorter, fatter man was holding a handkerchief to his nose. "You should know your place, girl," he said to Friday, "and stay there."

"In my land, I was a princess," Friday said quietly. Crusoe could hear an edge in her voice. He'd heard that edge before, and it usually meant trouble.

The taller man stepped forward. He raised his hand, and Crusoe could see that he was holding a walking stick. The silver top was knobbed and rounded. From the way the man was holding the stick—about a third of the way down its length—Crusoe realized that the top must be weighted, perhaps filled with lead. If that hit him, it could break a bone, or smash his skull open. He tried to step in front of Friday to protect her, but she stepped out from behind him and joined him, standing shoulder to shoulder, ready for a fight.

"You young whelp," the man snarled. "I shall teach you such a lesson, it will leave you limping for years!"

"Break his leg," the woman said. She was licking her lips. She obviously wanted to see violence occur.

"You will have to forgive these two," a calming voice said from behind them. Crusoe and Friday both whirled around. Their expressions must have been fierce, even murderous, because the man standing there took a step back and raised his hands defensively. He was small, with a dark wig and a suit that was well cut but dusty. He was maybe ten years older than Crusoe or Friday, with the pale complexion and slight paunch of a man who ate much and exercised little. He also carried a cane.

"Easy now," he said quietly. "I'm just trying to help." He turned to the two men and the woman who had been so insulting. "Surely you can see that these two are newcomers to these shores," he went on, louder. His hands were still raised, but now they were held out in an open, apologetic manner. "In their lands, things are done differently. Let me take them away and explain how things are done here in England. They will soon realize their error, but I will apologize now on their behalf."

"The boy needs to be disciplined," the taller man said, still holding his weighted stick up. There was a sick light in his eyes that suggested he actively wanted to hit someone and wasn't willing to be talked out of it. "He is disrespectful to his elders and betters."

"Perhaps," the newcomer said, "but his uncle is an important financier in this city. The boy and his . . . servant . . . are joining him here. You could break his skull to teach him a lesson, but his uncle would disapprove, and then you might find your own lines of credit are suddenly cut off. Is it worth it?"

The taller man stayed where he was for a moment, stick raised. It seemed to Crusoe that he was going to step forward and sweep his cane down on Crusoe's head.

Before he could, his fatter friend stepped forward and put a warning hand on his arm. "Best leave the young whipper-snapper," he said quietly. "We have business matters to attend to."

Abruptly the taller man lowered his cane. "See that you teach him appropriate behavior," he said to the newcomer. "I would not sully my stick with his blood." He suddenly turned and stalked off. The fatter man and the woman stayed for a moment and then walked off after their friend into the crowd. Crusoe could see that the woman was talking fast and gesticulating—obviously trying to encourage her companions to turn around and go back, but they kept walking away resolutely. Money obviously counted for more than the lure of violence.

"Well, that was interesting," the newcomer said, lowering his hands. "I suspect it would have ended badly had I not gotten here."

Friday was looking around, still tense. "Would nobody have interfered?" she asked. "Surely in this crowd, someone would have tried to stop a fight."

"People mind their own business in London," the newcomer said. He was smaller than Crusoe—closer to Friday's size. His features were sharp and intelligent. He seemed well dressed, at least in comparison to many of the people on the quayside. His hat, in particular, was large and topped with a feather. "But where are my manners? Permit me to introduce myself." He took his hat off with a sweeping gesture and half bowed. "My name is Daniel Defoe, Esquire, born in the parish of St. Giles Cripplegate, London, brought up in the village of Dorking, but recently returned to London to make my fortune."

"Aren't there guards here at the port whose job it is to stop fights—and thefts?" Friday pressed. "I thought this city was meant to be civilized."

Defoe glanced at her, eyes widening as he took in not only her unusually dark skin but also, it seemed to Crusoe, her extreme beauty. "Alas," he said, "the only thing approximating guards here in London would be the local wardens, but they are paid for by whatever businesses are in the area—including, I suspect, those two men—and besides, they are more concerned about stopping thefts of cargo than stopping fights." His gaze was fixed on Friday's face in a way that made Crusoe feel uncomfortable. "You need to look out for yourselves if you wish to survive here for long." He looked from Friday to Crusoe—reluctantly, it seemed to Crusoe. "I apologize. I should have gotten to you quicker, and stopped this from ever happening, but my journey was slowed by a brewer's dray that shed a wheel on the road nearby. Two of the barrels smashed, and there was beer all over the road. A terrible waste."

"'Gotten to us quicker'?" Crusoe repeated. "You mean you were looking for us?"

The man nodded. "Indeed I was."

"Why?"

"That," he said, "is a story in and of itself. Let me start by saying that I am a merchant both here in London and elsewhere in the country."

"What do you deal in?" Friday asked.

"I deal in many things, depending on the fashion of the moment, but currently I am attempting to secure a consignment of civet cats that I believe are being off-loaded from one of these ships."

"Civet cats?" Crusoe questioned. "Do people want to eat them, or keep them as pets? In my experience, they are generally untamable and inedible."

"Indeed." Defoe smiled. "I have tried both, and you are correct. They do, however, release a substance from glands on their body that can be used to make perfume that is more exquisite than you would believe. That is why I want to secure them—if I can set up a farm and breed them here in England, then I can corner the perfume market for the country's upper classes."

"We don't know anything about perfume," Crusoe pointed out.

"Or civet cats," Friday added.

"No." Defoe looked from one to the other and back. "You do, however, know about other things that I would wish to hear about. May I be permitted to buy you some luncheon and talk with you?" As Crusoe looked at Friday with a question in his eyes, Defoe added: "At worst, you will walk away with food in your stomachs. At best, we can come to a business arrangement that I shall explain to you."

Seeing curiosity in Friday's expression, and feeling the same curiosity himself, Crusoe replied, "All right—we'll listen to what you have to say."

Crusoe imagined Daniel Defoe would take them to some rough sailors' tavern—a place where the sawdust on the floor had already absorbed its fill of blood, vomit, and spilled beer, and whose clientele got thrown out by the landlord as often as they left of their own accord. Defoe surprised him by leading them through a maze of alleys, away from the quayside, and through a low doorway into a room that was surprisingly spacious and illuminated by light from a massive window in the far wall. Most of the men there were smoking pipes, and a haze of tobacco smoke filled the ceiling space and hung to about Crusoe's eye level. The place smelled of the aromatic tobacco smoke, of course, but also leather and spices and cooking meat, and something that it took Crusoe a few moments to identify. He finally realized that it was coffee. He remembered the smell from their time in Barbados, where he and Friday had left HMS *Inviolate*—the ship that had rescued them from the island—and taken passage on the *Stars' End.*

There were booths around the walls, and a mixture of wooden tables and comfortably stuffed armchairs and sofas in the middle of the room.

The people sitting and drinking glasses of wine and tankards of ale were mostly well dressed, with sober wigs framing their generally plump faces. Many of them either had open ledgers in front of them or were reading newspapers and making cryptic notes in the margins of the pages. Groups of two or three men together seemed to be discussing deals—as he watched, Crusoe saw two separate agreements being made, each one sealed by smiles and handshakes. This was the kind of place, he realized, where the cargoes from ships like the *Stars' End* were traded. It was, in short, as much a large open office as it was a coffeehouse.

Defoe led them across to an empty booth. Crusoe slid onto the leather-covered bench opposite him, and Friday moved to sit beside Crusoe. Her gaze was turned to the room, and she watched the various deals being made with interest.

"You mentioned food?" Friday asked boldly. "We've been used to ship's rations for months, and we haven't got any money to buy our own. You saw the robbery. You were in the crowd—I saw you."

Defoe gazed at her for a long moment before answering.

"Your English is very good," he said finally. "Your friend here has taught you well. I presume there was little to do on the island where you were stranded, apart from talking."

The word *island* hung there between them like the echo of a rung bell. Crusoe didn't look at Friday, and she didn't look at him, but he knew they both had the same question: How did Defoe know about the island, and their time there, when they had only just arrived?

CHAPTER THREE

"I see you are wondering how I know your history," Defoe said quietly. "I apologize for startling you. I spend so much time in places like this, where information is traded back and forth like corn, that I forget how strange it must seem to new arrivals." He gestured at the people in the center of the coffee-house. "These men are businessmen. They scour the newspapers for news of arriving ships. They also meet with arriving captains, eager to hear any gossip that they may have. For instance, a captain of a fast tea clipper coming in from India may have stopped off in Cádiz for supplies. There he may have talked to the captain of a slower ship heading for London with a cargo of cardamom and saffron. They leave Cádiz at the same time, but the tea clipper arrives here in London a day or so ahead of the slower ship. The captain of the clipper comes here as soon as he docks, and tells the businessmen that he has information on cargo that will arrive within the next day. The businessmen offer him money for that intelligence, which enables them to predict what they should be paying for cargoes now. If they know that there is a big shipment of spices arriving in the next day or two, then they do not have to offer much money to a captain trying to sell spices today. Alternatively, if they know that no teak wood will arrive for the next fortnight, then a captain who has teak wood now can command a fine price."

"I understand the principle," Crusoe said, "but I can't see how it applies to us."

"Before switching to the *Stars' End* on Barbados, you were on HMS *Inviolate*, I believe. Her captain spent a convivial night dining with the governor. There he told stories of the two young people whom he had picked up on an unnamed island, not marked on any maps. Another captain at that same meal was leaving the next morning. His ship was faster than the *Stars' End*—more sail and less cargo, and he arrived two days ago. I heard his story in this very coffeehouse, over a jug of very fine port, and I was interested in what he had to say about the two of you."

Before Friday or Crusoe could say anything, a serving girl arrived at the table. She gave it a cursory wipe with a damp cloth before asking, "And what will you be having, gentlesirs?"

"Three bowls of the oyster stew," Defoe replied, "and a tankard of coffee."

"You haven't explained," Friday said as the serving girl left, "why the information that we had been rescued from an island was so interesting that it raced ahead of us from Barbados to London. It is not as if we can provide any information on likely cargoes, or possible changes in prices."

"Or civet cats," Crusoe added.

Defoe looked around. "This city runs on two things," he said, "and they are both information."

"I don't understand," Crusoe said.

"I have already told you that these men are desperate for intelligence concerning what cargoes are turning up and which will be delayed. Given your time in the Caribbean, you may well be aware of facts which they would pay highly for—facts about the likelihood of piracy in the region, the lack of British naval vessels, or the increasing frequency of storms. That is the first kind of information. The second is entertainment—stories about survival against the odds, about the spirit of man triumphing over nature, about wild beasts that have never been described before, and native tribes with habits and tastes that would seem bizarre to our ears. I trade in things such as perfume in order to make a living, but more and more I have become aware that entertainment is the true currency, the one thing that will survive the ages. If I can tell a decent story and charge a few pennies for it, but sell hundreds or even thousands of copies, then I can make a fortune—simply put."

Friday glanced at Crusoe. "And what makes you think that our story is worth telling?"

Defoe leaned forward in his seat. "It contains all the right elements. Two children, one shipwrecked and one the daughter of a pirate king, coming together to form an alliance against the depredations of man and the elements—I could make you famous!"

"How?" Crusoe asked simply. "An entertainment, such as Shakespeare or Jonson might have written, with actors playing the two of us? I don't think so!"

Defoe shook his head. "I think not. I am much more enamored of the form known as the pamphlet—a few pages, printed with words, folded together and sold as a work in several diverse parts, each part ending at a dramatic moment so that persons who buy it will be desperate to read the next edition, just to find out how you managed to escape from the lion, or the tiger, or whatever threat the previous issue ended upon."

"There were no tigers on the island," Friday said quietly. "Nor were there lions."

"But there were threats," Defoe pressed. "Things must have been bad for you. There was starvation, yes? Animals such as wild boars, perhaps? And the pirates, of course. And then there is the whole story of how Mr. Crusoe here rescued you from your pirate father. 'Red Tiberius'—wasn't that what they called him?"

"You obviously know about my father," Friday said. Her hand, below the level of the table, clenched into a fist. Crusoe knew that she was very protective when it came to information about her father, her family, or the crew of pirates with whom she had traveled. "How much do you know?"

"That story belongs to us," Crusoe interrupted firmly. "It will never be told."

"I will pay," Defoe said simply. "We can come to an arrangement as to how many shillings your story is worth. Perhaps you wish for a fraction of the money accruing from the sales of each pamphlet, in which case we can discuss likely sales figures, but I would urge you to take a straight fee for telling your story. That places all the risk on me, and my ability to spin a convincing tale of daring from your words."

Crusoe was about to refuse completely and pull Friday away from the table when the serving girl returned with three bowls of stew, three spoons, and a single metal tankard filled with dark, steaming liquid, all balanced carefully on her arm. The smell of the stew made Crusoe's mouth tingle. Food on the *Stars' End* had been basic, boring, and infested with worms and weevils.

Friday, knowing what he was thinking, put a restraining hand on Crusoe's arm. "The least we can do is take advantage of Mr. Defoe's hospitality," she said carefully. "And perhaps give him a story or two while we are eating."

Crusoe couldn't help himself—he grabbed a spoon and took as much stew as he could fit into his mouth. Friday did the same. The stew was flavored with pepper, and the oysters were juicy and thick. For a moment he luxuriated in the taste. It was like heaven.

"Very well." Defoe nodded. "I'm intrigued as to how you came to be on such a perilous voyage in the first place." He leaned back in his seat. "You must have been, what, eleven years old when you set out on the ship? Twelve when it was wrecked and you found yourself the sole survivor? That's very young for someone to be thrown on their own resources."

Crusoe took another spoonful of the oyster stew while he thought about Defoe's question. He still wasn't sure why the man wanted to know so much about his and Friday's adventures. Yes, perhaps there were people in London who would pay a few pence for a series of printed pamphlets telling their story, but enough to make it a viable business proposition? He wasn't convinced. But then again, what other reason could Defoe have for wanting to know everything about what had befallen them?

"Yes, I was a young boy when we set out," he said finally. "My mother had died, and my father was employed to provide advice to an expedition that was sailing out of London for the Caribbean. I was young enough that I didn't really understand what it was that he did, or why they wanted him, but he had no choice other than to take me with him. That's how I ended up on the ship. For a young boy, it was like heaven and hell combined—all kinds of things to climb, all manner of new things to see, but the food was simple, the portions were small, and there was always the possibility of accidents and sickness. I know my father was doing something on the ship—he had maps and diagrams that he used to spread out in the captain's cabin, and he used some kind of brass instrument to take readings of the stars at night, but I still don't know the details. I—"

Friday rested a hand on his forearm, and he stopped talking.

"How did you eat on the island?" Defoe asked, leaning forward expectantly. "Obviously you found some way of catching fish and animals."

"Eventually," Crusoe said carefully. "I had to. It was either that or starve."

Defoe nodded. Crusoe presumed that he was filing all this information away in his mind so that he could write it down later. "And what about the island itself?" Defoe asked. "Did you manage to do much exploring?"

Friday glanced at him sharply, probably wondering why he was moving from food and survival to the relatively boring subject of exploration. Crusoe noticed the switch in subject, too. "I would have thought," he said, "that you would be more interested in our struggles to survive, rather than the local layout of the island. After all, we were there for five years, and it was, when all is said and done, just an island. There are thousands of them in the Caribbean."

Defoe took a swig from the tankard. "As to the local geography of the island, it would be an advantage for the pamphlets I intend to sell, telling your story, if we could also have some kind of map drawn up. That way our readers can follow your progress, knowing where you are at any time in relation to the main features—hills, ravines, sheltered bays or other points where a ship might drop anchor safely." Finally he turned to look at Friday. "After all, your father's ship of pirates must have made shore safely somewhere."

Again he was pressing her about the pirates and her father. Defoe's insistence on asking the same question in different ways was beginning to irritate Crusoe—as was the way the man kept staring at Friday, his gaze roaming over her face as if he was fascinated by her. Crusoe felt an almost overpowering urge to put his arm across her shoulders, or a hand on top of her hand, to warn Defoe off, but he stopped himself. He wasn't sure what Friday's reaction would be. She might move away or look at him questioningly, and he would be embarrassed.

"I have already said that I will not speak about my father or my background," Friday said firmly. "It occurs to me," she went on, "that we're giving you details of our story now, but we haven't discussed financial terms. You intend to make money from what we tell you, but you haven't told us what we get out of it—apart from this lovely stew, of course. We have to find a way to survive here in England."

"You make a good point," Defoe said, nodding. "On the one hand, I do intend to make some money from the sale of these pamphlets, and it is only right and proper that you get some of that money. On the other hand, the pamphlets may not sell as well as I anticipate, and if I pay you too much in advance, then I end up out of pocket." He paused for a moment, gazing at Friday appraisingly, realizing that she had business sense as well as beauty. Crusoe wasn't surprised— Friday was a survivor, and business dealings were another form of survival. "Let me suggest the following arrangement," Defoe continued. "One-tenth of every penny and every shilling that I earn from the sale of these pamphlets, I give to the two of you."

"One-fifth," Friday replied. At Defoe's raised eyebrow, she went on. "I often watched my father negotiate for supplies, or for the sale of the various treasures he acquired from piracy. Of course, he often ended up negotiating with his sword at the throat of the other party."

Defoe swallowed.

"And," Crusoe added while Defoe was on the back foot, "you also pay us a fee before we start, in case for some reason your pamphlets never get printed, or don't sell well."

"That fee to be an advance on the monies earned from the pamphlets," Defoe countered. By his expression, it was obvious that his opinion of the two of them was rapidly changing.

"Everything to be set down in a written contract, which we will all sign," Crusoe said. Friday leaned back and folded her arms.

Defoe nodded. "Agreed, but the contract will specify how many meetings we are to have, and that there will be full disclosure of everything that happened to you, and everything you did, on the island. Nothing to be held back."

Crusoe felt Friday's gaze as she looked sideways at him. "I think Robin and I need to talk," she said. "Can you allow us a few moments?"

"I shall go outside," Defoe said, placing his hands on the table and levering himself up. "I need to check whether my civet cats have arrived yet. I shall return in, say, ten minutes?" He took a swig of coffee from his tankard.

Crusoe and Friday nodded together, and Defoe left the booth and headed for the door. It seemed to Crusoe that he glanced to one side as he went, nodding briefly at someone sitting on a divan in the center of the room. Someone he knew from his business dealings, Crusoe assumed.

"What do you think?" Friday asked as soon as Defoe was out of earshot.

"I'm not sure," he said. "On the one hand, we haven't got any money. On the other hand, he asks too many questions for my liking, and he already knows more than he should, based on a report back from something that was mentioned at a dinner party half a world away. He seemed strangely interested in your background—the pirates, and your father. Is that interest in a story that he expects to make his fortune, or is it more?"

Friday shook her head. "He makes me uneasy."

"So it's agreed." Crusoe looked into her eyes, seeking reassurance that they were together on this. "We say no, we leave with thanks for the stew, and we make our own way in England, beholden to nobody."

"And we don't tell anyone our story, unless we trust them," Friday added.

Crusoe glanced away so that Friday didn't see his scowl. "I think he's taken with you. He certainly spent more time looking at you than he did at me, and I don't think it's the color of your skin. He doesn't seem to care about that the way those imbeciles on the quayside did." He dropped his gaze to the table. "I'm sorry about that, by the way. You are strikingly unusual, and some people in England will have a problem with that. I'd hoped it wouldn't matter, but it obviously does."

"Well, I'm not taken with him," Friday said quietly, "and as for those idiots—if they can't cope with someone whose skin is different from theirs, then they don't deserve even a second's consideration from me." She smiled. "Ironically, where I come from, it is the white-skinned people who are stared at."

In the silence that followed the decision, Crusoe found himself suddenly aware of the hubbub of conversation in the coffeehouse. The voices of the various traders, sea captains, and other customers all blended together into a continuous racket, with the sound of rattling metal tankards and plates from the kitchens and the clinking of cutlery as people ate. It was like the noise of the forest that covered most of the island—so many layers of sound from the thousands of different animals, underpinned by the roar of the surf, the thunder of waterfalls, and the sound of the frequent rain pattering against the flat leaves of the trees . . .

⚍⚍

Two Years and Three Weeks
Since the Shipwreck

"It's all a mess of sound," Crusoe said, defeated. "I know that you can tell things apart out there, but I can't!" He lashed out in frustration, his fist connecting with the rocky wall of the cave in which the two of them had taken shelter. He could feel the skin of his knuckles tear against the rock, but he didn't care. He was exhausted and starving and near the end of his tether.

"*You must learn,*" *Vijaya said patiently from beside him. Her English had improved significantly during the weeks that had passed since he had rescued her. His Sanskrit—Vijaya's native language—was still pretty basic, however.* "*You must know which birds are easy to catch and which are not, so you do not waste . . .*" *She screwed up her eyes in frustration.*

"*My energy,*" *he suggested.*

"*Yes—so that you do not waste your energy on chasing something that you will not catch. Also you need to hear what is animal and what is man.*"

"*How?*" *he asked simply.* "*I didn't grow up in a place like this. You did!*"

"*You have ears, I think.*" *Vijaya shuffled closer to the mouth of the cave and pulled on Crusoe's shoulder until he did the same.* "*Listen! Listen to all that you can hear.*"

Crusoe closed his eyes as he had been instructed. He tried to quiet the criticizing, panicking voice that ran through his thoughts all the time. He became very aware of his own breathing and of the rush of blood in his ears. There was another similar sound close by, and he was startled to realize that he was hearing Vijaya's breathing as well. She was inhaling and exhaling more slowly and more deeply than he was, and he tried to match her respiration with his. Gradually a sense of calmness spread through him.

"*Now,*" *Vijaya said quietly,* "*do you hear a noise like . . . like the sea, but different? More like breathing?*"

He did. Once Vijaya had directed his attention to it, he could make out something that sounded like a hundred people all whispering very softly.

"*That is the wind in the leaves of the trees,*" *she went on. She tapped her forehead.* "*Remember it.*" *She mimicked pushing something away from her.* "*Now, ignore it, the way you can . . .*" *She paused, looking around, then pointed to the scar that ran up the back of his calf. "The way you can ignore an old pain. Now, do you hear a sound like a whistle, far away?"*

There was a whistling noise. It reminded him of a musical instrument of some kind—a flute or an oboe—not playing a tune but moving up and down the musical scale.

"That is the wind again," she murmured, "but this time in the rocks somewhere in the caves." She tapped her forehead again, then pushed something invisible away. "Can you hear something saying 'peep-peep . . . peep-peep . . . peep-peep'?"

There was something out there making the noise that Vijaya had imitated. Crusoe could hear it clearly above the noise of the wind in the trees, although he hadn't been aware that he could hear it.

"That is a bird. It nests high in the trees. It is difficult to catch, but its eggs are good to eat. Now you can hear the bird, can you hear another one, more distant this time?"

He could. There were two . . . no, three birds making that distinctive "peep-peep" call. Crusoe was amazed to find out that he could even distinguish their directions—one, the closest one, was off to his left, while the other two, farther away, were more central.

"There is another kind of bird out there, in the trees," Vijaya continued softly. "It makes a sound more like 'caw . . . caw . . . caw . . .' Can you hear it as well?"

It was like seeing through sheets of gauzy material, all laid on top of each other, separating the various patterns out. "I can hear it!" he breathed. "It's off to the right."

"Good. That bird is a . . ." She closed her eyes briefly again, looking for the right word. "Parrot?" she said hesitantly. "It is easy to catch, but its meat tastes bad." She paused. "Now—what else can you hear?"

"A regular noise," he said, suddenly aware that the sound had been there all along, but he had missed it. "I think . . . is it an ax? Chopping wood?"

"A machete—a large knife." Vijaya's tone, which had been light and breathy, suddenly became darker. "It is one of my father's men, chopping his way through the bushes. He is looking for us. Now, where is he?"

"Nearby," Crusoe whispered. The "caw . . . caw . . . caw" noise suddenly stopped, and he heard the whirring of wings as the parrot took fright, and flight. "He's disturbed the parrot."

"Good. Once you get used to the natural sounds of the forest, you will be able to tell when something that does not belong there is present."

"What do we do now?" he asked.

"We wait until he has gone." She smiled. "Then I will teach you to tell apart a noise coming toward you and moving away from you . . ."

THE TRICKS THAT Friday had taught him had become second nature to Crusoe, and now he used them to set aside the noise of the plates, tankards, and cutlery, and to tease apart the various voices that he could hear, separating them by direction, by loudness or softness, and by whether the speakers were facing toward him or away from him. There were eighteen separate conversations that he could tell apart from one another. He let his brain move from one voice to another, highlighting the one he was listening to and ignoring the ones he wasn't.

". . . cargo of sandalwood and cedarwood due in tomorrow morning . . ."

". . . stiffed me for several shillings, he did, and I intend to get every single one back, with interest . . ."

". . . hear about the Countess of Lichfield? They say some ruffians attacked her carriage and were only driven off by her servants after a fight . . ."

". . . died three days ago, sitting in a tavern over near White-chapel, but nobody realized for three days. They thought he was asleep . . ."

". . . Fenny's Dock, burned completely to the ground. They say his dog knocked over a candle and set fire to a curtain . . ."

". . . looking for a warehouse guard over at dock nineteen. Pay's not the best, but there's a free room thrown in . . ."

He stopped listening, and let the conversations and background noise all meld back together into a morass of indistinguishable sound. He glanced at Friday. He could tell from her unfocused expression that she had been doing the same.

"Warehouse guard?" he said, raising an eyebrow.

"With a free room thrown in," she added. "Can we find out where?"

"I'm sure if we ask around, we can get directions. So—we might have an alternative to telling this Defoe our stories."

Crusoe indicated the bowls of stew. "If this is all we're going to get from this man, then we may as well finish it up."

By the time Defoe returned a few minutes later, they had both finished their bowls. He slid into the seat opposite them again and glanced from one to the other expectantly. "Well, my friends, what is your answer? Are we in business?"

Crusoe shook his head. "I'm afraid not," he said. "Our time on the island was a combination of hardship and friendship. The one is something we don't particularly want to recall, and the other is something private that we don't wish to share. In addition, Friday's origins and family are not something she wishes to discuss, and it seems to us that it is something you are particularly interested in. For all of those reasons, we do not feel comfortable having you tell our stories, or using what we know as intelligence that can be bartered around like grain. I am sorry."

Defoe nodded. "Very well. I understand what you are saying, although I obviously regret it. Perhaps more money? I could stretch to, perhaps, passing on one-quarter of the money I receive, and I could perhaps give consideration to making the monies I would pay up front a separate payment, rather than an advance on later payments?"

Crusoe shook his head. Beside him, Friday did the same. "Money doesn't sway us," he said. "Thank you for the offer, and thank you for the food, but the answer is definitely no. We will make our own way in this world."

"I understand." He held his hands out wide. "It has been a pleasure talking with you. Mayhap we will meet again."

Crusoe and Friday slid out of the booth. Defoe held out his hand, and Crusoe shook it. His grip was firm, but something on his little finger caught Crusoe's eye, a ring with an enameled design on the front. It was the letter W, with the main strokes in green and a shadow version behind it in red. Crusoe stared at it, incredulous. He recognized it. His father had worn a similar ring. Not similar— exactly the same.

Before Crusoe could say anything, Defoe turned to Friday and shook her hand as well, and it seemed to Crusoe that he held on to her hand for longer, and squeezed it. He was about to pull Friday away from the man when she took her hand out of his grip.

Crusoe hesitated, wanting to ask Defoe about the ring but aware that they had already made the decision to leave, and reversing it now would be difficult. They left the coffeehouse, feeling Defoe's eyes on their backs all the way to the door.

CHAPTER FOUR

Outside, in the weak sunshine, Friday turned to Robin. "Did you notice," she said, "that when Mr. Defoe left the coffeehouse, and also when he returned, he nodded to someone sitting in one of those chairs that look like soft rocks?"

"They're called divans," Robin replied. "And yes, I did notice. I assumed the man was some business associate of Mr. Defoe."

"That's what I thought, but he was looking at us. Not directly, but he was looking at our reflections in the glass of the window near him."

Robin thought for a moment. "That's . . . worrying," he said eventually. "It means there's more to this offer than we thought." He glanced back toward the doorway they had come out of. "They're probably talking about us now."

"I've got an idea," Friday said. "Nobody looks at a serving girl, and there were at least two others in there with my skin color. I could get an apron from the kitchen, then walk through the coffeehouse with a tray and see if I can hear what they're saying."

Robin smiled. "It's worth a try," he said. "I'll wait over by the broken wall there."

Quickly, Friday walked around the coffeehouse to the back. It was rougher around there, with piles of potato peelings and other less savory material. A fetid smell drifted out of the kitchen door, thick enough that she could have cut it with a knife. A girl was standing in the doorway, hanging her stained apron up on a rough hook on the kitchen wall. As she walked out, Friday walked in and took the apron before the folds even had time to settle out of it. She slipped it over her head, making sure to hold it over her face to avoid being identified as a newcomer as she walked rapidly through the kitchen, past the tables where men were gutting and chopping fish next to other men wiping dirty platters clean with stained cloths, past ovens and hobs and bubbling saucepans, through clouds of steam. At the end of the kitchen another door led into a short corridor, where rough tables held piles of dirty plates, tankards, metal platters, and trays. She scooped up a tray and passed through an arch into the coffeehouse.

Defoe was still sitting where they had left him, sipping at his drink. The mask of good cheer and friendliness that had formed his expression was gone now, not needed anymore. Instead, he was frowning.

As Friday watched, he drained the tankard and got up from the booth, but instead of heading toward the door, he walked across the coffeehouse to where an older man with a white wig and a long red coat was sitting on a divan, reading a sheet of paper covered in close, dark printing. The man didn't glance up when Defoe sat down opposite him.

Friday started to stack her tray up with discarded crockery and cutlery. She kept the tray up near her face, hiding it from Defoe and his companion, and moved closer to them, straining to hear what they were saying.

"I take it from the fact that the two of them have left these premises that they were not enamored of your offer," Defoe's companion said in a high, clear voice.

Defoe shrugged. "It was not entirely unexpected. They are cautious, and for good reason. They look out for each other, and they do not trust strangers." He smiled suddenly. "Actually, I rather like them. I will keep track of them over the next few days. They have been robbed and nearly attacked twice already. Whatever resources they have won't last forever. If they don't seek me out again soon, begging to tell me their stories, then I am no judge of character. Your Lordship need have no qualms about that."

A passing customer jostled Friday's elbow. Her tray nearly went flying. Desperately she tried to stop everything from spilling. Her sudden distraction meant that she missed the other man's question. The next thing she heard was Defoe saying, "No good card player shows all of his hand."

"You're not a good card player," the other man riposted. "Or so I am led to believe."

Defoe smiled. "The thing about really good card players, Your Lordship, is that you don't actually know they're very good until they take you for everything you have. I have spent a considerable amount of time, and lost a fair amount of money, over the past months in persuading various people around here that I am truly atrocious at card games. One day—and it will have to be a single day, otherwise word will get around—I will surprise everyone by winning every single game I play in every tavern, gin house, and coffeehouse within walking distance, and leaving with a fortune."

"Has it occurred to you," his companion said, smiling gently, "that the other players might be playing exactly the same game with you as you are with them?"

Defoe snorted. "It is . . . unlikely. I am, as you know, a very good judge of character."

The man in the white wig folded up the paper he was reading. Friday, who was standing on the other side of Defoe, turned her back and busied herself in picking up plates.

"I heard about the attempt to kidnap the Countess of Lichfield from her carriage," Defoe said. "What is the world coming to?"

Friday took the risk of turning partially around so that she could see their faces. More importantly, she could see their lips. The background din in the coffeehouse made it difficult to tell just by the sound what they were saying.

"Most people know, although nobody ever talks about it, that the countess is actually King Charles's illegitimate daughter," the other man replied. "He is very protective of her. She reminds him of her mother, whom he loved very much. I am expecting a letter from the palace any time now." He frowned. "The quicker we can get those two working for us, the better. I hope you have a plan to get them to return to you, over and above your natural optimism and the fact that you are, by your own admission, a fine judge of character." He climbed to his feet—not without some difficulty—and picked up a cane whose top was a silver wolf's head, snarling. "Keep me informed," he said, resting his weight on the cane. "I will be traveling back to the ship, to await the king's messenger. Join me when you are able."

Friday realized that she couldn't spend too much longer standing there without arousing suspicion. She moved away, carrying her stacked tray. There was a great deal in that conversation that she had to think about.

Outside, in the sunshine, Crusoe listened as Friday explained what she had heard.

"We need to know more—" he started.

"Look!" Friday interrupted. "It's Defoe—he's leaving!"

"Let's follow him," Crusoe said. "We need to find out more about where he goes and what he does."

Defoe walked through the winding lanes and wider roads of the city in an easterly direction, heading toward the outskirts rather than the center, but always staying near the river. After a while the houses, warehouses, and business premises thinned out, with patches of marshy open ground becoming more and more frequent. Crusoe was worried that Defoe might turn around and see them, but he kept on walking, swinging his cane and whistling. Crusoe and Friday tried to stay as much as they could in the shadow of any walls or stacks of barrels they could find. Fortunately there were enough people on the road—locals and sailors both—that they could blend in.

Just as Crusoe was about to suggest giving up and looking instead for some food and somewhere to sleep, Defoe diverted from the road onto a path that led off into an area of overgrown grasses between the road and the river. There were fewer people around now, and Friday and Crusoe hung back so they couldn't be seen. Defoe seemed to be heading toward the wreckage of a large ship that had obviously been stranded in the marshes after some particularly terrible storm. Winds had blown it completely over, so that its barnacle- and lichen-covered hull was pointing toward the sky like some massive turtle's shell, while its deck was hidden beneath its bulk, and its masts and sails were missing completely. It was in no condition to ever be refloated—there were holes in the hull, and its timbers were obviously rotten. Why was Defoe heading for it? What business could he have there?

The bushes and grasses that surrounded the overturned ship looked like some strange sea upon which it floated. Gulls and other birds were nesting in the holes in the hull. Defoe's head vanished into the vegetation.

"Where has he gone?" Friday whispered.

"I have no idea," Crusoe whispered back.

"Surely he can't have gone into that wreck? Why would he want to do that?"

"Maybe he's living there," Crusoe said. Friday glanced at him skeptically, and he went on. "I know he's nicely dressed, and he obviously keeps himself clean, but he might have fallen on hard times. It's possible that he's sleeping here, in the wreck, and keeping his stuff here, so that he doesn't have to pay for accommodation and can save up his money."

"Even so," Friday replied, "the rain must get in. He must have friends he can stay with. Maybe he stores cargo in there, and he's come to check on it. Or maybe he's meeting with someone that he wants to interview for his pamphlets." She laughed suddenly, and Crusoe was pleased to hear the noise. She had a beautiful laugh. Hearing it made him feel like . . . like taking her hands and swinging her around. "Maybe this is where he keeps his civet cats," she said.

"Let's get closer," Crusoe replied. "See if we can see what's going on."

"Stop where you are," a voice said from behind them.

Crusoe felt Friday instantly move away from his side, surreptitiously opening up some space between them in case they both needed to turn around fast and fight. He braced himself on the ground, bringing his feet beneath his body and shifting his weight forward to his toes so that he could leap away into the bushes if the need arose. Friday quietly did the same.

The vegetation in front of them rustled, and two figures stood up, one to either side. They were men, both in the prime of their lives, both heavily muscled and without an ounce of fat on them. They were wearing ordinary clothes—moleskin trousers, linen shirts, cloth jackets, with scarves around their necks and caps on their heads—but there was something about the clothes that gave the impression they'd all been made at the same time, in the same way. The men looked like they were in uniform, even if they weren't.

They were also standing exactly where Crusoe and Friday would have jumped, if they'd had the chance.

Crusoe straightened up carefully. The two men watched him with dead, flat eyes. Their hands were held out of sight, in the bushes, but Crusoe was fairly sure they were each holding something—a wooden stave, perhaps, or a knife.

He turned around. The man behind him, the one who had spoken, was standing about ten feet away—far enough that it would be impossible to get to him before he brought up the knife he was holding and slashed with it. He was similar to the other two men, except for a scar that crossed his face from the right side of his forehead to his left cheek. There was something about him, and the two other men, that screamed "soldier."

"What are you both doing here?" he asked in a flat voice. "Answer the question or die."

CHAPTER FIVE

"We're just wandering around," Crusoe said calmly. "Someone said there was work available down this way."

Instead of doing what any ordinary, innocent man would have done—saying "There's no work here" or "There's a position open at the farm down the road"—the man looked at him expressionlessly. For a moment Crusoe thought this was another robbery, more violent than the last, or some kind of attack based on the color of Friday's skin, but he realized quickly that this was different. The three men didn't seem to be particularly interested in Friday, any more than Crusoe, and they weren't trying to make themselves look tougher or more violent so as to frighten the two of them into giving up any money—money they didn't have, he reminded himself. They seemed to be watching for something.

"You were following someone," the man in front of Crusoe said.

"Why would we be following someone?" Friday asked innocently.

"A good question," the man said levelly. "Perhaps we should find out." He gestured with his knife. "Follow those two. Don't resist, or it will go bad for you."

"What happens if we don't follow them?" Friday asked. Crusoe could tell from her tone of voice that she was tensing up, ready for action. He did the same.

The man held his knife up, the point aimed for Crusoe's heart. "Don't even try to run. It's not worth it."

"Running wasn't on our minds," Crusoe replied darkly. His attention was snagged by the man's right hand. There was a ring on the little finger. The angle was wrong for Crusoe to see what design was on it, but he could see a flash of red and green.

The man smiled. The point of his knife didn't waver. "Fighting would be an even worse move."

"For who?" Friday asked. "Us or you?"

"Either way, there will be blood." The man gestured toward the overturned ship's hull with his knife. "Now move, before someone does something that results in someone else being harmed."

Crusoe glanced sideways at Friday. She nodded. The odds were against them—these men were dangerous—the more so because they were obviously trained professionals. There would be no hesitations, no uncertainties to exploit. They would fight quickly and harshly.

Best to go along with them and see what happens, he thought reluctantly. Once they were inside the ship—if that was where they were being led—they might have more opportunity to run or fight. And at least they might find out what Daniel Defoe was doing in there.

As THEY GOT closer, and as the curve of the overturned hull loomed above them, Friday noticed that the ship was partially buried in the muddy ground, with its bow pointed inland and its stern pointed out toward the Thames. Shrubs and weeds surrounded it, blurring the line where it met the soil, but Friday was familiar with the way plants liked to grow and spread, and she could tell that this had all been *arranged*. Perhaps the ship being wrecked had been an accident, but what had been done to it since was deliberate.

They walked up to a bush that looked no different than the rest, yet seemed to be their destination. Friday and Robin were in the middle of a triangle formed by the three armed men. The men held their knives loosely but professionally.

Their feet squished into the ground as they walked. The earth here was damp, almost marshy. One of the men sped up, moving to the side of the bush and pushing it away. Behind it Friday could see a door set into the hull—but instead of being upside down like the rest of the boat, the door was the right way up. The man knocked on the door—a complicated rhythm, obviously a code. Moments later, the door opened.

The men gestured them toward the opening. Two of the men flanked them while the one who had spoken, the one with the scarred face, took up the rear.

Friday expected that the interior of the hull would be dark and damp, like the ground beneath. Instead a small stairway led up to a comfortable wood-paneled corridor. The wood was fresh as well— not part of the original ship's design. Lanterns hung from the walls every ten feet or so, casting a warm light. There was even carpet on the floor. Well, the ceiling. Friday kept telling herself that this entire thing was upside down, and they were effectively walking along the underside of the upper deck.

They turned a corner and walked along another corridor—this one lined with closed doors. At the end they turned again, into a third corridor, but this ran along the curved inside of the ship's hull. On the ships that Friday was used to, the hull was wider the higher up—the farther away from the surface of the water—it went. This was the reverse: the reducing curvature made the corridor wider at the bottom than at the top.

Ahead of them was a set of stairs that led downward to a short corridor and a single door. The guards fell back and formed a line across the corridor. When Robin and Friday stopped at the doorway and looked backward, the men just stood there, watching them.

Robin glanced at Friday, shrugged, and knocked on the door.

"Enter," called a high-pitched but clear voice.

Robin pushed the door open, and the two of them went in.

They were at the back of the ship, and the room they were walking into had probably been the captain's quarters when the ship had been seaworthy. The room was dominated by a large window at the far end that looked out over the Thames, where ships were passing back and forth. The window went almost from floor to ceiling, and incredibly the lower third of it was actually underneath the murky water of the Thames. Fish were quite happily swimming around outside, unbothered by the fact that there were people a few feet away from them. Apparently the overturned ship was set so far into the ground that its lower sections were actually below the level of the Thames—depending on whether it was high tide or low tide, she supposed. There was no trace of water, or even dampness, around the window frame. It wasn't original to the ship; there was evidence that it had been specially built, and built strongly enough to keep the water from flooding in.

She looked around. As with the corridor, the room was wider at the bottom than at the top. Hooks that had been left attached to the walls from the ship's previous existence all faced downward, and there was a circular feature in the floor that had perhaps once held a small chandelier. A large table sat in the center of the room, surrounded by chairs, and there was an ornate desk at the far end. Friday almost expected the table, the chairs, and the desk to be attached upside down to the ceiling, but they were the right way up.

It was only then, having exhausted the wonders of the room, that Friday noticed that a man with a tall white wig and a red brocade coat sat behind the desk. Beside him stood Daniel Defoe.

Defoe smiled at Friday. "My dear lady, while I am happy that the two of you have decided to continue our brief relationship, I do wish that you had done as I asked and met me back at the coffee-house. It would have made things so much simpler."

"Why?" Robin challenged. "So you could keep lying to us about civet cats, perfume, and wanting to hear our stories so you could publish them as pamphlets?"

"I apologize for that. However, in my own defense, I would point out that I *am* a businessman, I *did* take a delivery of a consign-ment of civet cats, and I *do* fully intend to take your stories and publish them, with perhaps some appropriate dramatic alterations. However . . ." Defoe glanced down at the man in the wig and the brocade coat. The man's wig, Friday noticed, was so tall that its top was at the same level as Defoe's head, even though the man was sitting and Defoe was standing. The man nodded almost imper-ceptibly, and Defoe glanced at Robin. "I . . . we . . . also needed to establish whether or not the two of you could be trusted. We had to establish your *bona fides*, if you like. To be assured that you can indeed do the things that you have said you did, and survive in difficult circumstances."

"And you also wanted to ask us specifically about the geography of the island," Friday pointed out, not wanting Defoe to distract attention from that point. "Why was that?"

A pause, and then Defoe continued smoothly: "There are many things about your adventures that we are interested in, but we can come to that." He smiled slightly. "The fact that you have followed me here, and done it without me knowing, tells us something. It tells us that the stories about the two of you on that nameless island are perhaps not exaggerations. You are resourceful and intelligent, and you can take action quickly. You can follow a man without him realizing that you are following. I also know, from the incident when your purses were stolen, that you have quick reactions and do not fear violence. I also know, from the incident with those idiotic people who assumed that Friday was your servant, that you do not resort to violence when confronted—you know when backing away is the better option."

A movement above the lapping surface of the water outside the massive floor-to-ceiling window attracted Friday's attention. A ship was sailing past: four masts and an ornate bow. It suddenly occurred to her that the *Stars' End* would have passed by this very place earlier that day.

"You were watching us, even before we knew you were there," she said.

"I was," Defoe admitted. "I have been watching you since you left the *Stars' End*." He glanced toward the window and smiled. "And yes, we did watch the *Stars' End* as it passed by this point on the river."

"Did you arrange those confrontations?" Robin asked angrily, stepping forward. "Were they some kind of test?"

Defoe shook his head firmly. "Absolutely not. That would have been morally wrong, and besides, I am not a recruiting agent. My role is more like a collector of intelligence and information. But this is London—unrest is only a step away in any direction."

"This country is troubled, divided, and weak," the seated man said suddenly, surprising Friday. "We have indicated to our enemies abroad, and even to our friends, that we are vulnerable. The only thing that has stayed them from taking advantage of us is that they have been involved in fighting one another, but we remain a largely Protestant country surrounded by Catholic countries. That is not a safe position to hold. The king, may God bless him and keep him safe, has thought long and hard about this. He has determined that if this great nation were a human body, then he and

Parliament would jointly be the head, the church its heart, and the army its muscles. This has led him to the realization that a body also needs senses—it needs to see, hear, and touch. It needs to know when danger is approaching, so that its head or its muscles can decide upon an action and ready themselves for that action."

Friday glanced at Robin. He was staring at the two men on the other side of the table with a frown upon his face. "I understand that the king and Parliament together are like the head of a body, the church could be considered to be like its heart, and the army like its muscles. That's just a poetic description, though. What about the people themselves—what are they? The fat? The tissue? The bones? And yes, a body also has eyes and ears and so on, but if England is a body, then what are those senses?"

"We are," Defoe said simply.

"I don't understand."

Defoe drew himself up and brushed unconsciously at the front of his coat. "We are Segment W—an organization set up by the king and reporting directly to him, but financed by a secret act of Parliament. It is our job to look for threats to the king, both internal and external. We do that using agents based in other countries, or based here in England. These agents might be ordinary people who report back to us what rumors they hear, or they might be people who have trusted positions in useful places, like foreign courts, or in the hierarchy of the Catholic Church, in Parliament, or even in the houses of the great families who support the king, but are paid secretly by us to provide information. We collect intelligence from all over the world, and we filter it, analyze it, looking for threats."

"Mr. Defoe has been working for Segment W for two years now," the seated man interrupted smoothly. "In his role as a businessman, he often hears things that may be of interest to us—rumors about the French building up their navy, perhaps, which might signal a possible war, or about Dutch traders who spend more time looking at our coastal defenses than they do buying or selling things, which may indicate they are, in reality, spies. As a pamphleteer, he can ask questions of people without arousing their suspicions, and he can, when necessary, use his pamphlets to spread rumors that we wish to be spread for our own purposes."

"Not," Defoe said with a grimace, glancing at Crusoe and Friday, "that I was particularly effective in not arousing *your* suspicions."

"And what happens then?" Friday challenged. "What happens with all this intelligence that you collect? Do you send the army in to deal with the threats?"

"Sometimes, perhaps," Defoe admitted. "But we are beginning to realize that there may be another course. Muscle is all very well if a body is being attacked from outside, but what if the attack comes from inside? What if it is fighting a sickness that can cause fever, rather than a ruffian causing bruises and cuts? Both can lead to death, but muscles can't fight sickness."

"We need an army inside the body of England," the man in the wig interrupted. "Something that can fight sickness and destroy it without the body even realizing that a battle is going on. That is the true purpose of Segment W. We are to be a secret service whose task is to keep England healthy." He stood up, his hands pressed against the desk. He was impressively bulky. "My name is Sir William Lambert, and I want you to join us."

The offer hung in the air like the echo of a rung bell.

"Just because we've learned to be resourceful, and to survive?" Robin asked eventually. He didn't seem angry, or indeed surprised. Based on his tone of voice and the way he held his body, Friday could tell that he was intrigued. She wasn't so sure.

"Exactly," Sir William said. "You are obviously intelligent— speaking with you confirms that. You have a quickness of mind to match your quickness of body. There are few in England who could match that combination."

"There is something else, isn't there?" Robin said thoughtfully. "It's to do with the fact that my family is all gone, I've been away for the past seven years, and Friday has never been here before. We have no allegiances, no ties. We are not beholden to anybody."

"Very good," Sir William said, smiling. He turned his head toward Defoe. "You were right—they are quick-witted." Turning back, he said, "Given the turmoil of the past decade or so, it is difficult to know whom to trust. Loyal Englishmen might be accepting money from the Dutch, and apparent Protestants can hold secret Catholic opinions, while those who now vehemently support the Royalist movement might covertly long for that time when there was a commonwealth declared, and no king. Neither of you have any previous links to these movements. We know that we can trust you."

"If we are talking about trust," Robin said suddenly, "then I have a question." He stared at Daniel Defoe. "I saw yesterday that you wore a ring—one with a sign on it like the letter W."

Defoe held his hand out. The ring was still there. "It is a symbol, a method of identification," he said. "It means that if I meet up with someone, I have a way of knowing that person is a member of Segment W, and they can do the same with me. Why do you ask? I would not have thought that the ring was that obvious—in fact, I am worried for our security if you remarked it so easily."

Friday reached out and took Robin's hand. She knew, from earlier, how sensitive this would be. If there was one thing that penetrated the wall of apparent invulnerability that he tried to project, it was memories of his family.

"My father wore a ring like that," he said.

Defoe frowned. "Are you sure? It was several years ago, and the ring might have been similar rather than identical."

"Your ring—does the stone turn around to hide the symbol?"

Defoe stared at Crusoe for a long moment without saying anything. Eventually he slipped the ring from his finger. Carefully he held it between the thumb and forefinger of one hand, while with the other, he fiddled with the central stone that had been incised with the W mark. To Friday's surprise, the stone turned on some hidden pivot. The reverse side was just a plain stone.

"Obviously," Defoe said, "if anybody realized that various people scattered through England and outside its borders all shared the same sign on their rings, then it might cause suspicions. Therefore we have a means of disguising the symbol when we are not among people we trust." He frowned again as he slipped the ring back on. "Segment W is a new creation," he said. "It has come into existence since you and your father left England for the Caribbean. I cannot see any way that the symbol we use—in fact, the very type of ring that we use—could have been in his possession."

"So my father was not a member of Segment W?"

"Absolutely not," Defoe said. "There was no Segment W when he left this country. I take it you do not still have his ring?"

"It went down with the *Rigel*. It was lost along with him, and the rest of the crew."

"I am sorry about your father," Sir William said, "and I wish I could help explain the ring that he possessed, but I am unable. I'm afraid we can spend no more time discussing it. We have more important fish to fry." He looked around the table. "There is likely to be some confusion when the king dies, and others both inside and outside this country will seek to take advantage of the fact. Our task will be to try to ensure that the ground is prepared, and that things take the easiest course they can."

"The succession to the throne is an important concern of ours," Defoe added. "The king has many children by many different mistresses, but there has been no legitimate issue from the queen. Indeed, it is suspected that she is barren and will never have a child."

"In that case," Sir William said, "the monarchy would in theory go to the king's brother, James. He is currently king of Scotland, but he is a Catholic and would prove unpopular. The closest acceptable alternatives are his illegitimate son James Scott, the Duke of Monmouth, and James's Protestant daughter, Mary." He frowned. "And then we have the problem of Charlotte Lee, the Countess of Lichfield."

The name rang a bell in Friday's mind. She tried to remember where she had heard it recently.

Robin got there first. "There was an attack on her carriage, wasn't there?" he asked.

Friday suddenly remembered overhearing someone at the coffeehouse talking about it. Obviously Robin had remembered, too.

Sir William and Daniel Defoe both looked impressed. "Your knowledge of recent events does you credit," Sir William said. "I doubt that nine-tenths of London have heard that news yet. Where did *you* hear about it?"

"We have our intelligence sources, too," Robin said cagily.

"If it were just an attack by a group of roughs for money, then, terrible as that is, we would not get involved," Defoe answered. "However, there have been rumors over the past few months that there might be an attempt to kidnap her and extort ransom money from the Crown, or even to influence the king's decisions. If that happens, then we would very definitely become involved." He glanced at Sir William. "The best tactic is prevention, of course. If we can stop any kidnapping from happening, then so much the better."

Robin looked around. "I would have expected an organization such as yours to be based in the center of London—the Whitehall Palace, perhaps, or St. James's Palace, not in an abandoned hulk on the banks of the Thames."

"Basing ourselves close to the seat of power would make us too obvious," Defoe responded. "Our faces and names would become known, through our close association with the king. How then could we conduct our secret business? No, it makes much more sense to place ourselves somewhere we cannot be observed."

Sir William, who had been standing since his request for Friday and Crusoe to join Segment W, sat back in his chair. He waved a hand around, indicating the walls of the room and, by implication, the overturned ship around them. "This wreck has been here for some years, but we have turned it into a base of operations. Being on this side of London, closer to the coast, means that our agents and messengers can get to us without being spotted and marked."

"So," Defoe said. "What is it to be—join us, work for us, help make England a safer place? Or make your own way in the world?"

Friday glanced at Robin. He was looking at her, the same question in his eyes.

"It's up to you," she said. "This is your world."

He turned back to Defoe and Sir William. "We're in," he said simply.

Friday felt a shiver run up her spine.

=*◈◈◈*=

Two Years and a Day Since the Shipwreck

The girl looked around the cave that Crusoe was living in.

She glanced at the chair that he had built out of driftwood, and the rough table he had constructed. She seemed amazed that he'd even bothered.

He shrugged defensively. "I made it out of the wood from the shipwreck," he said. Now that the danger had passed, now that they were hidden, he found it difficult to talk. He hadn't spoken to another living being since the Rigel sank.

She moved on to the wicker baskets that he had woven. They were filled with various fruits that he had picked over the past few days. She seemed particularly taken by the coconuts.

"Fruits and vegetables—I've worked out which ones are safe," he said, knowing that she didn't know what he was saying, but feeling forced to say something. "I also eat wild pigs if I can bring them down with a slingshot and a stone. I gut them and cook them the way the butcher did in the village where I came from. Oh, and fish." He pointed to the net that he had woven, which was hanging from a spur of rock to dry.

She nodded, as if she understood. She looked around the cave, noticing the large, flat stone where he had been painstakingly drawing his map of the island. She moved to look at it, nodding again.

He moved closer to her. "You know this place?" he asked, seeing the light of recognition in her eyes.

She nodded.

Next to the map stone was his fishing line, hanging from a rocky projection on the cave wall. She inspected it critically.

"I taught myself how to weave lines from vegetable fibers taken from vines or from large leaves," he said, "and I made hooks by pulling nails from the wooden wreckage of the ship and bending them into shape." He realized that he was beginning to babble, but he wasn't sure he could stop himself. "I used worms from the soil as bait. Worms, and flies that I caught. It wasn't easy, and I nearly starved to death before I caught anything, but it worked in the end." He glanced at her. A brief smile touched her face.

She was the most perfect thing he had ever seen.

A range of expressions flickered briefly across her face. She seemed to come to some kind of conclusion. She reached out and took his sleeve, pulling him softly toward the mouth of the cave.

"No," he said, pulling back. He gestured toward the outside. "Too dangerous."

She stared at him uncomprehendingly. How could he make her understand?

He moved to the mouth of the cave and cautiously looked out, shielding his eyes with his hand even though the sun was going down. He looked around in an exaggerated manner.

She nodded. Tapping him on the shoulder, she pointed to the sun—low in the sky—then made a scissoring motion with her fingers pointed downward. She kept repeating it, moving her hand in the direction of the bay where he had found her, and then wafting her hand in a wavelike motion.

"Those men—the ones who were looking for you—they've gone back to their ship?" He searched her face for some sign that she understood. "They've gone back because it's getting dark? They don't want to search at night, because it's too difficult?" He understood. It made sense.

She pointed at the sun again, and mimed it rising in the sky as if it were morning, then made the walking gestures again. This time the gestures were heading back toward the cave—toward them.

"They'll start looking again in the morning?"

Again she nodded. Taking his arm, she pulled him out of the cave. Reluctantly he let himself be moved. She seemed to know what she was doing.

He followed her, still limping thanks to his injured leg, but the girl's treatment had worked incredibly well.

They walked together down to the beach. The sun was low on the horizon, turning the sky purple. She gazed at the sea and the beach. "The tide's on the turn," he observed. "It's going out."

She walked down to the edge of the sea, where the waves were trickling in. She looked around, obviously trying to locate something. Her gaze caught on a pile of rocks deposited in the same place by eddies in the tides. She pointed to them. When she saw that he had followed her gaze, she started to walk toward them. She picked up one of the rocks and waited until he did the same.

It took them until the sun had dipped beneath the horizon to fetch a pile of rocks big enough to make her happy, and Crusoe still didn't know what she wanted them for. The tide was going out now, and there was a line of wet beach.

Taking a rock, the girl waded out until she was thigh-deep in the water. She bent down and put the rock beneath the surface. She straightened up and drew a shape in the water with her hands— three sides of a square, with the open end facing the beach.

Standing there, with the sunset behind her, she looked . . . different from anything Crusoe had ever seen. He felt a twinge somewhere inside him and didn't know what it meant. He felt strangely as if something in his life had shifted. Despite having survived on the island for two whole years, he felt for the first time as if he was actually growing up.

He waded out to join her with another rock and placed it beside hers. She nodded. Fish were swimming around their legs—too fast and too slippery to catch, Crusoe knew. Some of the fish were swimming around the rocks that they had placed, and suddenly he realized exactly what she was doing. It was as if a picture had been transmitted from her mind to his. If they built a three-sided structure out of rocks, just as she had outlined with her fingers, then fish would swim in and out of it. As the tide went out, the water would drain away, between the rocks. Eventually it would leave the rocks there on the beach, with a small pool of water trapped between the walls. And if they were lucky, there would be fish trapped in the water, unable to get back to the ocean—ready to be picked up, killed, and eaten.

This was going to work out well.

If she stayed.

CHAPTER SIX

They ate in a galley on the *Great Equatorial*: plates heaped with steaming meat and vegetables. It was a small area with copper pots and pans hanging from the ceiling and a roaring stove on which various things were being cooked. It opened out onto a large room with several long tables in it. There were a few men, and indeed a couple of women, sitting at the tables and eating from dishes. The normality of the scene was bizarre in comparison to the life-and-death struggle they had both been engaged in only an hour or so before.

"You need to keep your strength up," Defoe said. "We can't have our agents suffering from malnutrition."

"We will need somewhere to stay," Crusoe pointed out.

Defoe nodded. "There are rooms for you here." He leaned back in his chair and glanced around the galley. "But now we need to see Isaac Newton. As far as anyone else in the country knows, Professor Newton is the Lucasian Professor of Mathematics at the University of Cambridge. A very intelligent, very well-read man. He has published extensively in the fields of optics and mathematics. He is also a member of the Royal Society of London for Improving Natural Knowledge, and so he spends a great deal of his time here in the city. Unknown to anyone else, he provides us with the fruits of his experience and his intelligence. He is an adviser, rather than an agent, but he is invaluable to us."

The journey took about an hour, through streets rutted by the wheels of carriages and carts and by the hooves of horses. Crusoe stared out the carriage's window for the entire journey, marking the new buildings that had been erected since he left the city. Friday's attention was taken up more by the crowds of people who thronged the streets; it seemed to Crusoe that she was checking each face to see if she recognized it. He suspected that she worried about bumping into one of her father's pirates, even here in the center of the largest and most heavily populated city in the world. He reached out and put his hand on her arm reassuringly. She glanced at him and smiled, touching his hand with hers and sending a shiver through him that he desperately hoped she couldn't feel.

Gresham College was a collection of redbrick buildings on a street that was, as far as Crusoe could see, only a short walk away from the notorious hovels and slums of Holborn. Defoe led them through an arch into a quadrangle, and then up some stairs to a doorway. He knocked, and it seemed to Crusoe that the knock was overly complex. Maybe it was another code that would tell the man inside they were friends, and members of Segment W.

Something moved in the shadow of the stone steps. Crusoe looked down and saw a dog. It was curled up, but its eyes were open and watching Crusoe warily. A rope was tied around its neck and attached to an iron ring set into the stone wall beside the door. Strangely it had a folded linen cloth held against its stomach by a long strip of material tied tightly around its body. Crusoe thought he could see a bloom of fresh blood on the folded linen pad. Who would injure a dog like that? More interestingly, who would treat an injured dog for its wounds?

"In!" a voice called. "Quickly!"

Defoe pushed the door open, and they entered. The dog watched them go.

The room was large and airy, lit by the sun streaming through a massive arched window at the opposite end. Its walls were lined with bookcases that reached up to the absurdly high ceiling. There was no space at all on the shelves; they were filled with leather-bound books and journals, piles of paper, rolls of parchment, and what Crusoe assumed—based on descriptions he'd heard—to be Egyptian papyri.

There were things hanging by chains from the high ceiling, filling the space inside the room so that not one square inch was wasted. Looking around with amazement, Crusoe saw stuffed reptiles larger than any he'd ever seen, kites, metal spheres, detailed model boats, and things that he had no idea about at all. It was like a kid's playground of wonders, all hanging in midair.

The benches and tables that jostled for space on the floor all had things on them. Some had collections of glassware—flasks and beakers and all kinds of shapes, all connected together by glass tubes and corks. Some of the beakers rested on trivets, and beneath the trivets were candles or burning oil lamps. Liquids bubbled and moved through the glass tubes: blue, red, green, black, and muddy brown. Other tables held more stacks of books, collections of rocks, rows of bottles, and the dead bodies of animals that had been pinned down and then cut open so that their innards could be examined. Crusoe guessed that the room would be hot and very smelly if it hadn't been for the fact that the far arched window had various panels that were hinged so they could be opened or shut by pulling strings—and most of them were open at the moment.

"Close the door!" a voice yelled. It was coming from the other side of a bench stacked high with seashells.

Defoe pushed the door closed and called: "Isaac! It's Daniel!"

"Mr. Defoe—always a pleasure!" A head popped up from the other side of the table, followed by the upper half of a body as the man crouched there stood up. He was, Crusoe thought, in his late thirties, with a mass of curly and prematurely gray hair that cascaded down onto his shoulders. His face was thin and his chin pointed. He wore a black gown, beneath which Crusoe could see the collar of a white shirt. Well, it had been white once, but now it was stained with various chemical substances.

"I want to introduce you to—" Defoe started, but Isaac Newton sprang out from behind the table and grabbed his shoulder, interrupting him.

"Defoe—come and look at this," he said rapidly, not even glancing at Crusoe or Friday. "Tell me what you think." He spoke quickly, and he had an accent that Crusoe thought came from Norfolk, or somewhere in that direction.

He led the way across the room, robes billowing behind him. He found his way through the maze of benches to one near a book-lined wall. The table was surprisingly empty—all it had on it was a tray filled with black stones, a wooden tripod, and another pebble suspended from a piece of string whose top end was tied to the tripod.

And the stone was moving.

It wasn't being disturbed by the breeze, because there wasn't any breeze in the room. It wasn't just slowing down after having been disturbed earlier on, because each time it moved it went as far as the last time and the time before that. It wasn't responding to some rocking motion of the bench or even the room, because it wasn't going back and forth in the same direction each time. Instead it seemed to jerk sideways every time it swung over the middle of the tray of similar stones, sometimes left and sometimes right. It appeared to have a mind of its own. It seemed to Crusoe like the little wild pigs that he and Friday had hunted on the island. They would run in a straight line for a couple of seconds, then jink sideways, then back again, trying to evade their hunters.

Friday was gazing at the swinging pebble with wide eyes and a smile on her face.

Isaac Newton seemed to see her for the first time. He glanced at Crusoe as well, registering his presence. "Who are you?" he asked.

"This is Robinson Crusoe and his friend Friday," Daniel Defoe said. "They are working for . . . us." He touched the ring on his little finger—the enameled ring that Crusoe noticed earlier. It was as if even thinking about Segment W caused him to want to check it was still there.

Newton was wearing a similar ring, Crusoe noticed, and the robed man reached to touch it as well.

Newton had noticed Friday's fascination. "That is a lodestone," he explained, "suspended above other lodestones. Look at how they all fight to push it away or pull it close."

Instead of inquiring about the swinging stone, Friday asked, "Is that your dog outside?"

"It is," Newton said. "Why do you wish to know?"

"It's injured," she pointed out.

"Yes. I stabbed it with a knife."

Friday stared at him. She wasn't squeamish at all—Crusoe had watched her kill, gut, and skin wild pigs on many occasions on the island—but she didn't like needless suffering. She had seen enough of it on her father's pirate ship. "Why did you stab a dog?" she asked levelly.

"I'm glad you asked," Newton said. He moved rapidly across the room, toward the big arched window, turning halfway to check that they were following him. "Come on! This way—quickly!"

Newton scooped up a dagger off a table as he passed. He also picked up a leather bag. When he got to the window, he turned around and showed them the knife in one hand and the bag in the other.

"An ordinary knife," he said, raising it. "I used this knife to stab the dog earlier today." Seeing Friday's expression, he added rapidly, "It was a small wound, barely a scratch, and it was covered with a cloth immediately. The dog will survive, believe me. I will even give it more food than usual tonight as an apology." He held up the leather bag. "In here is what is called a 'powder of sympathy.' It is difficult to make, and requires . . . special ingredients . . . but when this powder is applied to a weapon that has made a wound, it will cause that wound to hurt again."

"That sounds like magic," Crusoe said.

"Alchemy," Newton corrected.

"Why would you want to hurt a dog once," Crusoe asked, "let alone keep hurting it from a distance?"

Newton frowned. "Apart from the sheer intellectual interest of the experiment," he said, "there are practical applications. Imagine each ship that leaves the London docks carries with it a dog that has been injured with a knife such as this." He hefted the knife again. "At noon each day, a man here in London sprinkles the knife with the powder. On the ship, the dog barks in pain. The captain knows that it is midday in London, and by looking at the sun, he can tell how many hours he is ahead or behind that time, and so work out his distance east or west. Would that not be a boon to sailors and merchants everywhere?"

"It is true," Defoe said, shaking his head. "Many are the ships that have been lost at sea because their captains could not tell where they were."

With a flourish, he used the point of the knife to prize open the neck of the leather bag, and then dramatically thrust the blade inside. A puff of powder emerged from the bag, like a coil of smoke.

Nothing happened. The dog outside made no noise that anyone could hear.

"I am still evaluating the principle of the powder," Newton said unapologetically. "It may be that I have the exact formulation incorrect."

"May I make a point?" Friday asked.

Newton nodded.

"Dogs bark all the time," she said. "They bark at seagulls, they bark at shadows, and they bark if anyone comes near them. Even if the 'powder of sympathy' works, how will the captain know which bark is caused by the knife touching the powder in London and which is caused by any other event?"

Newton stared at her for a long moment. "It is still an experiment in progress," he said stiffly.

His mind suddenly seemed to catch up with something Defoe had said earlier. "These children are members of Segment W?" he asked.

Defoe nodded. "Sir William Lambert has selected them personally," he said.

Newton frowned. "Why? We have numerous agents already—men of strength, men of cunning, and men of wisdom. What do these two bring to the organization?"

"They are survivors," Defoe explained. "Robinson Crusoe here was shipwrecked on an island in the Caribbean when he was twelve. While he was there, he rescued this girl, who goes by the name Friday, from a crew of pirates who had landed on the island. Between the two of them, they managed not only to survive but to thrive. They have learned how to live without the aid or assistance of anyone else—finding and killing their own food, building their own protection from the elements, and so on. They have survived the worst that the elements can throw at them, as well as attacks by wild animals and by other human beings. They have learned skills of survival and self-reliance that others—not only of their age but older—have not." He paused. "More importantly, they appear to have established some kind of link between them—a way in which, although separate, they each can be assured of what the other is doing. Sir William believes that such a link provides them with a strong tactical advantage when they are threatened."

Of course Crusoe knew that he and Friday shared a link, but he hadn't thought it was so obvious to others. He glanced sideways at her, but unusually she didn't glance immediately at him. Instead she was looking fixedly ahead, almost as if she didn't want to look him in the eye or acknowledge the truth of what Defoe had said.

"Such a link would do away with the need to use a powder of sympathy and dogs in order to determine the time on a sea voyage," Newton mused, staring at Crusoe curiously. "If we could establish what the nature of this link is—how it works, what provokes it, how much information can be conveyed through it—then one could foresee a time when two people with such a link between them could be recruited for every sea voyage—one to be on the ship and one to stay behind on shore. Through their link, the captain of the ship could establish exactly what time it was in London, and so determine the ship's position."

"I wouldn't let Robin go on a voyage if I wasn't with him," Friday said, moving to Crusoe's side. He felt her hand on his back. The skin beneath her hand tingled warmly.

"And I wouldn't stay on shore if Friday was leaving on a ship," Crusoe added. He made his voice calm, but he could feel a seed of anger growing in his heart. Newton seemed to be treating them no differently than he would a dog, or a lodestone—as objects rather than people.

"Indeed," Newton said. "Your words indicate the strength of the bond between you." He was staring at Crusoe's head now, seemingly examining the shape of it. "I wonder how such a link could be tested."

"By watching us," Friday said warningly. "Not by hanging us from a piece of string, or stabbing us with a special knife, or any other of your strange experiments."

"Attraction at a distance," Newton said. His gaze had moved from Crusoe's head to Friday's.

"Sorry?" Crusoe said.

"I have become convinced that many of the things we take for granted are due to an attraction at a distance. Take an apple, for instance. It stays on the tree because its stem is growing from a branch, but if the stem breaks, what happens?"

"The apple falls to the ground," Friday said.

"Exactly, but why? Why should it fall? Why should it not stay exactly where it is? The answer is, there is an attraction between the apple and the ground, but the ground, being much bigger than the apple, moves less, and the apple moves more."

"So when an apple falls downward from a tree to the ground, then the ground is also falling upward to the apple?" Crusoe asked.

"I believe that to be so, although the exact mechanism is unclear." He paused for a moment. "Or consider light from a candle—why is the light attracted to our eyes whereas the smoke is attracted upward? I believe that the whole world can be explained by reference to the attraction across emptiness. One day I will find the rules that lie behind these effects."

Newton suddenly sprang toward Friday. She partially raised her hands to defend herself, and Crusoe moved to help, but Defoe held up a hand. "Please, my friends . . . Isaac can be forgetful of the fact that he is dealing with people, but his heart is in the right place. Please allow him a little . . ." He smiled. "A little latitude in his actions."

Friday dropped her hands, and Crusoe stepped backward. Newton ran his fingers across her scalp, gently. Her hair moved beneath the pressure. He stepped back, then reached out to a table. He picked up a device that consisted of two metal bars that came to points at one end and were connected together by a hinge at the other. He opened the device out and started making measurements of Friday's head: temple to temple, front to back, and then between various things on her scalp that only he could see, or sense. Each time he made a measurement, he referred back to a graduated ruler on the desk, putting the points on the ends of the bars against the ruler and memorizing the distance. Leaving Friday, he raised his metal device and started measuring the distances between points on Crusoe's head. "Intriguing," he muttered. "I detect a distinct similarity between the widths of your foreheads. I do wish I could see your brains."

Crusoe glanced across the room toward the tables where various animal carcasses, from frogs to rats to birds, had been splayed out, pinned down, and opened up. Newton obviously had a long-term obsession with investigating the source of various things in animal bodies.

"You're not going to see our brains unless we're dead," he said firmly, "and even then I'll leave instructions that our heads are to be left intact when we're buried."

Newton frowned and pursed his lips, but he seemed to understand Crusoe's point. He stepped back, put down the hinged metal instrument, and glanced at Defoe. "What news from Sir William?" he asked. "Is my intellect and experience needed by Segment W, or can I return to Cambridge? I have lectures to give, and students to teach."

"Sir William is concerned about Charlotte Lee, the Countess of Lichfield," Defoe answered. "Have you heard the news?"

Newton shook his head. "I do not read the *London Gazette*," he answered, "and neither do I frequent taverns or other places of ill repute where rumors and gossip are spread. I deal only in facts, and in neither of those locations can facts be found."

"There was an attack," Defoe said, "on her carriage. She was uninjured, but Sir William is concerned. He believes that the attack wasn't just carried out by disaffected commoners, but by agents of some power. He is worried that they might try again."

"That would be unfortunate for the poor lady," Newton countered, "but in the great sweep of events, it hardly raises a bump. People live and people die. It is the immutable rule of things."

"Sir William was wondering," Defoe asked casually, "whether you could use . . . the object that Segment W possesses . . . in order to predict what might happen."

Newton stared at Defoe. "Such an investigation is not to be done lightly," he pointed out. "The . . . object, as you call it, is not a lens or a window through which events can be seen clearly. It requires careful handling, and it takes its toll. Using it can be . . . tiring."

"Nonetheless," Defoe pressed, "Sir William would be obliged if you could at least try."

Newton shook his head and turned away. It seemed to Crusoe that he was suddenly more nervous than he had been before. "I do not see the need," he said curtly. "Woman are attacked in this city every day, whether they are duchesses or fishwives, whether they are in carriages or in taverns. It is what happens. The only thing that can be predicted with any certainty is that such attacks will continue to happen in the way that they always have. I do not need the . . . the object to tell you that."

"But the political implications of the death of a member of the aristocracy at the hands of foreign agents—" Defoe continued.

Newton waved a hand, cutting Defoe off. "Immaterial. You are adding assumption to assumption, and making of it a structure that has no foundations. I will not use that thing unless there is a pressing need."

Defoe seemed to Crusoe to be trying to hold back his temper. "You are paid by Segment W, Isaac. I think you owe us a little of your time and your ability."

"I owe you nothing," Newton snapped, turning away. "The money you pay me is a mere stipend, barely enough to buy wine. I do what I do for England, for the king, and to advance my own experiments." He turned back and fixed Defoe with a hard stare. "There are some things that can make use of powers that we barely understand. That object is one of them. Its use is risky at best, dangerous at worst, until I have evaluated it properly and scientifically."

"And how can you do that unless you use it?" Defoe asked.

"There is using it in controlled conditions, and then there is using it because Sir William wants to know the answer to a question, but he can't be bothered to ask anyone. Come back to me when you have something serious that you want to know."

As they left Gresham College and walked into the crowded streets of London, Defoe hailed a passing hackney carriage. "I think," he said, "it is time to call on the Countess of Lichfield. You two may be able to make some suggestions concerning her safety that have not occurred to us."

"With the best will in the world," Friday said. "We're not adults, and we've only just gotten here. I doubt that we can help much."

"We're too civilized here in London," Defoe answered. "The two of you have had to survive pirate attacks and all kinds of adventures on your island. That kind of instinctive approach to safety is what we value you for."

The carriage stopped, and Defoe engaged the driver in conversation, telling him not only where they were going but also the route he wanted the man to take. It occurred to Crusoe that Defoe was, despite his optimistic and friendly exterior, a very cautious man. He needed to be in control of any situation he was in.

Friday started to climb into the carriage. Defoe reached out a hand to help her. She shook it off.

"She doesn't like to be helped," Crusoe said to Defoe.

"So I see. I was merely being . . . chivalrous."

"Her experience of being manhandled is that it is usually followed by a punch or a kick."

Defoe glanced into the carriage at Friday, then back at Defoe. "For my own safety, I shall try to remember that," he said. He gestured to Crusoe to climb in, and then joined him in the relative darkness as the carriage began to move.

CHAPTER SEVEN

The journey to the Countess of Lichfield's residence took over an hour and led them out of London's environs and into the tended countryside of Hampstead Village. The carriage labored uphill, through parkland and past sculpted gardens and large houses. Eventually they passed through a set of gates and arrived at a large mansion made of red brick and set in its own well-cultivated grounds. There were men standing at the gates who stopped the carriage, interrogated its driver, and looked in at Defoe, Crusoe, and Friday before they would let it continue onto the grounds of the house. They weren't wearing uniforms, but like the men who had stopped Crusoe and Friday before they got to the overturned hulk where Segment W was based, they looked as if they should have been.

The carriage eventually stopped outside the impressive portico of the mansion, and Defoe got out. He extended a polite hand toward Friday, then snatched it back as he obviously remembered the previous conversation with Crusoe.

The manservant who opened the door was slightly put out by their casual clothes, but he let them into the house and led them through a hall, lined with suits of armor and with swords and

shields hanging on the wall, to a visitors' room hung in pink brocade and silk curtains.

"The countess will join you shortly," he murmured, so quietly
that Crusoe strained to hear him.

The three of them stood there for a few minutes in silence.
Defoe seemed to be inspecting the paintings on the walls. Crusoe,
for his part, was listening to the distant sound of music being
played: plucked notes that seemed to hang in the air and shiver.

"What is that?" Friday whispered.

"I think it's a harpsichord," he answered.

"It's like angels are playing music," she said, and there was an
expression of awe on her face that Crusoe had never seen before.

The music stopped after a while, and a few minutes later, the
Countess of Lichfield swept into the room. She was wearing a
long robe of blue satin that brushed the floor. The sleeves were
bell-shaped, and ended around her elbow. Her face was wide at
the forehead and pointed at the chin. Her shoulders and neck
emerged from the robe as if she were walking shamelessly out of a
calm blue sea.

"Mr. Defoe," she said.

Defoe took her extended hand, bowed over it, and kissed it.
"My lady," he said, "thank you for seeing us. May I present my col-
leagues, Mr. Robinson Crusoe and Miss . . ."—he hesitated—"Miss
Friday."

Crusoe kissed the countess's extended hand as well. Friday
smiled at her and bobbed slightly—not enough to be a curtsy but
just enough to show respect.

"His Majesty sent a messenger informing me that you would be
visiting," she said. Her voice was pure and quiet, like a struck bell.
"This has to do with the attack on my carriage?"

"It does, my lady," Defoe answered. "Mr. Crusoe and Miss Friday
here are very experienced in matters of protection. I would be

grateful if you would let them look over your house and make some suggestions about how it might be better made safe."

The countess frowned: a near-invisible wrinkling of her perfect, porcelain-smooth white brow. "Surely the attack was an aberration," she said. "Just a few discontented commoners who have been listening to too many street corner sermons by persons who still desire the return of Oliver Cromwell and the Commonwealth. People who are rich are always the target of people who are poor—it is the way of things, even though none of us have a choice in the matter. Some of us inherit money from our families; some are born into poverty. Taking offense at this would be like taking offense at having red hair or freckles. God has decided that this is the way things will be divided up in this world."

"Perhaps," Defoe replied diplomatically, "but we need to be sure, if your safety is at stake. His Majesty would require nothing less."

She smiled at Crusoe. He felt a shiver of warmth run through him. "If my safety is in the hands of a man such as this," she said, gazing into his eyes, "then I shall be happy to listen to any advice." Her eyes were a lavender color, and the light seemed to strike them and make them flash as if they were jewels. Crusoe could feel himself sinking into them like he had submerged himself in pools of warm water on the island.

Friday stepped forward. Her elbow seemed to accidentally hit Crusoe in the ribs. "Perhaps we could both take a look around—if that is acceptable to you?" she said tersely. Crusoe wondered what was irritating her.

The countess kept staring into Crusoe's eyes, but she replied to Friday's question. "Of course—go anywhere, and ask any question. Just promise you will come back and tell me what you think." She turned to Daniel Defoe. "While your colleagues are checking over the house, perhaps you and I could speak about what happens when I leave it, and how I can keep myself safe."

"I would be deeply honored," he said.

Friday grabbed Crusoe and pulled him away. "Come on—we've got work to do."

They spent the next hour checking over the various windows and doors that gave access from the house to its extensive grounds. The doors were all closed and bolted from the inside, unless they were being used, and the windows were all fastened with catches. From every window, Crusoe could see men wandering the grounds, searching bushes and trees. If the king had provided this level of protection already, what else could he and Friday do?

"Does everyone in your country live like this?" Friday asked as they walked down yet another corridor whose floor was covered in expensive-looking carpets and whose oak-paneled walls were lined with paintings of landscapes, people, and horses.

"Not everyone," he responded. "You've seen the hovels out by the docks."

"I know," she said, "but—all this! How many possessions does one person need?"

"It's not how many you need, it's how many you can afford. The reason rich people have so many possessions is to demonstrate to other rich people just how rich they are."

Friday sighed. "Pirates are the same," she admitted. "The main reason my father attacked so many ships and took so much gold and jewelry wasn't because he needed it—he had so much the last time I looked that he could have bought an entire country, if he'd wanted to. The real reason he had so much was to make the other pirates respect him and fear him."

"So—not that different from rich people in England," Crusoe said.

"Except for the violence," Friday pointed out. "On my father's ship, and between ships, it was obvious. Here it is more subtle."

Every time they had looked through the house's windows, the sun was lower in the sky. As it grew darker, servants began to appear with candles and lamps, lighting all the rooms—even the ones that weren't being used. By the time they had finished, the sun had set, and the sky was a dark indigo color.

"Any weak spots that you've noticed?" Crusoe asked Friday. "Anything your father could have taken advantage of to get in, for instance?"

"Not that I can see."

He sighed. "I'm not convinced that we're doing any good. I think Sir William made a mistake in wanting us to work for Segment W."

Friday punched his arm. "If he's willing to pay us just to wander around some rich aristocrat's house, then I'm willing to do the wandering," she said. "Come on—let's check the roof."

They stopped a passing servant with a candelabra and asked him how to get onto the roof. He led them to the top floor and a narrow wooden stairway, unpainted and uncarpeted, that led upward. A door at the top opened onto a balcony that ran around a pitched length of tiles.

It was night now, and the stars were shining down on them. A cold wind was blowing uphill from the Thames, bringing with it the smell of the river and the distant sound of shouting and music. The city was only visible as a series of windows lit by candlelight and lamplight and fires that had been lit in areas of common ground. It seemed as if there was a warm yellow or orange light in the city for every cold white star that shone in the sky.

Except that there was a large dark patch in the sky to the west. For a moment, Crusoe thought it was a cloud. Then he realized three concerning things: it was circular, it was getting larger, and there weren't any other clouds around.

"What's that?" he said, pointing.

"I don't know," Friday replied quietly. Crusoe could hear the tension in her voice.

The shape got larger, blocking out more and more of the night sky. Crusoe felt a strange, crawling fear take hold of him. What was this? Some kind of huge silent flying creature swooping down on them?

"Father had a first mate from China for a while," Friday said quietly. "He used to tell us that his people, back home, built bags out of waxed silk and filled them with hot air from fires. The hot air made them rise, if the night was cold enough. People could hang from them, and fly, way above the ground. Sometimes they even had baskets hanging from them."

"I think," Crusoe said, straining his eyes, "there's something hanging underneath that . . . that thing. I think there are *people* in it!"

Before Friday could say anything in response, the black shape seemed to swoop over their head with an audible *whoosh*. Ropes suddenly appeared, and men were sliding down the ropes. They hit the tiled roof—three of them, no, four of them. They pulled swords from their belts, the metal suddenly bright in the starlight. Their heads were encased in black cloth, leaving only slits for their eyes. Their clothes were black as well. They glanced at Crusoe and Friday, as if wondering what to do with them, and then without any sound or any word, they ran for the doorway that gave access to the house.

"We need to stop them!" Crusoe shouted.

Above them, the black object swept on, its ropes trailing across the roof. Without the weight of the men, it started rising. Crusoe remembered what Friday had said about hot air making it rise. Without thinking, he rushed forward, grabbing for one of the ropes. Friday was beside him, leaping and taking hold of another one just as he got his hands around his own. The rope was slippery, and he felt the skin of his palms burning as he began to drop and the rope ran through his clenched fists. He held on harder, wrapping his legs around it as well to stop himself from slipping any more.

The black object passed over the edge of the roof. Crusoe suddenly realized that he and Friday were hanging three stories above the ground. He could see the gravel of the drive and the stones of the front steps far below. At that height, if either one of them fell, they would break their backs and both legs.

He glanced upward to see a pale blur looking down at him from the basket that was hanging from the floating shape. Someone was still on board.

He looked down again. The ground was closer now. Their weight was bringing the flying thing down again, just as the weight of the black-clad passengers had done.

He released the rope just before his feet hit the flagstones. Friday did the same. Once they had let go, the black shape leveled out, hovering above the ground.

Crusoe raced for the main door into the house. He knew that Friday would be doing the same thing.

They crashed through the door together. The entrance hall was empty.

"Defoe!" Crusoe yelled.

"What's happening?" Defoe called from a side room. Crusoe ran across the hall toward where the voice was coming from. Friday followed, taking up a position in the doorway.

Defoe and the countess were standing in what had to be the music room. A large harpsichord stood in the center, dominating the space. Defoe was looking alarmed; the countess was looking mildly concerned.

"Men, attacking!" Crusoe snapped.

Defoe frowned. "How did they get past the guards in the grounds?"

"Some kind of aerial device. They floated past them! They floated over them!"

"How very ingenious. I shall have to ask Newton about that."

"What do you suggest we do?" Crusoe asked.

"I suggest we defend the countess at the cost of our lives, if required," Defoe said. His normally cheerful demeanor had been replaced by an expression of absolute grimness and certainty. He glanced at Crusoe and shrugged apologetically. "This one of the drawbacks of working for Segment W, I'm afraid. There are dangers, and sometimes we risk our lives for others."

"So—no different from the last five years of my life," Crusoe pointed out. He glanced around. "This room is defensible," he said, "but we don't have any weapons."

"There are swords and shields out here in the hall," Friday called. "If you hurry."

Crusoe glanced around the music room. There were no other doors apart from the one he had come in by.

"You stay here," he told the countess. "We'll guard the door."

She nodded. Her face was white, but she didn't seem to be on the verge of a nervous collapse. "Do what you need to do," she said, raising her pointed chin in defiance. "And be careful—don't die on my account."

Crusoe and Defoe rushed out into the hall. Crusoe pulled a sword from the wall. It had a slightly curved blade and a metal basket handle that protected his fist. Ignoring the weapons on the wall, Defoe took hold of his cane, twisted the top, and pulled a slender straight blade from inside what was apparently a wooden scabbard. Friday had already removed an ax from the wall.

Together, the three of them waited for the attackers to arrive.

———⟨◦∕◦∕◦⟩———

Two Years Since the Shipwreck

Crusoe stepped out from shelter and waved at the girl. "Here! Quickly!"

She saw him and almost tripped in surprise. She managed to catch herself and kept running, but the stumble had cost her a few precious seconds, and the pirates made up some of the ground between them and her. She stared at Crusoe, wild-eyed, as she kept running. Obviously she could tell he wasn't a pirate, but she didn't know whether she could trust him or not.

Crusoe quickly looked around. Some fist-size rocks were lying on the sand. He picked one up and threw it as hard as he could. It sailed over the girl's head and hit one of the pirates, a man whose hair was braided into hundreds of rattails. Surprised, he tripped and fell to the sand. The other pirates glanced at him, then at Crusoe, scowling in fury.

The girl was only a few seconds from Crusoe now. He picked up another rock and threw it. This time the pirates had to twist out of the way so that it missed them. That cost them a little bit of time.

"Here!" Crusoe yelled, indicating a gap between two fingers of rock. He knew this part of the island like the back of his hand. If he was lucky, then the two of them could hide out among the folds until the pirates gave up.

The girl raced toward him, her feet sending little sprays of golden sand up into the air every time they touched the beach. She had to be about the same age as him: slim, athletic, and a couple of inches shorter than he was. As she got to him, Crusoe grabbed her hand and pulled her sideways, into the gap between the rocky outcrops. He dragged her along the slanted sandy ground to where he knew that a crack had forced the rock on their left apart into something like a narrow cave. He pushed her shoulder to get her to go into the crack. She turned, eyes blazing. Obviously she didn't like being told what to do. Crusoe held his hands up defensively, knowing that the pirates were just a few seconds behind her. "Get in!" he said urgently. "It's safe, I promise."

She stared into his eyes, then past him to where the pirates would appear. She seemed to make a sudden decision, then dropped to her hands and knees, and scrabbled into the crack. Crusoe went in after her. The darkness swallowed them up, but only for a few seconds. They emerged into bright sunlight again, but on the other side of the finger of rock. Crusoe pointed to the right, uphill. "That way!"

They ran together, feet splashing in the few inches of water that was running down the center of the channel between the rocks. Crusoe realized after a few moments that they were holding hands, although he didn't remember either of them reaching out to the other.

They got to a place where a series of small ledges marred the rock wall on their right in a pattern like a ladder. Crusoe pulled the girl toward the rock. She resisted, eyes wide.

"Nīṅkaḷ mēlnōkki cella vēṇṭum," she said urgently in a language Crusoe didn't understand. He stared at her and shook his head.

She punched him in the chest, hard. She closed her eyes for a moment. "Up!" she said finally in English so accented he hardly understood. She pointed along the channel just to make sure he understood.

Crusoe shook his head. "If we climb up those ledges, we can get over the top of the rock and into a channel that comes to a dead end as it goes downhill. They won't know it's there."

She looked at him for a second, then shook her head. She didn't understand. Her English was obviously fragmentary at best.

He pointed along the channel, in the direction they had been heading, then shook his head violently and made an X shape with his hands. "Danger!" he said. He pointed to the ledges on the rock, nodded hard, and said, "Safe!"

She looked at him for a long moment, then scrambled up the rock. Crusoe followed, knowing that for a few seconds, they would be exposed. He listened desperately for any shouts, any sign of pursuit, but there was nothing.

The girl rolled across the top of the rocks and half climbed, half fell down into the sandy channel on the other side. As Crusoe had promised, the channel headed uphill in one direction, protected by rocky walls on either side, but stopped dead in the other, where the walls narrowed together to a point.

"You live this place!" she whispered accusingly in bad English.

"I know where it's safe," he said. "We need to go uphill, then east."

The girl looked down at his leg and frowned. It was only when Crusoe followed her gaze with his own that he saw he had caught his leg on some sharp point of stone. He had ripped the skin of his thigh open. Blood was streaming down his leg and dripping steadily on the ground. At the same time he saw the wound, he suddenly felt it: like someone had drawn a red-hot knife along his leg.

He looked back at the girl. She looked at him. He knew what was going through her mind: with him injured that badly, and leaving a trail of blood wherever he went, she was better off without him.

CHAPTER EIGHT

The black-clad men rushed down the staircase from the upper floors, the nails in their heavy boots sounding like staccato drumbeats on the marble steps. They all clutched swords in their hands, ready for action. There was no hesitation in their movements, no uncertainty. They knew what they wanted, and they would do anything to get it.

Crusoe and Friday spread out to either side of the doorway into the music room, leaving Defoe to guard the door itself.

Crusoe did a quick count, just to check that nobody else had joined the fight. Four attackers, and three defenders. The odds weren't in their favor.

Instead of splitting up and engaging each of them when they got to the bottom of the staircase, the attackers all rushed Defoe at the same time. They had obviously worked out that the countess was in the music room, and they were intent on rushing past Defoe and getting ahold of her. As Crusoe braced himself for action, something in the back of his mind couldn't help wondering why the men wanted her so badly. Were they just trying to kill her, or did they want to take her away and then ask for a ransom?

The four men headed for Defoe, swords raised. Crusoe and Friday attacked them from the sides. Two of the men—the ones on the outside—turned, ready to defend themselves. The middle two engaged Defoe simultaneously.

Within moments, Crusoe found himself in the midst of a sword-fight with a man whose features were completely obscured by black cloth. Friday had taught him to always watch an attacker's eyes, never his hands or his weapons. Those things could lie, but faces never did. They always gave away an attacker's intentions. The problem was that this man's face was totally hidden. Even his eyes were in shadow.

He slashed at Crusoe's face. Crusoe parried, the blades crashing together and sending a shock up Crusoe's arm to his shoulder. The man pulled his blade away, its razor-sharp edge grating against the nicks in Crusoe's old blade. The man slashed low, trying to cut Crusoe's legs from under him. Crusoe parried again, forcing the man's blade to the floor, then stepping on the point of the blade to trap it. The blade bent. The man tried to pull it away, but Crusoe lashed out with the basket grip of his own weapon, striking the man's nose with the sword's pommel. The man jerked his head away, blood splattering from beneath his hood, but he managed to pull his own blade out from under Crusoe's foot, sending Crusoe falling backward.

As he fell, Crusoe's gaze went to Friday. She was backing away from her attacker, who was raining a flurry of blows down on her. The ax had proved to be a bad choice—it was an impressive weapon, but it was unwieldy.

Crusoe's back hit the floor hard enough to knock the breath from his lungs. The back of his head smashed against the stones a moment later, and a cascade of red sparks shot across his vision. His opponent took the opportunity to step toward Crusoe, blade raised to bring it crashing down. Crusoe lashed out with his feet, catching the man on his black-clad shins. He fell forward. Crusoe rolled desperately sideways, getting out of the way just as the man crashed to the flagstones on his hands and knees. Miraculously he was still holding on to his sword. Its blade sent chips of marble flying from the tiles as it smashed into them.

The two of them were both on the ground now: Crusoe on his right side, and his opponent on his hands and knees. The man brought his sword around and thrust it toward Crusoe's face, balancing himself on his left hand. Crusoe tried to block the thrust, but his right arm was pressed against the floor, and he didn't have much freedom of movement.

The point of the blade came fast toward his eye. He raised his head from the tiles, and the blade passed beneath his cheek.

Crusoe rolled onto his back, freeing his sword arm. He could feel the flat of his opponent's sword hard and cold against the back of his head. He brought his own sword back across his body and then swung it at his opponent. The man pulled his sword roughly from beneath Crusoe, slicing Crusoe's hair and cutting his scalp. He tried to block the swing, but the effort twisted his body, and his left arm slipped, sending him crashing face-first onto the tiles.

This could go on until one or the other of them got too tired and made a mistake. Crusoe needed to stop it quickly, if only so he could help Defoe, who had two opponents to deal with. He glanced around wildly. There was no sign of Defoe, and the doorway was empty, but there was a suit of heavy armor posed by the door to the music room: all dark metal, sharp-cornered plates, and spikes. Crusoe rolled closer and shoved his sword sideways beneath the podium upon which the armor was standing, close to the wall. He strained. For a long moment, the podium didn't seem to want to move. Crusoe was painfully aware that his opponent was trying to get back to his feet again. He strained harder, throwing all of his strength into the effort. The podium rose up an inch, tilting the armor forward. It began to topple, falling onto the black-clad man. When it hit his head and his back, it bore him down, right onto the tiles again, burying him in heavy metal. The helmet, gloves, and various other extremities scattered away across the floor with a sound like a hundred metal buckets hitting something hard. He didn't move, apart from a twitching of his fingers.

Crusoe climbed to his feet and glanced across to where Friday was fighting her own fight. As he watched, the man she was fighting came in fast, thrusting at her heart with his blade. She spun her ax around, catching his blade and twisting it out of his hands. The blade fell to the floor. Instead of swinging her ax around again until the edge was upright and she could use it, she jerked the inverted ax upward, handle-first, catching her opponent beneath the chin. His head snapped backward with an audible *crack*. He fell heavily to his knees, then face-first to the tiles. The sound of his forehead and nose hitting the tiles was another *crack*.

"Defoe!" Crusoe called.

Friday nodded. Together they ran toward the music room.

Inside, amazingly, Defoe was still fighting with both of the intruders, backing away from them while his sword was a blur, first knocking away one and then the other. The Countess of Lichfield was cowering behind him with her arm up to protect her face.

Crusoe and Friday each picked a different opponent and came up behind them, ready to attack and save both Defoe and the countess.

"Quick, help him!" the countess called. Alerted by her words, the two attackers whirled around and intercepted Crusoe and Friday's weapons before they could do any damage. The black-clad men backed away, each toward an opposite wall of the room, luring Crusoe and Friday toward them. Their swords flickered left and right, like snakes' tongues, ready to block a blow.

Abruptly, Crusoe's opponent raised his sword above his head with both hands and brought it down toward Crusoe's skull. Crusoe stepped to one side. The blade swished past his face and his shoulder. Crusoe brought his sword up, aiming for the man's heart, but the man suddenly reversed the direction that his blade was going and knocked Crusoe's blade away. The point of his sword ripped upward through Crusoe's jacket and shirt, drawing a thin, stinging line of blood on his chest.

From behind, Crusoe could hear the clash of metal as Friday engaged her own opponent.

Crusoe's foe pressed forward, his blade a blur as he rained blows on Crusoe from all sides. Crusoe parried as best he could, but he was forced backward, into the center of the room. His opponent seemed to have no plan other than to keep Crusoe heading backward, but his blade was moving so fast, and coming at Crusoe from so many directions, that Crusoe had no time to think about what the man's strategy might be.

Something made him step to his left as he reached the center of the room. He suddenly realized that Friday was beside him, facing the other way and stepping to her left. Her opponent had been forcing her back as well. It had been a plan to try to get the two of them to collide—a plan that would have worked had each of them not somehow known where the other one was.

Crusoe whirled around, catching Friday's opponent by surprise. Friday did the same with Crusoe's opponent. Crusoe lunged, blade extended, and caught the man in the shoulder. His black jacket tore open, revealing white skin and blood. Strangely, Crusoe thought, he could see something blue on the man's skin, like a tattoo.

Crusoe could hear Friday's heavy breathing behind him as she tried to heft the ax. She should have taken a blade like he had, but she'd always had a fondness for axes, even on the island.

Crusoe pressed his foe back against the wall. The man's head jerked right and left, looking for the best way out, but stone plinths with sculptures on top blocked him in. Instead, surprising Crusoe, he dropped his sword to the carpet and held up his hands. Thinking he was surrendering, Crusoe relaxed, letting his own guard down. The man turned around and reached out toward the wall. For a moment, Crusoe couldn't work out what was going on—did the man expect Crusoe to search him?—but the man gripped the bottom edge of one of the massive framed paintings that lined the room and strained, trying to lift it up.

Crusoe glanced upward. The top of the painting was pulling away from the wall. The man had somehow lifted it off its fastening. As he watched, horrified, the painting toppled forward. The black-clad man gave it one final heave, raising the base far enough that he could duck underneath and press himself against the wall.

The painting fell, slowly at first but quickly gathering speed. Crusoe raised his hands to protect himself, but if the heavy wooden frame didn't split his head open, then the painting itself would flatten him to the carpet, where his opponent could easily stab him through the paint-encrusted canvas.

Which gave him an idea.

Desperately he slashed with his sword, back and forth, up and down, as the painting fell toward him. His maneuver cut a cross in the canvas. The painting fell around him, leaving him still standing in a hole in the center of the blank reverse side, facing his surprised opponent.

The man's gaze flickered sideways, checking what was happening in the rest of the room. Abruptly he bent and grabbed the base of the carved wooden frame where it lay in front of him. He pulled it up to waist height and pushed it away from himself, toward Crusoe. Crusoe tried to raise his sword, but the canvas and the frame were blocking him. The heavy wood caught Crusoe in the stomach, knocking him backward. His feet caught in the ripped canvas, and he fell. He raised his sword, trying to block whatever attack was coming.

When no blade appeared, he scrambled out from beneath the painting. He stood up, trying to work out where the next attack would come from, but there was nothing. The man wasn't there. Crusoe glanced toward the door, where he saw not only his attacker but Friday's as well running out.

And in front of them were the two intruders whom he and Friday had left incapacitated in the hall. They had obviously recovered and sneaked into the music room while Friday and Crusoe were occupied.

They were dragging the countess with them.

Crusoe glanced back toward the harpsichord, dreading what he might see. Defoe was lying facedown on the carpet. His sword cane was embedded in the wood of the instrument.

Friday was climbing to her feet from where she had been knocked down.

Crusoe caught her gaze and glanced sideways at Defoe's prostrate body. He knew she would understand the message: she needed to check whether or not their friend required help while Crusoe went after the countess.

He ran for the hall. The four intruders—the two whom he and Friday had fought in the hall and the two who had fought Defoe—were just leaving through the main door. The ones whom he and Friday had fought were staggering, probably injured, but they were still able to move. He followed.

Outside, the darkness was an intense velvety black, peppered with the distant fires of London and the pinpricks of the stars. He couldn't see the retreating men in the darkness. He quickly stepped to one side, desperately waiting for his eyes to adjust, and aware that he made a perfect target silhouetted against the light from the doorway.

A flickering orange glow that he thought was one of the fires of distant London was, he suddenly realized, closer. Much closer.

A huge black shadow hung above it like a pall of smoke, blotting out the light of the stars. It was the floating object they had seen earlier, the one that had delivered the attackers to the rooftop.

The basket beneath the floating blackness was touching the ground. As Crusoe watched helplessly, the four men threw the struggling countess inside and clambered in after her. A fifth man, the one Crusoe had seen earlier looking down from the basket, fiddled with whatever it was that contained the fire. The flames roared to life, and the black shadow suddenly lifted away from the ground. The wind caught it, carrying it away from the house.

The ropes that Crusoe and Friday had clung on to earlier were still trailing from the basket. If Crusoe ran fast, he thought he could get to them and hold on before the thing rose too high to reach.

Crusoe realized that Friday was standing beside him. "Defoe?" he asked.

"He'll live."

He indicated the rising shadow. "We should—" he started to say, then stopped.

"What can we do?" Friday said angrily. "They would know we caught hold of the ropes, because our weight would bring that thing back down again. All they would need to do is cut the ropes, and we would fall—and that might hurt us badly."

Crusoe felt his own anger bubbling inside his heart. "You're right—there's no point in giving chase. We have to let them go."

"For now," Friday murmured.

They watched as the dark object, kept up by the heat from the fire that now so obviously glowed below it, soared away, diminishing in size until it vanished in the darkness between the stars.

Defoe's strained voice sounded from behind them. "We need to go. Sir William needs to be informed of what has transpired. I will send a message to Isaac Newton to join us as well."

"What about the countess?" Crusoe asked, turning. Defoe was standing in the doorway, leaning against the frame. A bruise was already beginning to darken his forehead.

"We will track her down," Defoe answered grimly, "and we will make her abductors pay for their actions."

Within ten minutes, all three of them were in a carriage, heading away from the scene of the countess's kidnapping and heading for the Thames and the *Great Equatorial*. The mood in the carriage was bleak. Each of them was staring out of a window, not wanting to talk.

"That was some good sword work I saw back there," Crusoe said to Defoe eventually as they rattled along the road. He was more interested in breaking the uncomfortable silence than actually having a conversation. "Good for a businessman and a pamphleteer, at any rate."

"I have had good training," Defoe admitted. "You met John Caiaphas, I believe?"

"I don't think so."

"He was one of the men who intercepted you outside the *Great Equatorial*. He has a scar on his face, running from his right forehead to his left cheek."

Crusoe thought back, remembering the man. "Yes, we did. Who is he?"

"John is in charge of Segment W's own defensive force: a small number of former soldiers working for us. We call them the Increment. They are partly bodyguards, partly a military force, partly . . ."

He trailed off. Crusoe glanced across at Friday. She mouthed the word *assassins* at him. He frowned and shook his head. He didn't know much about Segment W, but he didn't think they went in for that kind of thing.

The carriage rattled on, through streets lit by oil lamps on poles. A few people watched as they went past: drunks, insomniacs, and ladies of the night.

It took them most of an hour to get to the waste ground of Tilbury, where the wreck of the *Great Equatorial* lay. Several of the Increment were standing outside, ready and waiting. John Caiaphas was at their head. He nodded to Daniel Defoe, then acknowledged Crusoe and Friday with a lift of his eyebrow.

"You heard?" Defoe asked.

"I heard," he confirmed, voice harsh. "So has Sir William. So has the king."

Defoe nodded. "It was to be expected," he said.

Defoe led them inside the overturned wreck. As they entered, Crusoe noticed that security had been ramped up. More of the Increment were standing not only outside the entrance but inside as well. They had small crossbows, primed and ready. Their eyes were watchful.

Defoe led them back through the ship and into Sir William Lambert's room. Sir William was behind his desk, staring out into the darkness of the Thames. The lower half of his window was black with the lapping water outside. He turned as they entered.

"What went wrong?" he snapped.

Crusoe stepped forward before Defoe could say anything. "They attacked from the air," he pointed out. "I don't think anybody could have expected that."

Before Sir William could respond, there was a flurry of activity at the doorway. Crusoe turned to see Isaac Newton striding into the room. He was as unkempt as he had been in his own rooms, with the addition of a patched coat of old design and many buckles over his clothes.

"I hear there was a flying device," he announced. "I must know about it. Who saw it? Who can describe it?"

Friday stepped forward. "It seemed to be like a very large bag," she said, "open at the bottom. There was a fire that made hot air, which filled the bag up. That made it rise. I think they came down on us from the hills behind the house."

"Parliament Hill," Defoe murmured.

"They probably filled the bag with air and let it rise," Newton mused, "then set it drifting toward the house. I have seen it done before, but on a much smaller scale. I am intrigued to hear that the effect can be scaled up. Obviously such a device cannot be steered properly—one would be dependent on the direction of the wind. Rising can be accomplished by means of, as you say, a fire producing hot air, although the risk of the device catching fire must be taken into account."

"This does not," Sir William snapped, "help us find the countess."

Newton wasn't listening. "In order to descend," he continued, "one presumes that the occupants either let the air inside lose its heat, as all things do in the end, in which case the device would descend of its own accord, or they have some way of opening flaps which would let the hot air out faster." His hand, Crusoe noticed, was twitching, as if he wanted to start making sketches of possible designs there and then.

"I have heard about similar things used in China," Friday told him.

Newton nodded. "The Chinese are very much in advance of us in many respects, including mathematics and science. They are, however, very reluctant to give their secrets away to anyone who is not Chinese. It's very frustrating."

"Were those Chinese men who attacked the manor house and took the countess?" Sir William demanded.

Defoe shrugged. "Difficult to determine," he said. "Their faces were covered. They fought like Europeans, however. I think—"

He seemed willing to go on, but Sir William banged on his desk.

"Enough," he said. "Much has happened in a short space of time, and I wish to make sense of it, but I am aware that all of us have been awake for many hours, and some of us have been subject to considerable exertion. I need to brief the king, and check to see if any of our agents have heard anything. I suggest, therefore, that the three of you take the next few hours as a period of rest, and we reconvene at sunrise." He glanced at Crusoe and Friday. "Rooms have been arranged for both of you here on the *Great Equatorial*. Get as much sleep as you can, and meet us here at sunrise. I will ensure that breakfast is provided. If you need food now, the galley can provide it, as it can any time of day or night."

Crusoe nodded his thanks, and he and Friday headed for the door. As they left, Crusoe heard Sir William say, "Defoe—stay for a moment, so that we may speak. I think—"

Newton interrupted, "I wish a quiet room, some paper, and a pen. I need to make some calculations."

"Very well," Sir William agreed. "As long as you are ready for a conference at sunrise, your time is your own between now and then. Do not leave the ship."

The door closed, and they could hear no more.

One of the—Crusoe wanted to say "crew," but that probably wasn't the right word for an upside-down ship that had been stripped and used for a different purpose. Staff? Servants? Whatever—one of them led him and Friday to an area of the *Great Equatorial* that was set aside for living quarters. There they found two adjoining rooms aleady prepared for them. The floor area, as with most of the ship, was larger than the ceiling, given that the vessel was upside down and the hull grew narrower as it went up. They had hammocks instead of beds, but both of them were used to that by now.

A few moments after entering their rooms, they were both out in the corridor again. Crusoe smiled at Friday. She smiled back, and they both went in search of the galley, and food.

A man in a grimy apron came out of the galley as soon as they entered.

"I can do venison stew or oyster stew or roast beef or roast lamb," he announced. "I can also do various vegetables. What would you like?"

"What have you got the most of?" Crusoe asked.

The man thought for a moment. "There's lots of lamb," he said, "and a great deal of boiled carrots."

"Then we'll have that, and thank you for it."

He nodded and returned to the galley.

Crusoe and Friday sat side by side at an empty table. There was silence between them for a while, but it wasn't a strained silence. It was the kind of silence that exists between two people who don't need to say anything, rather than the kind that exists between two people who cannot think of anything to say.

Or perhaps the silence that exists between two people who were each absolutely exhausted by what they had been through.

"A strange day," Friday said eventually.

"Lots of things happening," Crusoe agreed.

She glanced sideways at him. "Are we in the right place, Robin? We could have died tonight."

He thought for a moment. "It's better than a lot of the alternatives," he pointed out.

"The food's certainly higher quality. So is the accommodation. I'm not sure about the price."

"Nobody's mentioned a price," he pointed out.

She gazed up at him with deep brown eyes. "There's a price," she said. "There's always a price. Here . . . it's the fact that we have to risk our lives for our food and our rooms."

"Things don't come for free," he said. He knew what she was getting at, but he didn't want to think about it. Not now, not this late at night, and not after everything they had been through.

Once they had eaten, they went back to their separate rooms.

Crusoe didn't even bother getting undressed, he was so tired. It seemed like an eternity since the last time he had slept—back on the *Stars' End*. So much had happened in the intervening time, and tiredness seemed to have seeped deep into his bones.

He lay there on the hammock, staring at the ceiling, but sleep did not come. Instead he found himself thinking about Friday, in her hammock in the room next to his. He wondered if she was lying there sleepless, like he was. He wondered if he should go in and see if she was all right. Twice he started to get up and go next door, but something kept stopping him.

He wondered if she was thinking the same thing.

Eventually he slept. Given what he and Friday had been through that day and that night, it wouldn't have been any surprise if he dreamed of violence, fighting, and fire. But if he did dream, then he didn't remember.

—◦◦◦—

Two Years and Two Months
Since the Shipwreck

There was a hill on the island where a colony of snails had made their home.

The snails weren't the small ones that Crusoe remembered from his family garden back home. These were massive things, the size of his head. Their shells were gnarled and rough, and their glistening, moist skins were striped in orange and grayish green. They congregated in a small dip in the ground near the top of the hill, covering the rocks and the trees in a slowly shifting mass. Crusoe would have just left them there, untouched, if it hadn't been for Vijaya. A few weeks after they had met, she led him up there one day and picked a couple off the rocks. She gave one to him, and the two of them carried the snails back to the cave, where she quickly constructed a little pen out of branches tied together with vines.

"We're not keeping them as pets, are we?" Crusoe asked uncertainly.

"Don't worry—we're going to eat them," she said. "I just need to flush their stomachs out first." She glanced up at him from where she was crouching by the makeshift pen and caught his puzzled glance. "Snails eat pretty much anything they can get, so they taste pretty horrible if you just cook them straight away. You have to feed them on something that tastes good for a few days—like herbs, or certain kinds of tree leaves—before you cook them."

"Are you sure?" he asked dubiously. "They don't look edible. They actually look poisonous."

She looked away defensively. "You don't have to believe me," she said.

"I do believe you. It's just that . . ." He paused, thinking about the best way to phrase what he was going to say. "Look, we've been together here on the island for a while now, and I still don't know where you came from or how you learned so much about what to eat and what not to eat. All right, you've told me that these snails are edible, and I believe you, but I wish I knew how you know that." He paused.

She turned to gaze up at him again, and she was smiling, but there was something behind the smile, something pained. "I know there are things I haven't told you," she said, "but you already know a lot of it. You know I was on a ship, and I ran away."

"You were on a pirate ship," he pointed out. "I saw the men who were chasing you. I assumed . . ." He paused and swallowed. "I assumed you were their prisoner, and you managed to get away, but I don't know where you were before the pirates took you."

She straightened up. "Come on," she said. "Let's go and find something for these snails to eat."

It was obvious that he had hit a nerve, and he didn't want to make her too uncomfortable. He'd grown used to her presence, and the last thing he wished was to frighten her off. Instead he glanced at the snails. "Can we leave them here safely?"

"We'll be back before they can escape," she pointed out. "And it's not like they're going to knock a candle over and set fire to the cave."

She led the way outside and paused. She looked at the ground. "Do you trust me?" she asked softly.

"With . . . my life," Crusoe said. For a moment he'd been going to say "with all my heart," but the words had gotten tangled up in his mouth before he could say them, so he said something else. Something safer.

"I know where we can get some good moss for the snails to eat, but it's across the island, near where . . . where you rescued me. Do you mind going there?"

"Wherever you go, I'll go," he said.

It took them several hours to make it around the island's central peak and to the south side where Crusoe had been looking for lobsters when he had first seen Vijaya. They talked little as they moved through the patches of forest and across the open areas of rocky ground, and as they got closer to the beach where he had first seen her, they said nothing at all. Usually, when there were silences between them, the silences were natural and unstrained, but this time there was a tension. Something was not being said, and Crusoe didn't even know what it was.

They stopped just on the other side of the small, rocky hill whose fissures and cracks had hidden them when they were running away from the pirates. Instead of heading down to the beach, Vijaya headed sideways, to a point where the hill dropped steeply away to a calm, sheltered bay that Crusoe had found nearly a year before, during his explorations of the island.

She settled herself in a gap in the rocks and gestured to him to slide in beside her. He did so, conscious of the heat of her body and the softness of her skin. She didn't seem to mind their closeness, and he tried to stop his heart from beating quite so fast.

She indicated the glittering waters of the bay, a few hundred feet below.

A ship was anchored a little way out, still in the bay but away from the beach. It was a two-masted schooner, not pretty but obviously seaworthy. Its sails had been tattered by storms and the corrosive effects of sea salt, and patched several times with different materials, but they were intact.

"The pirate ship," Crusoe breathed.

"My father's ship," Vijaya said quietly.

It took a moment for her words to sink into Crusoe's head. "Your father is a pirate?" he whispered, amazed.

"My father is the captain of the ship." She sighed and shifted against his arm. "I didn't want to tell you because I wasn't sure what your reaction would be."

"I'm just amazed that you survived for so long in a crew of pirates!"

She laughed softly, but there was no humor in the sound. "My father would have ripped to shreds any man who dared touch me, and they all knew it." Her eyes glistened slightly, as if they were filling with unshed tears. "My father's name is Vijaya Dinajara, the same as mine, but the name he has taken as a pirate is Red Tiberius."

"You and your father have the same first name?" he asked.

She shrugged. "It's Sanskrit—the name can be used for a girl or for a boy. Anyway, my mother died when I was very young, and my father took me to sea with him. I have spent years traveling from island to island and port to port, and I've learned a lot from his crew—how to survive at sea, how to survive if I was cast up on an island, and how to fight. But the older I got, and . . ."

She stopped, with a catch in her throat.

"And the things you've seen," Crusoe continued, realizing what she was trying to tell him. "The things you watched your father and his crew do—they made you want to leave."

"I grew to hate him, and them," she went on, still staring down at the schooner, "but you don't leave the crew of a pirate ship—not alive, at any rate."

"I would have thought," he said, choosing his words carefully, "that you would have chosen to get away at an occupied port, not an island."

"When I joined the ship, I was six," she said. "If the crew noticed me at all then, they saw me as just a child. But recently, they've been looking at me differently. The ship's first mate—Mohir, his name is—asked my father if he could take me as his wife." She shuddered against Crusoe's shoulder. "I've seen what happens to his wives, so the first chance I got, I dived overboard and swam for the shore. I thought I could get away from them before they saw I was gone, but Mohir spotted me and launched a boat." She glanced downward at the rocks and said softly, "But you found me, and here I am."

"Your father's name is Vijaya Dinajara, and your name is Vijaya Dinajara." He stared at her until her gaze moved up from the rocks and locked with his. "Every time you think of that name, you'll remember him."

"I know," she whispered. "I need a new name."

He smiled. "What about if I call you Tuesday, because that's the day we met? I've made a mark on the cave wall for every day I've been on the island, and I know that we met on Tuesday, the seventeenth of April, in the year of Our Lord 1686."

"I like the name Tuesday," she said, smiling. "But your calculations are wrong. We met on a Friday."

CHAPTER NINE

The events of the previous night might almost have been a dream, if it hadn't been for the fact that Friday's arms and legs ached, and she thought she might have sprained something in her hand. She was painfully aware that the weeks on board the *Stars' End* had softened her, just a little. She needed to get back into shape.

Just as long as it didn't involve going back to the island.

There was a pail of fresh water outside her door, and she used it to splash her face and arms to wake herself up and to freshen herself a little. She knocked on Robin's door to see if he was ready, but there was no answer from inside. She thought about going in anyway, on the basis that he might still be asleep and need waking up, but something inside her made her flinch at the very thought. Maybe he wasn't dressed. Maybe he'd be embarrassed. She'd noticed that he was acting oddly around her, more so since they had been in London than on the island.

Instead she headed for the galley, following the smell of fresh bacon and bread.

The galley was significantly more full than it had been the night before. There were more cooks as well, preparing a variety of meals. Steam formed a layer in the air, close to the ceiling.

Robin was sitting over near a doorway, Defoe sitting opposite him, and his back was toward the wall. Even there, in the heart of friendly territory, Friday was pleased to see that he still took care about not leaving his back exposed, and always knowing where the exit was.

The bruise on Defoe's forehead had developed into a purple lump the size of a duck's egg. His right eye was surrounded with bruising to match.

If this *was* the heart of friendly territory. Friday supposed that the matter was still unresolved.

She sat down beside her friend. Robin glanced sideways. There were dark shadows beneath his eyes. Defoe smiled at her from across the table.

"You look the way that I feel," Robin said.

"Then you must feel pretty bad," she answered. "Last night—did we . . . I mean, was there a . . . ?"

"We did and there was." He held up his right hand and wiggled the fingers. "My hand feels like I hit a wall."

"I think someone kicked me. Oh, and I think I pulled a muscle throwing that ax around."

"That ax was a bad idea—you know that."

She grimaced. "It was the first thing that came to hand. And it was sharper than the sword that you were using. That blade was so rough, it could have been used as a saw."

"If anyone is interested," Defoe observed, "my head hurts."

Robin smiled. "Returning home was supposed to be easy," he said.

"I don't think we would know 'easy' if it was served to us on a plate," Friday replied.

One of the cooks slapped two plates down in front of all three of them: bacon, eggs, mushrooms, oysters, and thick, crusty bread. They all fell on it ravenously. Another cook followed with heavy mugs of coffee. The menu for breakfast was apparently fixed, but she wasn't going to complain.

"Do you miss the wild pigs?" Friday asked, mouth full of bread and eggs.

"I suppose." Robin thought for a moment. "I miss the plantains more. They were delicious. I never got tired of them. And the pineapples."

"I should be making notes," Defoe said, mopping up the food with a handful of bread.

"For what?" Robin asked.

"For my pamphlets." At Friday's surprised expression, he added, "I was serious about telling your story, you know."

"We thought that was a ploy to get us into Segment W," Robin said.

Defoe shook his head. "I am a man of many talents: businessman, entrepreneur, writer . . . and secret agent."

They finished eating and got up, taking their plates and mugs to a table at the end of the room where they were being stacked, ready for washing. The moment they left their table, three more people moved in and sat down. Obviously there was a premium on space in Segment W's headquarters.

They all headed for Sir William Lambert's office, as they had been instructed. When they got there, Sir William was sitting at the head of the meeting table, with Isaac Newton on one side. They looked as if they had been there for all the time that Robin and Friday had been asleep.

There was a flask for coffee on the table, several empty bottles of wine, and three trays with plates that had once been stacked with food but were now covered with crumbs, grease stains, and small bones. There was also something underneath a black silk cloth—something that looked to Friday to be spherical, or nearly so.

Sir William had taken his wig off and left it on his desk. He was nearly bald underneath: just a fringe of white hair running around the back of his age-blotched scalp, from ear to ear. He smiled at them. "Feeling better?"

"Yes—thank you." Friday's attention was caught by the large window behind Sir William's desk: thick glass crisscrossed with a grid of wood. The water was lapping about a third of the way up the window now. Above it, she could see the fresh blue sky as background to the masts of boats and ships out on the Thames, and gulls flying nearby. Below it, the water was dark, but fish were swimming past and staring in through the glass.

"Please, come and sit with us."

"You have an impressive base of operations here, Sir William," Robin said.

"It serves," Sir William said. "We have spent most of the night discussing what has happened."

"Is there any news of the countess?" Robin asked.

"Nothing. Nobody saw the flying device after it left the manor house, and there have been no reports of it landing anywhere. She and her kidnappers have disappeared."

"Has there been any ransom demand?" Friday asked.

It was Defoe who answered. "Nothing, but it is still early days."

"And what about the attackers?" Robin asked. "What have you found out about them?"

"We have considered the problem from all angles," Sir William replied, "but I regret to say that we have not come to any definitive conclusions." He grimaced. "Not definitive enough to tell His Majesty about, anyway."

"We might be able to find out more information," Defoe said, looking toward the window and idly drumming his fingers on the desk. Robin noticed that his fingers were near the thing on the table. Defoe gave the impression that he wanted to pull the cloth away, revealing it to everyone. "There is, however," he said, dragging his fingers away, "a reluctance on the part of one of us to use all the resources at our disposal."

Isaac Newton looked up angrily and was about to make a retort when Sir William raised a hand.

"This has been discussed at length," he said. "Isaac is not willing to risk our . . . asset. Nobody else can use it, and so it is his decision whether it is used or not."

"What is this asset?" Friday asked, remembering a similar discussion between Defoe and Newton back in Gresham College. "Is it a person, or a thing?"

"That is not for discussion now," Sir William said. "I have asked John Caiaphas to join us. He has some questions for you about the events of last night."

As if on cue, there was a knock on the door.

"Enter," Sir William called.

John Caiaphas pushed the door open. His eyes were like chips of blue stone, and his face could have been a carving, it was so emotionless. He carried himself stiffly, as if he were standing at attention but still moving.

"I believe you have met our new members—Robinson Crusoe and Miss Friday," Defoe said, waving a hand at the two of them.

Caiaphas sat down. He even seemed to sit at attention. He glanced from Friday to Robin and back.

"Yes," he said simply. "We have met."

For the next hour or so, Robin, Friday, and Defoe explained to Caiaphas, each from their own point of view, what had happened the previous night. Each of them had a slightly different take on what had happened, but Caiaphas had a way of asking simple, direct questions that cut through any confusion and established the exact sequence of events.

"What do you make of it, John?" Sir William asked when it was clear there wasn't anything left to remember.

The soldier leaned back in his chair, thinking. "The men were obviously well trained and well organized," he said in his gravel-dry voice. "The way they mounted their attack—from the air—concerns me."

"It was certainly inventive," Isaac Newton interrupted. He had been making sketches on a sheet of parchment in front of him. "We have nothing like that ourselves, and I would like to know a lot more about how that flying object—"

"That isn't what I meant," Caiaphas interrupted. "What concerns me is that the object seems uncontrollable. Correct me if I am wrong, but it goes up when filled with hot air, it will go down if the air cools, and it drifts with the wind."

"That is largely correct," Newton admitted.

"It's what I heard about the Chinese devices," Friday added.

"Then it is largely useless, from a military point of view," he said. "I can see how it could be used for observation, perhaps, but as a means of transporting men on a mission? As a means of extracting those men after their mission ends? It's useless!"

There was silence in the room for a few moments. "What are you suggesting?" Friday asked eventually.

"If the mission had not been such an obvious success," he mused, "I would have said at the very least that the purpose of the attack was not to kidnap the countess at all. There was no clear and reliable means of getting her away."

"But they did kidnap her," Robin said. "Your analysis is wrong."

Defoe frowned and glanced at Sir William. "Do you recall," he asked, "a year or so ago, hearing reports of an organization that called themselves the Circle of Thirteen? There was some intelligence at the time that they were opposed to the Crown, but the trail went cold, and we never heard any more. Could this attack have been carried out by them?"

John Caiaphas shook his head. "Secret organizations spring up all the time, and fall apart just as easily," he said. "I never gave much credence to this Circle of Thirteen. I thought at the time that it was just a way for disaffected nobles to let off steam in secret." He reached out for the flask of coffee, but his hand accidentally brushed against the black silk that was shrouding the object on the table—at least, Friday assumed it was an accident. Perhaps he had done it deliberately. Whatever his motives, his fingers pushed the cloth away from the object it had been shrouding.

Friday caught her breath and leaned forward, amazed.

It was a black orb about the size of a grapefruit. A silver base with feet carved into the shape of claws prevented it from rolling away across the table. It seemed to be hollow and filled with viscid black oil on whose surface rainbow swirls could be glimpsed. Deep into its heart, Friday thought she saw a small red glow that seemed to pulse like a heartbeat, although she quickly told herself that it was a reflection of the sunrise outside.

"Is that a jewel?" Robin asked, amazed. "An opal, perhaps?"

Daniel Defoe reached out and took the silk cloth from the table. "It is not a jewel," he said, flicking the cloth over the sphere and covering it again. "It is . . . a nodule of a kind sometimes found on the ocean floor, by sailors."

"A pearl?" Friday breathed. "A black pearl?"

"Alas, no—merely a special kind of rock. Interesting to a natural philosopher such as Isaac Newton here, but nothing more." He glanced at Newton.

"Indeed," Newton said, picking up on Defoe's cue. "As a constituent element in alchemical studies into how to transmute lead into gold, it has some value, but as an adornment—I think not."

"Let us move back to the attack last night," Sir William said, tapping the table. "There may be some detail we have missed—something that can be learned from the way these men operated, the way they fought."

As the debate went on, Friday found her attention wandering. All this dry talk of tactics, strategies, and motives was alien to her. She was more concerned with knowing where the enemy was and when they would be attacking. That was what mattered.

She gazed toward the window. The sun was a little way above the horizon now, and the masts of the various ships and boats on the river cast long shadows like clutching fingers toward the *Great Equatorial*. The sunlight penetrated a few feet beneath the surface of the water, turning the drifting motes of refuse and vegetation into black specks against a bright background like the exact opposite of the night sky.

Something caught her attention, and she focused her gaze on an odd movement. The stern of the *Great Equatorial* looked out sideways onto the river, which meant that most of the shipping was going from left to right and right to left. One boat, however, was heading directly toward them—crossing from the far bank of the river and aiming for the near bank. In fact, it seemed to be aiming directly for the *Great Equatorial*. Friday assumed for a few moments that it was an optical illusion—the boat was a ferry, perhaps, and it would pass them by to one side or the other. It was hard to tell, with the sun behind it, but the longer she watched, the more it looked like the boat was heading directly toward the window. It wasn't veering off at all. Its sharply pointed prow—looking from that angle more like a single vicious horn pointed straight forward—was aimed right at them.

"Excuse me . . . ," she said hesitantly.

The talking around the table continued as if she hadn't said anything.

The dark shape grew larger as she watched. She could see the water froth as the bow of the boat cleaved through it.

"Excuse me!" she said, more loudly.

"My apologies," Sir William said. "Did you have something to contribute, my dear?"

"I only wanted to ask—is that boat heading right for us or not?"

Sir William, Daniel Defoe, John Caiaphas, Isaac Newton, and Robin turned to look at the window.

"Get out of here!" Caiaphas shouted, leaping to his feet. "It's an attack!"

Sir William and Defoe sprang up and moved together toward the door. Robin moved to Friday's side, catching her as she stood up and trying to pull her in the same direction. Newton made a grab for the black sphere in the middle of the table.

It was too late.

The pointed prow of the boat seemed to accelerate right at the last moment. It hit the window toward the top, smashing through the glass with a sound like a cannon firing and grinding along the roof of the cabin, gouging splinters and chunks of wood out of the paneling. The wooden detritus fell like hard rain on the carpet. The *Great Equatorial* lurched like a stunned ox.

The bow of the boat followed, crashing into the glass in a line all the way down to the surface of the river and below. The glass seemed to explode into the room, as hard and as transparent as ice but sharp-edged and dangerous. The river poured into the room through the hole in the window. Within moments there was a maelstrom of muddy water, fish, and bits of vegetation lapping around the legs of the table. The boat appeared to pull back, but it was just a momentary retreat caused by the lapping of the waves, and a second later the boat rammed right back into the stern of the *Great Equatorial*, wedging itself more tightly in the gap. Water poured around it and beneath it, coming up almost to the level of the table's surface, and pushing the door closed just as Caiaphas got to it. The roar of the water was deafening.

Caiaphas grabbed the knob and strained to pull it back open again. Defoe and Sir William joined him, but it was only when the guards on the other side of the door added their weight to it that it began to move. Everyone was shouting, but Friday couldn't hear anything over the roaring of the river and the grinding of the ship's timbers.

Friday and Robin had the same thought at the same time: get out through the window and past the boat, rather than try to get the door open. Clutching each other for safety, they moved toward the smashed stern of the *Great Equatorial.* The bow of the invading boat loomed over them.

"Accident?" Friday mouthed.

Robin shook his head violently. "I doubt it," he mouthed back. "That boat was aimed at us!"

They both turned back toward the smashed window, looking for the safest way out, but the bow of the intruding boat suddenly and shockingly split open like a pair of barn doors. Men dressed in black, just like the attackers at the manor house, jumped out of the revealed interior. They pushed past Friday and Robin, heading for the middle of the room.

Reacting instantly, without thought, Friday grabbed one of them by the collar and pulled. He fell backward into the water, his jacket ripping open and revealing pale skin covered with what looked like a mottled blue pattern. Robin had already pushed another one sideways. He fell with a splash. Robin picked up one of the chairs and smashed a third man over the head with it.

The men had knives, however: wickedly sharp things curved like crescent moons. The next three emerged from the bow of the boat, sloshing through the water toward Friday and Robin and slashing expertly at them in an attempt to get them to back away. Robin still had the chair and parried with it. His opponent thrust his knife right through the seat of the chair. Friday, meanwhile, picked up a metal platter from the table and threw it at the man who was heading for her. It caught him beneath the chin and he doubled over, hands clutching at his throat.

Water was pouring backward now, into the revealed interior of the attacking boat, reducing the water level in the *Great Equatorial*'s cabin significantly.

The combined efforts of Caiaphas, Sir William, and Defoe on one side and the guards on the other side had finally pulled the door open against the reduced weight of the water. Caiaphas urged Sir William and Defoe out to safety, then turned around and joined the guards, who were pushing their way in and engaging the attacking men: swords against knives. Wherever Friday looked, a fight was going on.

Beside her, Isaac Newton surfaced from beneath the water, his unkempt hair plastered to his scalp. He was holding the black sphere in his hands.

"Thank Providence!" he cried. "I have it!"

One of the black-clad men grabbed the orb from out of his hands, turned around, and ran past Friday and Robin, back into the gaping bow of the boat. Two more men grabbed Isaac Newton, hauling him from the water and pulling him away. Bizarrely, from somewhere inside the boat, a trumpet sounded. At that signal, every single black-clad intruder disengaged from the fight they were engaged in and backed away, forming a protective line between the advancing Increment guards and their own retreating companions.

Friday and Robin were on the wrong side of the line.

Daniel Defoe's face was horrified as he stood by the door, holding the frame for support. He pointed at the retreating intruders and shouted, "They've got Newton and the scrying orb! Stop them!"

Friday looked past him. In the doorway, Sir William had turned around and was trying to get back in. He caught her eye. "Get them back!" he shouted over the general tumult. "For the sake of everything you hold dear, get them back!"

Friday tried to grab the arm of the man who was sloshing past her with the orb, but he pushed her away. Her foot caught on something beneath the surface of the water, and she fell. Just before her head went under, she saw Robin grabbing for Newton as he was pulled away, but one of the two men who had grabbed Newton let go of him for a moment and punched Robin in the stomach. Robin doubled over. Friday's head went under the water. She grabbed hold of Sir William's desk and climbed to her feet.

When she wiped the water from her face, she saw Robin throwing his chair at the line of attackers who were trying to intercept the approaching Increment guards, catching two in the back of the head. Then he turned and ran with Friday into the darkness of the boat that had rammed them.

They were sloshing through knee-high water in what looked like a crude staging area, with benches to sit on and leather straps to hold. This was where the attackers must have been waiting in darkness while their boat hurtled toward the *Great Equatorial*. At the far end was a set of rough wooden stairs leading into the light. The men they were chasing were climbing the stairs two at a time. The one with the orb was holding it in the crook of his right arm to prevent it from falling.

The water was slowing them down. Friday jumped onto one of the benches and ran along it, leaping for the stairs just as the man with the orb vanished out of sight. Robin followed her, grabbing her legs and boosting her up the stairs faster than she could have climbed.

Friday emerged onto the sloping deck of the boat like a jack-in-the-box. There was nobody there apart from her, the three retreating attackers, and a shocked-looking Isaac Newton. The men were running down the slope, past the sails that had caught the wind and smashed the boat into the *Great Equatorial*. They were heading toward the boat's stern. For a moment, Friday thought they were going to dive into the water, taking Newton with them, but she realized that there was a small ship tied to the rudder. Its sails were full of wind, ready to carry it away as soon as the men climbed aboard.

Behind her, Robin hauled himself out of the stairwell and onto the deck. He obviously realized immediately what was going on. He had picked up one of the curved knives from the seat of the chair he'd been using as a weapon, and he threw it at the farthest man—the one who had the orb. It caught him in the shoulder, embedding itself deeply into his flesh, but he jumped over the stern of the boat and into the waiting vessel. The attackers who had taken Isaac Newton threw him over the stern of the boat, into the attached ship. Newton hit the deck with a *thud* that Friday could hear even over all the tumult of the fighting that was happening behind them, and slid across the wet timbers to the far side, where more black-clad men caught him and hauled him away. More men appeared at the side of the vessel, slashing through the holding ropes. At the bow of the ship, other men were hauling up its anchor. Like a greyhound released from a trap, the ship began to move away, downriver and toward the sea.

Friday and Robin reached the stern at the same time, but the gap between it and the receding ship was too great to jump across. All they could do was to watch in frustration and anger as it cut its way through the turbulent water, increasing its speed and racing past the other boats and ships on the river.

She suddenly realized that only three of the attackers had gotten onto the escaping ship. The others were still behind them—still leaving the *Great Equatorial*. She whirled around, just in case they were about to be attacked from behind, but the black-clad attackers were diving off the side of the boat, into the waters of the Thames. Obviously their plan of escape was different from that of the men who had the orb—and Newton. It must have been important that they got away quickly.

Friday glanced around desperately, hoping that there was some vessel nearby that they could get to and give chase, but they were all too far away or going in the wrong directions. Their sailors were pointing at the *Great Equatorial* and shouting to one another, trying to work out what was going on.

"There's no point," Robin said as they watched their quarry vanishing into the press of vessels on the Thames, jinking port and starboard to avoid them as it raced away. "Let's go back and see what the damage is."

Friday nodded. "Up or down?" she asked, indicating the upside-down hull of the *Great Equatorial* that loomed like a cliff face above them. The rotted remains of its rudder would provide decent foot- and handholds, but it would take time to get up, and they would have to make their way down the curved hull. No, she had a feeling that they needed to get back and find out what they had lost before too much more time went by.

Together they made their way back down the stairwell, through the staging area and out through the open bow of the boat into the captain's cabin. John Caiaphas and his guards had removed any of the attackers whom they had managed to capture, presumably to some form of captivity. Sir William and Defoe were standing calf-deep in the water. They looked dejected.

"Did you—" Sir William started.

Robin shook his head. "They had an escape ship at the rear of this one," he said, indicating the boat that had rammed them. "They got away with Isaac Newton and the orb. I'm sorry."

"We were outnumbered and surprised," Defoe said bitterly. "And not for the first time."

"I suggest we retire to the galley," Sir William said. "At least there we can dry ourselves off." He turned to Defoe. "Send out word all the way down the river to the estuary—I want to know where the escape ship goes. Oh, and make sure that some suitable story is circulated among the sailors out on the Thames. A boat went out of control when its rudder snapped and managed to crash into the wreck of a once-great warship—something like that."

Defoe nodded and headed for the door.

"Wait!" Robin called.

Defoe stopped and turned around.

"Can you send out some men to the other side of the river?" Robin asked. "Get them to check the banks directly opposite the *Great Equatorial*."

Defoe frowned. "Why so?" he asked.

Robin glanced at Friday, then back to Defoe. "Something occurred to me," he said. "I'll explain later, if they find anything."

Defoe nodded and left. As he did so, Sir William glanced at Friday. "Your warning gave us just enough time to prepare for impact," he said. "You have my thanks."

"But they still got away with the thing they came for," Friday pointed out.

Sir William nodded. "The scrying orb, yes." He shook his head. "A grievous loss."

"And Isaac Newton," she pointed out.

He glanced at her and raised an eyebrow. "Natural philosophers I can replace," he said quietly. "That orb is unique."

"Why?" Robin asked, joining the conversation. "What does it do?"

"I'll tell you," Sir William replied, "but first we need to evacuate this place and find somewhere safer. And I am afraid that the king will require a full briefing. That is not a conversation I relish having."

CHAPTER TEN

―◦◦◦―

Three Years Since the Shipwreck

Sitting on the branch of a tree, Crusoe listened as Red Tiberius's pirate crew searched the jungle for them.

It had been a trap. Just before sunrise, the pirates had gradually surrounded the cave where the two of them had been sleeping, some taking the high ground, some approaching from the forest below. How they had found the cave was a mystery, but it was only when one of the pirates had triggered an alarm that Crusoe and Friday had realized an attack was in progress.

The alarm had been simple: a length of vine stretched across a trail and hidden by grasses, set to pull a peg from a hole in a tree trunk if disturbed. The plug was holding a bent branch, preventing it from springing back into shape. The branch, when released, would fling a bunch of metal tankards and cutlery into the air. They were detritus from the shipwreck that had been retrieved by Crusoe from the beach where they had washed up. Tied together with more vines, they would make a loud metallic clattering when they came back down to earth—a sound that could not be mistaken for anything else on the island.

Friday had shown Crusoe how to set many such traps around their cave. Animals would instinctively avoid them, but humans wouldn't notice them.

The alarm triggered, waking Friday. She shook Crusoe's shoulder until he was aware of what was happening. Within moments, they were out of the cave and scrambling up the side of the hill, Friday had pushed Crusoe toward a particular tree. By the time he had climbed up into the branches, she had vanished into the underbrush, heading for her own place of safety.

Crusoe drew himself in, closer to the tree trunk, so that no part of him could be seen through the leaves. He listened as the pirates—warned by the alarm that their stealthy approach had been spotted—rushed the cave. He heard their curses as they discovered it to be empty, and then the guttural orders given by Red Tiberius's second in command to search the jungle until the two of them were found. He was the ugliest and strongest of the pirates. At some time in the past, he had lost an ear—torn off in a fight, Crusoe assumed—and the side of his head was a landscape of rutted scar tissue. Both of his cheeks had also been branded by a burning iron with an H shape. He was a brute, and Friday was terrified of him. So was Crusoe.

Crusoe listened, trying to use the lessons that Friday had taught him to work out where the pirates were. He shut his eyes and concentrated, gradually filtering out the noises of the birds, the wind in the leaves, and the distant crash of waves on sand. What was left was a series of noises in different directions: six—no, seven—men moving through the bushes in a rough circle around them.

Except that Crusoe wasn't at the center of the circle. The cave was, and he was off to one side. One of the men was closer than the rest. That, he thought, gave him a chance. Gave both of them a chance.

Staying in the trees wasn't an option—the pirates would be peering up into the foliage, looking for them, and if they didn't find Crusoe and Friday on the ground, then they would send the lightest of them up into the branches to see if he could see them. If that didn't work, then they would set fire to the trees to drive them out, ignoring the possibility that they might burn down the entire jungle in their eagerness. Red Tiberius was so desperate to get his daughter back that he would risk anything.

Crusoe was located near the edge of the circle of pirates. Friday would be somewhere close at hand. They both had to act together, otherwise one of them might be left behind or caught, but how could they coordinate their actions? If Crusoe dropped onto one of the pirates and ran, then the rest of them would run in his direction, and Friday would be trapped in the trees. At best they would be separated; at worst she would be caught.

Crusoe had noticed that when they were hunting for food, he and Friday seemed to share a mutual understanding. Each of them knew, without words, what the other would do. Often, when they were sleeping, they would wake up at the same time, each opening their eyes and yawning to find that the other one was doing the same. They even had the same dreams, or so it seemed when they tried to remember them. If that connection held true, if there was that strange link between them, then he and Friday might be able to act at the same moment—each knowing what the other was doing. It was worth a try.

The sound of the nearest pirate pushing through the bushes was getting closer. Crusoe peered through the leaves, pushing them to one side carefully. He wanted to wait until the man was directly beneath him.

Eventually the pirate came into sight. He was muscular, with a shaved head and tattoos on his hands and forearms. He held a sword in his hand—a wickedly curved length of sharp metal—and had an ax strapped across his back. He was using the sword to probe the bushes as he passed. Every so often he would stop and suspiciously stare upward into the foliage.

Crusoe waited, holding his breath, until the pirate was directly underneath him. If he was right, then Friday would know, as soon as he jumped onto the pirate's back, that he was taking action. She would instantly leap down herself, and the two of them could run together.

Crusoe readied himself.

The pirate got closer, and closer . . .

And stopped. Something had attracted his attention. He moved a few feet sideways, poking his sword into a low-hanging mass of leaves and twigs. Nothing was there, and after a painfully long moment, he moved back to the path he had been following.

Crusoe tensed, sliding his body forward so that it was just his bare feet and his hands on the rough branch that was stopping him from falling.

He leaped.

And just as he did, just as it was too late to go back, he saw a second pirate walking through the bushes toward the first. He couldn't take out two of them. The moment he landed on the first pirate, the second one would join the fight and he would be killed—or worse, captured and tortured for stealing Red Tiberius's daughter away.

The thoughts took less than a second to go through his mind as he was falling. The second pirate saw him and turned his head.

The pirate's mouth opened, ready to shout a warning.

And Friday dropped out of the tree above him, landing on his back just as Crusoe landed on top of the big pirate. He saw the flash of her teeth as she grinned at him. The big pirate crumpled to the ground. Crusoe fell sideways and rolled, grabbing for a rock he had identified from his position up in the tree. He grabbed it and threw it just as the big pirate pushed himself up on his two hugely muscled forearms. The rock caught him just above where his ear had been, once upon a time. His head jerked sideways, and he fell unconscious to the ground.

Crusoe glanced sideways. Friday was on the back of the second pirate. Her arm was around his neck, choking him. As Crusoe watched, his eyes rolled back in his head, and he dropped to his knees, then fell face forward as she released him.

"Ready to go?" she challenged, eyes bright.

"How did you know I was—" Crusoe started, but she interrupted.

"I just did," she said.

⌘

OUTSIDE THE *Equatorial*, a fleet of black carts and black arrived from some secret location and was carrying both people and possessions away. One carriage in particular, off to one side, was obviously waiting for Sir William. Daniel Defoe headed away to follow Sir William's instructions to look for where their attackers had made landfall, while Crusoe, Friday, and Sir William climbed into the carriage.

"Where are we going?" Crusoe asked.

The carriage lurched into motion, throwing Sir William back into the cushions. "To see the king," he said.

Crusoe's stomach felt as if the carriage had suddenly driven off the road and was falling into some pit. "Now?" he cried. "We're going to see the king *now*?"

Sir William nodded reluctantly. "He had already summoned me to brief him on our efforts to get the Countess of Lichfield back. I now have the unenviable task of briefing him on how we have lost the . . . the scrying orb and our adviser in natural philosophy as well. This is not something I am looking forward to doing."

"You'll be leaving us in the carriage, won't you?" Crusoe continued. "Or at least leaving us outside the royal palace?"

"No, you two will be coming with me." He grimaced and momentarily covered his eyes with his hand. "The king may be slightly more merciful if there are children present."

Crusoe still felt as if his stomach were significantly closer to his mouth than it had been a few moments earlier. He turned to Friday and whispered, "We're going to meet the king!"

She grinned widely, eyes bright. "I know!" she whispered back. "And I've only been in London for less than two days!"

As the muddy roads of Rotherhithe gave way to the cobbled streets of London, and as half-built wooden shacks gave way to brick houses leaning over the road as if conspiring together, Sir William's gaze moved between Crusoe and Friday.

"Before we get to the Palace I owe you an explanation, Mr. Crusoe and Miss Friday," he said. "There are things I haven't told you yet—not because I wasn't intending to, but because I didn't want to overburden you with too much information too quickly. But we have now been outmaneuvered not once but twice—we have lost the countess, and we have lost both Mr. Newton and the orb."

"What was that orb?" Friday asked. "And why was Isaac Newton so reluctant to use it?" She thought for a moment. "And how exactly does one 'use' an orb, anyway?"

Crusoe said, "Both you and Newton referred to it as a 'scrying orb.' Scrying is a way of trying to see the future, isn't it?"

Sir William nodded. "You have a fine mind, Mr. Crusoe," he said. He closed his eyes and pinched the bridge of his nose. "Very well. I don't believe I told you why Segment W is so called. It was named in honor of Sir Francis Walsingham, who worked for Queen Elizabeth a hundred years ago. He set up the first real official network of royal spies and informers, but he did it out of his own purse. He did, however, go further than that. Although he was a devoutly religious man, Sir Francis came to believe that it might be possible to see events at a distance, without having agents actually witness them. He also came to believe that it might be possible to see events that had *yet to happen*."

"Witchcraft?" Crusoe was strangely shocked. "But he was a religious man, you said. How could he reconcile doing that with a belief in God?"

Sir William smiled. "A very perceptive question. There was a man at the court at the time—a man named Dr. John Dee. The queen used him to provide her with astrological predictions— horoscopes, drawn from the movements and positions of the stars. It was . . . acceptable . . . to the clergy partly because the queen herself endorsed it, and partly . . ." He paused, glancing out the window at the passing buildings. "Partly because Dr. Dee himself claimed that he consulted with angels who visited him from heaven and not only told him what was happening elsewhere in God's realm but also allowed him to see what events were to come. The idea of angels interceding between God and man was acceptable. Sir Francis came to an arrangement with Dr. Dee—he would provide Dr. Dee with money if the good doctor would, on occasion, ask the angels questions that Sir Francis would provide, questions that touched on matters of state. In that way he believed—or at least he claimed to believe—that he was gaining insight into the actions and intentions of the queen's enemies."

"But that doesn't explain the orb," Friday pointed out.

"I am coming to that. After a while, Dr. Dee claimed that one particular angel had given him a gift that would allow *him* to see distant events and events to come, rather than asking the angels about them. It was a black sphere, like some huge opal, inside which lights could sometimes be seen glowing."

"The scrying orb," Friday said.

"The very same."

"I'm guessing that only Dr. Dee could use the sphere," Crusoe said. "That way he could keep control, and keep getting paid."

"That's correct. He said that using the sphere took great concentration, and interpreting the results took experience. He kept the orb to himself. Well, to himself and to his assistant, a man named Kelly. Sir Francis tried hard to get Dee to part with the orb, but he would not let it out of his control. He said that God himself had given it to him, through his angels, and that it would be a sin to allow anyone else to use it." He paused. "Dr. Dee became a rich man—or at least he could have done, had he and his man Kelly not gambled it all away."

"And the orb—it came into your hands?"

Sir William nodded. "It was lost for many years, but my agents located it eventually. When Dee died, his man Kelly took the orb and tried to sell it, but without Dee to work it, nobody was interested. Kelly died eventually, and the orb vanished from sight. We tracked it down, hidden in a secret cupboard in the house where he spent his last days. Isaac Newton has been trying to determine how it can be used. Newton is the most intelligent man I know— probably the most intelligent man in England at the present moment. If he cannot work it out, then I suspect nobody can."

"Was it really given to Dr. Dee by angels?" Friday asked, wide-eyed.

"I think it is fair to say that nobody knows where he got it from, so the angel explanation is as likely as anything else."

The carriage jerked as the wheels bumped over a pothole in the road.

Crusoe remembered the way Newton had acted back in Gresham College and in the *Great Equatorial*. "He doesn't like it, though, does he?"

"Very perspicacious of you." Sir William rubbed a hand over his face tiredly. "No, the orb worries him. He says that he sees things in it."

"I thought he was supposed to," Friday pointed out.

"Yes—he's supposed to see things that we want him to see. Things that we need him to see. The problem is that he says he sees . . . other things. Horrible things. Demons. Human bodies being tortured in terrible ways. Visions of hell. He is very reluctant to spend time in the same room with it, let alone look into it."

"And you believe him?" Crusoe exchanged glances with Friday.

"It doesn't matter whether I believe him or not. If he doesn't want to look into the orb, then I won't force him." He grimaced. "At least, I wouldn't have done, until—"

Friday finished the sentence for him. "Until the king instructed you to use all means necessary to rescue his illegitimate daughter, the Countess of Lichfield, from the clutches of her kidnappers."

There was silence for a few moments, then Sir William said quietly, "Oh, of course! That's what they *wanted*, isn't it? That's what they really wanted. Not the countess, but the orb!"

Crusoe looked from Friday to Sir William and back again. "You mean the attacks on the countess were just a ruse to force you to get the orb from . . . from wherever it was kept?"

Sir William nodded. "I wouldn't let Newton keep the orb in Gresham College while he was examining it. You've seen the state of his rooms? He has little conception of neatness, or organization. He would have ended up using it as a paperweight, or a doorstop or something."

Crusoe nodded. "You've got a point."

"We kept the orb in safety, in a locked cabinet in the middle of the *Great Equatorial*, guarded by John Caiaphas's men. It was safer than the crown jewels! And then the king sent a message telling us that we had to use any means necessary to find the countess, so we unlocked the cabinet, dismissed the guards, and carried the orb to my cabin so that Newton, reluctantly, could gaze into it in an attempt to descry the countess's current location. That was our mistake. That was my mistake, and I shall explain as much to the king." His face was pale, and Crusoe could see a thin beading of sweat on his forehead. "And I will suffer the consequences of his anger."

A thought surfaced in Crusoe's mind. "Why would these men in black want the orb? What is it to them?"

"And how did they know that you had removed the orb from its cabinet, whoever they are?" Friday asked.

He frowned. "I have no idea. That is, however, a very pertinent question."

"Do you suppose that they have an agent on board the *Great Equatorial* who signaled them that the orb was vulnerable?" Friday pressed.

Sir William's face darkened. "I will ask John Caiaphas to investigate that question, and most urgently."

"It would be unlikely," Crusoe said, thinking. He glanced at Friday, and she nodded, following his chain of thoughts. Sir William gazed questioningly between the two of them, and Crusoe continued, "If they had one or more agents on board, then those agents would have already tried to steal the orb from its cabinet or would have taken it by force the moment the cabinet was unlocked."

Sir William nodded gratefully. "An excellent point, most skillfully made, young sir."

The carriage kept moving, passing grander and grander buildings interspersed with fields of green. For a few minutes it drove past the same building: one constructed of white stone and lined with arches, colonnades, and towers.

"Whitehall Palace," Sir William commented.

Eventually the carriage stopped outside a larger arch. Soldiers in breastplates and armor with long pikes were standing on either side.

A man dressed in colorful clothes and sporting a velvet cap with a feather in it emerged from the darkness of the arch. He approached the carriage. When he saw Sir William through the window, he swept the hat off and bowed low over it, then gestured to the guards to let the carriage through.

"You're recognized," Crusoe observed.

"That's normally a good thing," Sir William said with a touch of nervousness in his voice. "Today I am not so sure."

The carriage's wheels clattered on the stone cobbles of a court-yard and came to a stop. The door was opened. Several footmen were waiting outside for them. They led Sir William, Crusoe, and Friday at speed through stone corridors lined with colorful tapestries, up steps, down steps, and around corners until they were disoriented and dizzy. That, Crusoe thought, may have been the point. He was amazed at the fact that his and Friday's identities seemed to have been taken on trust, just because they were with Sir William. The man in charge of Segment W appeared to have a great deal of power at the court, or at least a great reputation.

Crusoe was amazed as they walked along the edge of open areas in which he could see bowling greens, a pit for cock fighting, and a tiltyard for jousting. They also walked along a balcony looking down on an indoor court where several people were playing a game that involved hitting a hard ball with a bat back and forth, letting it rebound from the walls.

Eventually they entered a hall that was filled with a large number of people dressed in velvets and silks, doublets, stockings, and breeches. They were standing together in groups of three or four and apparently exchanging gossip. The hubbub echoed from the vaulted ceiling and filled the room. It was like a much richer version of the marketplaces Crusoe dimly remembered from his childhood. He was aware that everyone in the hall was watching them as they crossed from one side to the other, some obviously, and some from behind their hands or their handkerchiefs. A ripple of murmurs developed behind them like a trail. Interestingly, it wasn't Friday's skin color that was exciting their interest, although they had certainly noticed it. No, it was more a question of who they were, why they were there, and what influence they might have on the king. Crusoe suspected that everyone in the hall was constantly feeling threatened, and needed to reevaluate their position in the court every time someone new appeared.

From that hall they exited into a short corridor that led to another hall, smaller but with more expensive furnishings and tapestries. There were several people present, but rather than standing in small groups and talking, they seemed to be whispering to one another with half their attention fixed on the far end of the room, where a throne sat on a raised dais. And on the throne, the king.

He was wearing largely white—doublet, hose, and shoes—but the voluminous robes that fell like a waterfall of ice from his shoulders down to his feet and spilled onto the cushion upon which his feet rested, and then onto the carpet of the dais, were scarlet, edged with white. His arms emerged from gaps in the robes, and his hands were clenched on the carved wooden arms of the throne. He had thin lines of a mustache on his upper lip. A black wig on his head cascaded onto his shoulders and farther in the same way that his robes cascaded to the dais. On top of his wig was a crown made of gold and embedded with what looked to Crusoe like real pearls, rubies, sapphires, and diamonds. Any part of the crown that wasn't set with jewels was decorated with fleurs-de-lis and crosses. Crusoe couldn't help but wonder how heavy it was, and how long the king could bear to have it on his head.

There was a path through the people in the throne room to the dais. Sir William strode toward the throne, stopped, and made a sweeping bow with one leg placed before the other. Crusoe glanced at Friday and replicated the bow. Friday, whose boy-like leggings and jacket were already attracting some disapproving stares from the people of the court, did the same a few seconds later. Maybe the king's eyesight was bad, Crusoe thought. Maybe he would let Friday get away with a bow rather than a curtsy. He wasn't sure she even knew how to curtsy. He was pretty sure that she wouldn't want to.

"Sir William, we are most pleased to see you," the king said in a deep voice that cut through the subdued murmuring in the throne room.

"Your Majesty," Sir William responded, straightening up. "I have traveled posthaste to inform you of recent events which" —he glanced around the throne room— "are such as are not fit for the ears of any other than Your Majesty alone, being affairs of state and of great secrecy."

The king glanced behind Sir William, to where Crusoe and Friday were rising from their own bows. "And do you speak for the trustworthiness of your friends, Sir William?"

"I do, Your Majesty."

The king slowly glanced left and right. Crusoe supposed that it was difficult for him to do it any quicker with the weight of that crown and wig on his head. He raised his right hand. "We would have our court cleared," he commanded, "with the exception of our primary advisers."

Most of the people in the throne room turned and headed for the corridor that led to the larger hall. The king gestured to two footmen who came forward and reached up to take the crown from his head, placing it on a padded stool beside the throne. As the last person left the room, footmen closed the doors. Two more footmen then approached the king and carefully lifted the wig from his head. They carried it away through curtains behind the throne. Beneath it, his own hair—gray and short, with a prominent bald spot on top—was matted and unruly.

"We thank God for this relief," he said in a heartfelt tone. He closed his eyes briefly. "It is like sitting here with a large dog on our head—just as heavy, just as hot, and just as ridden with fleas."

Crusoe glanced at the king's remaining advisers. They seemed scandalized that the king had removed his wig in front of mere commoners. One of them bent to whisper in the king's ear, but he waved the man away.

"Sir William has known us for many years," he said, his rich voice filling the throne room. "He hid us when we were on the run from Oliver Cromwell and his New Model Army. Sir William has seen us in a worse condition than just being bereft of our wig. Besides, he is the custodian of many royal secrets in his present post, and we trust his discretion as we trust the discretion of those he chooses to employ." He waved to the three of them—Sir William, Crusoe, and Friday—to approach. "Your colleagues, Sir William—introduce them to us, if you please."

Sir William turned and gestured toward Crusoe and Friday. "May I present, Your Majesty, Mr. Robinson Crusoe and Miss Friday, both but recently arrived on these shores after several years cast ashore on a deserted island in the tropics, from which they were rescued by Your Majesty's own Royal Navy."

"Good to know the Royal Navy does something for the exorbitant amount it costs our royal purse," the king said. He glanced between Crusoe and Friday—spending considerably longer on Friday than he did Crusoe, Crusoe noticed with a flash of annoyance that he quickly tried to suppress. This was the king, after all. "Welcome, both of you, to our court. If Sir William trusts you, then we trust you as we do him." He turned to Sir William and raised an eyebrow. "Although recent matters that have been reported to us do force us to question the amount to which we *do* trust you."

Sir William hung his head. "I am ashamed to say, Your Majesty, that I have lost not only the Countess of Lichfield to forces unknown, but also the black orb that was passed down to us from the possession of Dr. John Dee."

"This would be the same black orb that we urged you to use to locate the Countess of Lichfield, whom we do love as though she were our own progeny, would it not?"

Crusoe glanced at Friday and looked quickly away. Based on the conversation they had overheard in the coffeehouse the day before, it was common knowledge that the Countess of Lichfield *was* the king's own progeny, albeit illegitimate.

"The very same, Your Majesty."

The king nodded. He seemed unconcerned, but Crusoe suspected he had spent many years cultivating that particular attitude.

"We will grant you another audience in two days," the king said. "At that time, you will tell us that you have recovered both the countess and the scrying orb. If you do not tell us that, then we shall be seeking a new head of Segment W, and you will be seeking a new head, having lost your current one to our own executioner as punishment for your monumental failure. Are we clear, Sir William?"

"Your Majesty, your words are as clear as the finest crystal." Sir William bowed low again and began to back away from the throne. Crusoe and Friday bowed and started to back away with him. Crusoe could see a bead of sweat fall from Sir William's brow to the marble tiles. "I shall return in two days with good news."

"We do not doubt it," the king said. He was already gesturing to his advisers to come closer. "Just make sure you *do* return. It would be tiresome to have to send people to fetch you from wherever you had hidden yourself." He smiled a kindly, regal smile. "We still remember from our time in exile how good you were at finding places to hide."

CHAPTER ELEVEN

O utside the palace, with their carriage trundling along past great houses and vast open spaces, the three of them were silent. Crusoe glanced from Friday to Sir William and back. He was still slightly stunned by the speed with which he had been catapulted to the highest echelons of society, but Sir William was caught somewhere between relief and panic.

Crusoe could tell, without her saying anything, that Friday wasn't particularly impressed. She had often told him, while they were on the island, about some of the potentates and island rulers that her father, Red Tiberius, had dealt with over the years. She had probably decided that the only difference between them and the king of England was that the king of England had a larger territory to rule. Judging by what she'd told him previously, the king of England certainly wasn't any more ornately dressed than some of the people she had seen her father meeting with over the years.

"Where are we going?" Friday asked, obviously wanting to break the silence.

"We have a mustering point on the other side of the river," Sir William said, snapping out of his reverie. "We will meet with John Caiaphas there and decide what to do next."

The carriage turned sharply. Gazing out the window, Crusoe could see that it was now passing across the very bridge that he and Friday had passed *beneath* the day before: the one lined with shops and houses. It seemed so long ago now. The river was actually visible in the gaps between the houses: like rolling brown fields that somehow glistened in the sunlight. So much had happened in the intervening time, and he felt a sudden pang of nostalgia for the simpler times on the *Stars' End*, and on the island.

At the other side of the bridge, they turned again, right this time, and continued along the side of the river.

"Southwark," Sir William said, nodding toward the part of the city that was passing by outside the window. "Not the safest place in the king's realm. Take my advice and do not venture here at night."

After a few minutes, the carriage stopped. At Sir William's nod, Crusoe opened the door and got out. Friday and Sir William joined him.

They were outside a round wooden building. It was three stories high, with a pitched roof, and must have covered an area of ground about the same distance from side to side as the *Great Equatorial* had been long. Two of John Caiaphas's Increment were standing by a large, square entrance. They glanced at Sir William as he approached. Friday saw him raise his hand and flash his enameled ring at them. They both nodded and turned their hands so that their own rings were visible to him.

"We'll have to get ourselves some of those," Friday murmured to him.

The three of them walked through a short tunnel into an open space surrounded by circular balconies. Groups of people were busy collating stacks of boxes that Crusoe couldn't help but notice were damp—rescued from the *Great Equatorial*, he assumed. Daniel Defoe was at the center of one of the groups, dispensing advice and orders liberally.

Directly ahead of them was a wooden stage.

"A theater?" Crusoe asked.

"It's called the Globe," Sir William answered. "Originally built by the Lord Chamberlain's Men, who were a group of actors who performed in London. One of them, William Shakespeare by name, attained some reputation as a writer of entertainments. Oliver Cromwell's Puritans ordered it to be pulled down, but it was saved when the monarchy was reestablished and King Charles II was crowned. It has more recently fallen into disuse. Official records show that it has been torn down and replaced by tenement housing, but in fact its use has been transferred to us. John Caiaphas uses it for training his men."

Caiaphas himself was standing near the stage. Having seen them, he crossed the intervening space. "Sir William—glad to see you are . . . still with us." He glanced at Friday. "Good work back there on the *Great Equatorial*. Things might have been a lot worse if you hadn't given a warning."

Friday nodded, embarrassed, but Caiaphas had transferred his gaze to Crusoe. "And you—Defoe told me that you asked him to have us check the riverbank opposite the *Great Equatorial*. What did you hope we would find?"

Crusoe glanced at Sir William and directed his answer to both of them. "Someone had to have known that the scrying orb had been taken out of safe storage, and alerted the attackers. We'd already eliminated the possibility of a traitor among your men"— he nodded at Caiaiphas—"on the basis that they would just have grabbed the orb and run with it. The window in Sir William's office was facing out over the Thames. Someone on the other side of the river could have been watching with a device like a telescope, such as some captains use at sea."

Caiaphas nodded. "You were correct. We found a man still there. He had constructed a hiding place in the riverbank, and yes, he did have a telescope. I have kept it for Newton to examine—when we get him back. The man I have tied up in a room behind the stage."

"Does the man know where the attackers have taken Newton and the orb?" Sir William asked urgently.

Caiaphas shook his head. "If he does, then he is not talking."

"Have you pressed him on the matter?" Sir William asked.

"He has been beaten, but he still says nothing." Caiaphas looked around. "We could press him further, but we have little here to use as tools. We could, I suppose, improvise with knives and suchlike, but I suspect that he is more worried about what his friends might do to him if he talks than what we will do to him if he doesn't."

"Let me talk to him," Friday said suddenly.

Caiaphas stared at her. "You? A girl?"

"Let her try," Crusoe said. Caiaphas and Sir William turned to look at him, and he went on, "Her father is a pirate captain—Red Tiberius, one of the most feared on the high seas. Do you think he got that reputation by accident? I know that Friday has seen things her father has done that she won't even tell me about. Let her try."

Friday gazed up at Crusoe. Her expression was a strangely uneasy mixture of guilt and gratitude.

John Caiaphas glanced at Sir William, seeking permission. Sir William nodded. "Give her a chance," he said. Looking at Friday, he said, "Do you need anything? A knife, perhaps?"

She frowned, thinking. "This is a place where entertainments are performed, isn't it? Actually, I'm not going to threaten him—I'm going to get him to trust me. I'm going to need some makeup, but it has to be blue."

"Blue?" Sir William questioned.

Instead of answering him, Friday turned and looked at Crusoe. "Did you notice some strange blue patterns on the skin of the attackers in the countess's house?" she asked. "And then again on the *Great Equatorial?* When their clothes were ripped?"

He nodded, remembering. "Like a rash, or a strange tattoo. I thought it was odd at the time."

"I think they might be some kind of identification. If all of them have it somewhere on their bodies, then it might be a way that they can tell who is a friend and who isn't."

Caiaphas interrupted, "When we searched the prisoner, we found that he had a strange marking, just as you describe, on the inside of his arm, near the wrist."

Sir William gestured to Caiaphas. "Take Miss Friday and Mr. Crusoe to the dressing rooms. She will find what she needs there, I believe."

Caiaphas led the two of them through a maze of corridors at the rear of the stage to the room where the actors obviously prepared themselves for their roles. There was a long table set against a wall with a mirror on it. The table was scattered with pots of makeup and brushes.

Friday rummaged through the various pots until she found a small one containing a vivid blue powder. Crusoe was no expert, but he assumed that it was used to highlight the eyes of the boy actors, making them look more like women when they were onstage.

"Do you think you can re-create that pattern on my arm?"

"I can try," he said honestly. "I used to paint in watercolors when I was on the *Rigel*, before I was wrecked on the island. Seascapes, mostly."

Caiaphas nodded. "You're going to trick him into thinking you're on his side. Clever."

Using some volatile spirits from a stoppered jar on the table, Crusoe quickly mixed up a thin paste with the blue powder. Using a small brush, he tested it on the back of his hand. The spirit and the powder combined stained his skin blue where he dabbed it. He blew on the stain to dry it, then showed it to Friday. "The spirit should wash it off again," he said. "If not, it'll fade with time."

Caiaphas, who had been watching the process, interrupted. "Her skin is a deal darker than yours," he pointed out. "Will the blue color show up properly? It might be best if *she* paints the colors on *you*."

Friday shook her head before Crusoe could agree. "I know I can pretend to be something I'm not. I spent a long time on my father's ship doing just that. Robin is too honest, too open. He can't pretend like I can."

Crusoe was going to put the coloring on Friday's arm, but she shook her head. "Too obvious," she said. "This needs to be hidden somewhere." She reached up and pulled the collar of her blouse away from her neck. "Do it here."

Crusoe glanced at Caiaphas. "A little privacy for the lady, please," he said quietly.

Caiaphas nodded curtly and withdrew.

With Friday sitting down and holding the material away from her skin, Crusoe used the brush to create a series of blue blotches, linked by thin lines, on the skin of his friend's shoulder. He was very aware as he worked of the closeness of her body, and the heat of her skin. Once or twice, as he bent over her, he realized that she was staring at him from just a few inches away. He felt . . . awkward. His hand trembled slightly as he worked. He didn't dare returned her gaze—not with his face so close to hers. He wasn't sure what might happen.

When he had finished, he blew on her neck and shoulder to dry the staining. Friday gasped.

"Sorry," he muttered.

"Just . . . surprised," she murmured.

He stood back, feeling a strange mixture of relief and regret. "That should pass muster, at least for a while," he said.

Friday gazed at him for a long moment. "You have a very delicate touch with a brush," she said softly.

"You should see my watercolors," he replied.

Friday stood up, adjusting her collar so that the staining was hidden. "Let's see if this works," she said.

John Caiaphas led them through more rabbit-warren corridors until they reached a door that was guarded by two of his men. Nodding to them, he gestured Friday forward. She took a deep breath, checked her collar again, then glanced at Crusoe.

"Wish me luck," she said.

"I'll be just out here," he replied. "If anything goes wrong—if he realizes he's being tricked and tries to do anything to you—I'll be in before he can do any harm."

She nodded. "I know."

She pushed the door open, stepped inside the darkened room, and closed the door again. Crusoe and Caiaphas pressed their ears against the wood. Crusoe kept his hand on the doorknob, ready to burst in if he was needed.

"Nobody can hear us," Friday said from inside the room. "I'm a friend."

There was a noise as if the captive was shifting position, but he said nothing.

"I said I'm a friend," Friday repeated, more insistently. "If you don't believe me, look at this."

Crusoe imagined Friday tugging carefully at her collar, revealing the blue pattern on her skin. He thought he heard an intake of breath from the captive.

"You're working on the inside?" the captive asked. His tone was suspicious. Crusoe expected him to speak roughly, but his voice was strangely cultured, as if he was a gentleman. "Why did we have to go through with the attack, then, if you could just *take* the thing?"

"Before I answer your question, or help you in any way, you must identify yourself to me," Friday said.

There was silence for a few seconds. Crusoe imagined the man pushing his sleeve up to show his own marking.

"The object was too heavily guarded," Friday replied levelly, "and I wasn't supposed to give myself away."

"You're here to kill me, aren't you?" He sounded resigned, rather than scared, as if he had been expecting something like this. "To stop me from talking. You don't have to do that. I won't talk, no matter what they do to me, I swear it!"

Friday said nothing, letting the man's panic grow.

"But I suppose whatever I swear or do not swear is not important," he went on, his voice strained. "I'm a loose end, and I need to be removed."

"Actually," Friday corrected him, "I need you alive for another task. I think that Segment W knows where the orb has been taken. They're organizing an attack now. I need to get you out of here so you can warn them. Can you do that?"

"Why isn't she asking him where they've taken the orb?" Caiaphas whispered, so low that Crusoe could hardly hear him.

"Because if she's with the attackers, then she should already know," Crusoe whispered back.

"Of course I can," the prisoner said. He sounded relieved, and Crusoe knew that Friday was relying on that feeling of reprieve from death to make the man careless. "What do you want me to tell them?"

"Tell them that they need to move the orb to one of the *other* bases of operations as quickly as possible."

"What other bases of operations?" the captive asked. He sounded surprised that there were bases he didn't know about. Crusoe mentally applauded Friday's ingenuity.

"There are many others," Friday said. She had put a suspicious tone in her voice. "If you don't know where they are, then I'm not allowed to tell you. I thought you were more . . . important . . . than that." She paused momentarily. "Which base did you come from?" she asked, even more suspiciously.

"The fort, on the Isle of Thanet," the captive said. "That's where they've taken the orb, isn't it?"

"Of course it is, but that's where the Segment are planning to attack. The orb needs to be moved."

There was silence for a moment. Crusoe imagined the man staring up at Friday, trying to work out if he could trust her or not. The thought of Friday so close to a ruffian like that, no matter how well-spoken he was and how well he was chained up, made Crusoe's flesh crawl. He wanted to burst in there and pull her away despite the consequences. These people were clever, and she was in danger when she was in there without him.

"You know that the orbs cannot be held together in the same place?" the man said dubiously. "They interfere with each other, and if they interfere with each other, then the plan cannot be completed—or so they say. I don't know for sure, I just hear things that they say. I don't even know what the plan *is*." He sounded like he was desperately trying to convince Friday that he hadn't overheard too much.

The plan? Crusoe thought. What plan? What did these people— the Circle of Thirteen, if indeed it was them, although John Caiaphas thought otherwise—want the orbs *for*?

"Of course," Friday said dismissively. "It will have to be taken to a base of operations that hasn't currently got an orb. Tell them that."

"His Lordship will not be happy about moving himself and his men." It sounded like the man was scared to convey such a message. Scared for his life.

"That can't be helped. Besides, he will be grateful to you for telling him about the planned attack." She was more reassuring now. "You lie here quietly. Don't tell them anything. I'll come back later, when it's quiet, and get you out of here."

"Bless you," the captive said, and Crusoe almost felt sorry for him. Almost.

Friday slipped out of the room and closed the door behind her. She glanced at Caiaphas and raised an eyebrow. "Did you get all that?" she whispered.

"I did. Very clever of you."

The three of them headed back to the central area of the theater. When Sir William saw them, he waved a hand at Daniel Defoe, who was working with a group of people on the other side of the open space but had been keeping an eye on what was going on. He quickly crossed to where the four of them stood.

"What did you find out?" Sir William asked.

Caiaphas quickly briefed him and Defoe on what the prisoner had said—that the orb had indeed been the focus of the raid, that this mysterious organization of traitors and criminals had more than one base of operations, that there were more orbs and that the orbs were part of a plan, although the prisoner didn't seem to know what the plan was.

"They took the orb and Newton to Thanet," Caiaphas finished.

Defoe thought for a moment. "Perhaps seventy miles," he said. "Separated from the mainland by the Wantsum Channel. That is all I know of it."

"We need to mount a mission, and quickly." Caiaphas's face was grim and dark. "As many people as we can muster. There is a fort on the island. We need to attack it with as much haste as possible. The problem is that many of my best men are scattered. The attack on the *Great Equatorial* caused a deal of confusion. I have but one boat ready to go, from a dock nearby, but it will take me several hours to get the other boats here and crew them with enough men."

Crusoe gazed at Friday. She gazed back at him. Although their expressions didn't change, they each knew exactly what the other was thinking.

"Let us have the boat," he said. "We can get there quickly, and at least scout the location out. Maybe we can get inside and identify where the countess and Isaac Newton are being kept."

Caiaphas looked to Sir William for guidance. Sir William immediately nodded.

"I could come with you," Defoe said quietly.

Friday shook her head. "Robin and I work best together, and alone."

"Isn't that why you suggested to me that they join Segment W?" Sir William said to Defoe. Defoe himself looked disappointed, but also relieved.

"Come with me," Caiaphas said, and strode toward the exit from the theater. As he walked, he gestured to one of his men to come across to him. They talked briefly, and then the man ran off.

Crusoe looked at Friday. She nodded, and they followed Caiaphas.

CAIAPHAS LED THEM across a muddy stretch of grass toward the nearby riverbank. He looked up at the gloomy sky. "We have perhaps two hours of sunlight left," he estimated, "and there is an easterly wind that will take you in the right direction. The tide will be in your favor as well. It will take you most of those two hours to get to the Isle of Thanet from here, heading down the Thames. One of my men is fetching a map from the documents that were retrieved from the *Great Equatorial*. I will mark on it where you will be going, and any landmarks you need to look for on the way."

At the riverbank, Caiaphas stopped. Across the river, Friday could see the irregular outlines of London's north bank through a haze of smoke. Boats plied the river, some going up and down, some going across from bank to bank. These weren't big ships like the *Stars' End* or the *Great Equatorial*—those stayed farther down river, at the docks—but smaller river craft that could head up toward Maidenhead and Oxford.

Bobbing on the brown waters of the Thames, tied to a wooden pier, was a small boat with a single sail and a rudder. It was just large enough for the two of them. Robin glanced across at Friday, who was appraising the boat with a knowledgeable eye. "Can you—"

She nodded. "I've used similar before. I'll handle the sail; you take the rudder."

A man came running across from the massive bulk of the Globe Theater, behind them. It was the man Caiaphas had spoken to on the way out. He was clutching a rolled sheet of parchment. Caiaphas took it and unrolled it as the man ran back again.

"Here," he said to Friday, pointing at the map. "This is where we are." He shifted his finger to the right. "This is the Isle of Thanet. The fort will be on the other side, here, facing the direction from which any French or Danish invasion might come. The main things to look for on your way will be—"

"I remember the landscape from the journey upriver," Friday said. "I think I remember seeing the Isle of Thanet as well."

Caiaphas nodded as he handed the parchment across to her. "Good luck to you. The Increment will follow on as quickly as we can. If you can do anything, then scout out the island and the fort for us. Look for points of entry and for sentries. If you can get inside the fort, then do, but make sure you have a way out. See if you can signal us from the ramparts, or from the riverbank."

Friday nodded. "We understand," she said.

"Then good-bye, and good fortune attend you." He stepped back and saluted, unself-consciously. Friday glanced sideways to where Robin was standing. She could tell he was resisting the urge to salute back. It wouldn't look as impressive as Caiaphas's version.

Friday scrambled down the bank of the river and ran lightly along the pier to the boat. She climbed into it and started checking the ropes on the sails. Robin joined her and moved to the stern. After a few moments, Friday nodded to him and untied the rope holding the boat fast against the pier. The boat began to drift into the middle of the river, carried eastward by the tide. Friday unfurled the sail, a disreputable and patched sheet of faded red canvas. It quickly bellied out, filled with the wind, and their speed increased. Robin, for his part, sat in the stern, holding the tiller and ensuring that they kept a straight course. The surface of the Thames was a foot or so away, and he let his fingers trail in it as they moved. The water was cold, and it smelled.

Their small boat might have been old and badly looked after, but it was fast. Within ten minutes they had left the last of London's bridges behind them and were passing the larger cargo vessels that had made their way upriver. Within another ten minutes, she could see the bulk of the *Great Equatorial* on her left. From outside it looked like any number of beached wrecks along the banks of the river. A sheet had been hung over the smashed window, disguising it. Friday found herself wondering whether the ship would ever be made habitable again, or whether Segment W would have to find itself a new home.

The sun dropped steadily behind them, turning the sky red and casting the shadow of their boat and its sail farther and farther ahead of them. They passed many craft that were tying up for the night wherever they had happened to find themselves. Sometimes the banks of the river were high on either side of them, higher because of the reeds that grew in profusion on top, and sometimes Friday could see across miles of flat, marshy ground that was distinguishable from the river only because thin grass and the occasional bush was growing out of the water. Whenever the banks appeared, however, they were farther apart than they had been the last time Friday had seen them. She and Robin were getting closer to the Thames Estuary, and to the sea.

"When was the last time we ate?" Robin called to Friday. His hair was streaming out behind him, blown by the fresh and salty breeze.

"Just before the attack on the *Great Equatorial*," she called back over her shoulder. "Why—do you want to stop for dinner?"

"No, but I'm beginning to wish we'd brought a loaf of bread and some cheese with us."

She glanced into the water as it flowed past them. "I could try to grab a fish."

"Don't worry, I'll survive. Maybe we could raid the kitchens in this fort before we look for the countess, Newton, and this orb."

She smiled. "Yes—maybe we could take a nap in their bedrooms as well."

The banks were so far apart by now that they were almost out of sight in the gathering darkness and the haze of wood smoke. Friday assumed they were getting close to the Isle of Thanet. The lights of fires twinkled orange and red on either side of them.

A few minutes later, she glanced over her shoulder at Robin. "Can you steer to port?"

He looked around. "There isn't a port."

"I mean"—she pointed left—"over there!"

"Oh." He hauled on the tiller, and the boat responded, carving a curved path through the water. They passed a small dock area with a series of piers projecting out into the water and several boats tied up. A group of men were standing on the bank, watching as their boat went past.

For a few minutes she wondered if she had made a mistake—they seemed to be heading directly for the dark bulk of the riverbank—but then she spotted what she had glimpsed before—a gap in the bank, a channel that separated what had to be an island on their left from the south bank of the river on their right. The dock area she had seen had been on the island.

Robin steered directly into the channel. The reed-covered banks rose up on either side, higher than the mast of the boat. This cut down the amount of breeze getting to the sails, and their speed dropped. That was a good thing—with the channel narrowing around them, there was a much greater chance that they might run aground. Friday kept a tight hold on the ropes, tacking when necessary to keep them on a straight and true course.

This, Friday assumed, must be the Wantsum Channel.

Ahead of them, the channel opened out into the width of the Thames Estuary. Somewhere in that direction was the North Sea. The bulk of the island curved away to their left, and the waves that buffeted the boat were higher now, driven by the increasing wind and the weather out in the open ocean.

Friday indicated left, and Robin steered the boat in that direction. They were curving around the far side of the island now. Chalk cliffs rose up from a shingle beach, gray rather than white in the encroaching gloom, and atop them Friday could see a dark stone fort glowering down upon the approach to the river. The top of the fort was crenellated, like big square teeth, and there were towers at each corner. Slits of light marked the position of windows.

There was no mistaking it—this was their objective.

Friday thought back to the dock area she'd seen a few minutes before—the one with the boats tied up and the hard-faced men watching as they sailed past. Those boats must have been the ones that attacked the *Great Equatorial*, and the men must have been the ones who invaded, who took Newton and the orb, and who before that had fought with Robin, Friday, and Defoe in the

Countess of Lichfield's mansion. There must be a path—or several paths—up the slope of the island to the fort.

"It would be easier to go all the way around the island and find a landing spot where we can get up to the fort!" Robin shouted.

Friday looked back. She shook her head. "We go up the cliff!" she shouted back. "They won't be expecting us from that direction."

"There's a reason for that—it's impossible!"

"No—just challenging!"

Reluctantly, Robin brought the boat around and headed for the shingle beach. As they approached, Friday furled the sail. Momentum carried them on until the bow of the boat hit the shingle and it came to a halt with a long *chisss* of stones knocking against stones.

Friday jumped out of the boat. There was nothing to secure a line to—they would have to take the risk that the boat would be there when they came back. If they came back.

She gazed up the gray chalk cliff face. The sun was setting on the other side of the island, so the cliff was in shadow. There were darker patches there, but it was difficult to tell whether they were holes that could be used as handholds and footholds or just discolorations.

It didn't matter. They had to do it. She headed straight for the foot of the cliff and started to climb.

Behind her, Robin sighed and followed.

The chalk was slightly crumbly beneath her fingers, but strangely that made things easier. The dust gave her traction, stopping her fingers from slipping. The chalk face was also rougher, rougher than an equivalent rock face would have been, meaning that her feet and hands could easily find places that would take her weight. Robin was above her, and off to her right. He was taking a different path than her. It was something they had learned on the island,

searching for gulls' eggs on the cliff faces to the west—don't follow
the same course, because if you do and one of you gets into trouble,
then the other one isn't in a position to help.

The wind was whipping in from the sea. Its questing fingers
kept trying to insert themselves between Friday and the cliff face,
pulling her away. In response, she pulled herself closer to the chalk,
feeling its grit against her cheek.

Small stones pattered on her shoulders. Maybe someone was up
on the top of the cliff, keeping watch, or maybe the wind had dis-
lodged some pebbles from the chalk. Friday paused in her climb,
head pulled back, gazing upward for a long moment. Eventually she
started climbing again, and Robin did the same.

She didn't look down. There was never any point in doing that.
You were either surprised and disappointed at how close the ground
still was, or you suddenly realized how high you were, and froze.

The line of hand- and footholds that Friday was following
was diverging from the line that Robin was taking. Her path was
easier, and rather than being above her and slightly to the right,
Robin was now almost parallel to her. She glanced over at him and
smiled. He smiled back. She knew that he, too, was remembering
the gulls' eggs and the island cliffs.

Her fingers and toes had found holds that were more secure than
previously, and she took the opportunity to lean back and look up
the cliff face to see how far they had to go. They were about two-
thirds of the way up; she could see the continuation of the cliff
face, a fringe of grass, and then the dark bulk of the fort rising up
above them. The sun had gone down now, and stars were beginning to emerge in the night sky behind thin wisps of cloud.

Friday reached up for the hundredth, or perhaps the thousandth
time, seeking a hole in the chalk that she could use to haul herself
farther up. Her questing fingers found an opening. She strained,

taking her weight on her fingers and her toes. She shifted her left foot upward to a small ledge that her fingers had abandoned a few seconds before, and pulled her right leg up.

She glanced across to where Robin was climbing, checking that he was all right.

As she watched, something burst out of the hole in the cliff face, knocking his fingers away from the chalk. He began to fall.

CHAPTER TWELVE

Crusoe's right hand clenched, trying to maintain a grip, as he slammed his left hand back against the chalk, clawing for purchase. Something hard struck him across the eyes, blinding him for a moment. He flinched away instinctively as feathers fluttered in a storm of white around him. The seabird lunged for him with its beak, catching his forehead and leaving a gash. He could feel warm blood trickling down his temple and across his cheek. He flailed with his left hand, trying to push the bird away. It pecked at his hand, screeching loudly. Desperately he grabbed at it, catching its neck. He could feel it struggling. It was defending its nest, protecting its eggs. He couldn't snap its neck— that would be wrong. Instead he flung it away from him, away from the cliff face. He heard the *snap* as it opened its wings, catching at the breeze. Before it could return, he hauled himself up, weight on his right hand and left foot. His left hand and right foot scrabbled for some kind of support on the cliff. For a long moment, they couldn't find anything apart from powdery chalk, but eventually his fingers found a stone embedded in the cliff face that they could grab on to, and his foot managed to catch on a ledge. He took a ragged breath, trying to calm his heart down.

His fingers pulled the stone out of the chalk.

The stone dropped away toward the distant beach, and he nearly joined it.

The weight of his left arm pulling away from the cliff nearly tore him loose. Exerting all his strength, he hauled his left hand back toward the chalk. His fingers hit it so hard that they embedded themselves in it, creating five new holes. He clenched his fingers desperately and hugged the cliff. His heart was beating so hard that he almost expected it to push him away from the cliff itself, but gradually it subsided. He could visualize himself, spread-eagled against the cliff face like some kind of giant spider.

He looked left, to where Friday was stationary against the chalk. In the meager starlight, her face was shocked, and her eyes were wide.

"Are you all right?" she whispered.

"No!" he whispered back.

"What can I do?"

"Pray!"

He sent his right hand questing up the cliff, looking for a hand-hold—preferably one that didn't have a seagull nesting in it. Once his right hand was secure, he moved his left foot, looking for a ledge that would take his weight. Having done that, he hesitantly pulled himself upward.

Somewhere around the level of his knees, he sensed rather than heard the seagull returning to its nest. Fortunately it had decided that the threat was over, and it would rather go back to sleep—or whatever seagulls did when they weren't flying. Did birds actually sleep?

He recognized that he was getting slightly hysterical, and he took several deep breaths before continuing.

A few minutes later, instead of finding chalk, his right hand touched damp grass. Thirty seconds later, he was lying on his back, staring up at the stars and trying to steady his breathing.

Friday hauled herself up to join him.

"Let's never do that again," he whispered.

"Yes, you say that now," she answered, "but the next time there's a countess to rescue, you'll be the first one climbing."

He laughed. "Jealous?"

"Should I be?" She said it casually, but there was an expression in her eyes that made him feel strange. Protective.

"Never," he said. "You and I will always be together."

She looked away, but he could have sworn that her eyes were glistening, as if she was about to cry.

Crusoe rolled over onto his stomach and pushed himself up to a crouch. He looked around. They were on a stretch of grassy land that extended sideways, bounded behind him by the cliff and in front of him by the wall of the fort. Left and right, the wall of the fort ended in a tower that projected outward, encroaching on the grass strip.

There were no guards in sight. Fortunately.

He looked the other way. Past the edge of the cliff, there was nothing but empty space, and the distant crests of the waves, which seemed to glow in the meager light. Far, far away was a straight horizon, a dividing line between one kind of darkness and another.

"Is it just me," he whispered, "or is this fort built too close to the edge of the cliff?"

"I think," Friday said, standing up beside him, "that when the fort was built, it was a lot farther away from the edge. There's been quite a lot of erosion taking place over the years—storms, probably." She glanced at him, smiling slightly. "This country of yours is gradually crumbling away, from what I can see. At least the island where we met was made of solid rock. It wasn't going anywhere."

"That's why *we* had to," he said.

Crusoe glanced upward. There were black gaps in the wall of the fort, but each gap had something projecting out of it. Something round and dark.

"Cannons?" he asked.

Friday nodded. "That's what they look like. They were built facing the sea to defend against invasion." She paused. "If this place is occupied by the people who took the countess, Isaac Newton, and the scrying orb, then they probably installed cannons facing *inland* as well. That's what I would have done."

Crusoe nodded slowly. "So if John Caiaphas and his men make an assault from the front, then they'll be cut down."

"We need to do something," she said.

He glanced at her. "Hey—we're the new people in the organization. Don't they have experts for this kind of thing?"

She smiled. "In the end," she pointed out, "isn't it always down to you and me?"

"You have a point." He gazed left and right. "From here we could take the easy option and look for an entrance at ground level, or . . ."

He looked up. Friday followed his gaze.

"Or we could take the hard option and keep going upward to see if we can find an unguarded entrance up there," she said, completing his thoughts.

"The front entrance is likely to be heavily guarded," Crusoe pointed out.

They shared a long glance. Both of them already knew what they were going to do. There was only one choice.

The stones of the fort had been put together fairly clumsily. There were gaps between them, and ivy was growing over most of the wall. It would, Crusoe thought, be an easier climb than the cliff. All they had to do was avoid the gaps where the cannons were sited, so they weren't seen by anyone who was inside.

Sighing, he started to climb.

It was easier, if only because, despite his initial concerns, he could use the lintels of the gaps in the wall as footholds to steady himself before continuing on up the stones. It seemed to take only a few minutes before he and Friday were hauling themselves up onto the crenellated battlements.

They kept themselves low, crouching between the battlements as they surveyed the flat top of the fort. It was a hollow square, with a large open space in the center. Towers at the corners seemed to hold observation points, but if there was anyone up there—and Crusoe was pretty sure there was—then they were looking out rather than down, and they probably had telescopes.

There were cannons on top of the fort, too, iron and wood contraptions covered in sacking. They looked like crouching animals, set back from the edge but able to be wheeled forward if they were required. There was nobody in sight.

"Well defended," he pointed out.

"They have a lot to defend," Friday replied.

She walked across to the inside edge and crouched down before looking over. After a few moments, she stood up and moved back to Crusoe's side.

"Parade ground or training area," she said. "Possibly both. Lots of troops down there, all wearing armor, a couple of campfires, and some things that look like black tents."

Crusoe noticed several dark rectangles in the stone roof. He guessed they were trapdoors leading downward, into the fort itself. Keeping low and to the shadows, the two of them moved to the closest black rectangle. As Crusoe had suspected, a wooden trapdoor was set into it. A metal handle was attached to the wood. He reached forward, took hold of the handle, and pulled, hoping that it hadn't been bolted on the other side. They were in luck; the trapdoor lifted up, revealing a stone corridor beneath.

He listened for one hundred of his heartbeats, making sure that there was nobody down there, nobody who could have heard them.

Silence.

Eventually he nodded to Friday. She swung herself into the rectangular hole. Crusoe took her hands and lowered her to the flagstones.

Looking down, he could see her head swiveling, looking for any sign of guards, or other people who could raise an alarm. Eventually she raised a hand, indicating to him that it was safe.

He slithered into the hole left by the trapdoor, lowered himself, and let go. His feet hit the flagstones, and he crouched, absorbing the shock. He straightened up so that he was standing with his back to Friday, facing one way down the stone corridor they had ended up in while she faced the other way.

The fort was silent.

The corridor stretched away in both directions. At both ends, a turn took the corridor out of sight. Openings along the length of the corridor, on either side, were sealed with wooden doors. Candles hung in lanterns from fittings attached to the stone at head height.

"What do you think?" he asked.

"I think that the countess, Isaac Newton, and the orb will be guarded. That means they're not along this length of the corridor."

"I suppose it would have been too much to ask." He hesitated. "Would they be held high or low? At the top of the fort, or in the dungeons, if there are dungeons?"

"Oh, there'll be dungeons. Nobody builds a fort without building dungeons." She considered for a moment. "Dungeons are a punishment. They'll be kept high rather than low, for the moment. If they're being kept to be traded for something, then whoever has taken them will want them to be kept relatively comfortable, so nothing bad happens to them by accident. If they're being kept because they can be useful for some reason, then the same argument holds true. They'd only be put into a dungeon if they'd refused to do something, and they haven't been here long enough for that."

Crusoe nodded. He looked up and down the corridor. "I want to check something," he said. He moved to one of the doors on the side of the corridor where the rooms would look out into the open. He put his ear against the wood and listened. Nothing. After a few moments, he took hold of the door latch and quietly raised it. He pushed the door open a crack and put his eye up against the gap.

The door opened out onto a room that ran perhaps half the length of the fort. It was dark inside. Starlight from outside shone through glassless windows, illuminating the shapes of cannons that were lined up in a long row. Barrels of gunpowder were stacked against the wall, along with pyramids of cannonballs and ram-rods—iron rods about six feet long with one end thicker than the other that would be used to tamp the cannonballs down inside the cannons before firing.

He let Friday look. She glanced up at him as she pulled back.

"How many cannons do you think this place has?" she asked.

"Hundreds. Let's hope they don't have enough men to fire them all."

He crossed the corridor and repeated the process at one of the inner doors—listening and then cautiously opening it. What he found was a storeroom: crates and boxes and barrels filling most of the space.

He moved back to where Friday was standing. "It looks like this is a storage floor, apart from the cannons. You head down to your end of the corridor and take a look," he said, "and I'll head to my end. Back here straight away."

Without saying anything, Friday moved off. Crusoe did the same thing.

Crusoe got to the corner of his length of corridor and cautiously edged his head around it. Another corridor extended along that side of the fort. In the middle he could see an open space facing into the fort. He assumed that it gave access to a stairway that led downward. Again, there were no guards.

He moved quietly back to the place where they had dropped down from the trapdoor. Friday arrived at the same time he did.

"Another corridor," she said. "There's a right-hand corner at the far end—that must lead to the fourth side of the fort. No guards."

"Another corridor, with a balcony that might lead to a stairway," he countered. "And a left-hand corner that must give onto the other end of the same corridor. No guards."

"We don't want to be seen on the balcony—let's go down my corridor to the far end and see what we can see there."

They moved quietly together back to where Friday had just been, then along that corridor to the far end. Crusoe peered around the corner of the fourth corridor.

There were two guards standing on either side of a doorway about a third of the way down. For guards deep inside what should have been considered safe territory, they both unusually wore a nearly complete set of steel armor, from helmet down to sabatons. Instead of swords or pikes, they were both holding what looked to Crusoe like crossbows without the bows: lengths of wood that had shoulder stocks and triggers, but no way of firing bolts. He wondered what they were.

He moved to let Friday take a look. After she pulled back, they shifted a little way down the corridor.

"Interesting—do you think that's where Newton and the countess are being held?" she asked.

Crusoe frowned. "I wouldn't have thought they'd have been put in the same room—not unless they're running a bit short of guards here. It might be one of them, in which case the other might be on a lower floor." He thought for a moment. "We can't take the risk of tackling those guards now if there's only one prisoner in there. The chances are we'd cause an alarm to be raised."

"That's what I was thinking." Friday gazed up at him, her face close to his. "We really need to check the other floors."

"We ought to split up," Crusoe said reluctantly. "We can cover the fort quicker that way."

Friday nodded. "I agree."

"You take the next floor down. I'll take the one below that—which should be the ground floor. We'll meet back here in"—he thought for a moment—"about half an hour. Your sense of time is pretty good—do you think you can do that?"

She smiled. "Hey—my sense of time is better than yours. I guarantee I'll be back here and waiting for you."

He reached out and squeezed her arm. "Just don't wait for too long. If I'm not back within ten minutes after you get back, then get out of here—go up to the roof and signal to John Caiaphas and his men when they get here."

She nodded seriously. "And the same goes for you—don't wait for me."

Together they slipped back the way they had come, around two corners and along the corridor that Crusoe had seen earlier. As he'd thought, halfway along was a stretch of stone balcony edged with a stone banister. The banister had a gap in the center leading to the stairs that went down in two directions—left and right. The other side of the stairs was open: a space that probably went all the way down to the ground.

Friday was about to go down the left-hand stairway, but Crusoe stopped her. He moved quietly along the rest of the corridor to the far corner and edged his head around. He was staring down the corridor that he'd seen earlier—the one with the two guards standing in front of the doorway—but this time he was looking from the other end, and the guards were about two-thirds of the way down.

He moved back to the balcony, where Friday was leaning over the stonework and listening. "I can hear voices," she said.

Crusoe indicated the two stairways, left and right. "I think they join back up on the next balcony down. See you there."

He moved right and Friday moved left. He lost sight of her for a moment. His stairs reversed direction at a small quarter landing, and he turned the corner carefully, listening for footsteps. Nobody was there, and as he descended the second set of steps, he saw Friday approaching him from the opposite direction, descending her own stairs. They met on a balcony that was virtually a mirror image of the one above, with a corridor leading away in two directions and two more stairways leading down.

The voices that Friday had heard were closer now—one more level down. Friday tapped her chest and pointed along one branch of the corridor. She pointed at Crusoe, then down one of the sets of stairs. Reluctantly, he nodded. They were going to have to split up.

As Crusoe headed down the stone stairway, the voices from down below became louder. One was a woman's voice, the other a man's. It sounded as if they were arguing.

He stopped halfway down the steps to the landing, where the stairway suddenly reversed its direction. If he went any farther, he ran the risk of being seen. His head was on a level with the first floor of the fort, and he could see across the balcony area to where the mirror-image stairs on the other side started.

"You know that Segment W will mount an offensive on this fort, Lord Sebastos?" the woman's voice said. He was sure that the voice belonged to the Countess of Lichfield. She sounded very self-possessed, very confident.

"I not only expect it, I welcome it." This voice was harsh and deep, but still well-spoken: obviously someone at a similar level of society to the countess.

Crusoe heard the sound of boots on stone, getting louder. The man—Lord Sebastos—was walking toward him.

"Where are you going?" the countess asked.

The footsteps stopped. "I need to speak with the good doctor for a few minutes," the harsh voice said. "He may have seen something in his new scrying orb that would tell us *when*, or indeed *if*, Sir William Lambert's pathetic forces will be preparing to attack. After that, I need to check on Isaac Newton." He paused. "You will be comfortable enough here, I trust," he said silkily. "Should I call for guards?"

"There is no need. I am perfectly comfortable here."

Crusoe could hear the sound of Lord Sebastos's boots start up again as he walked toward the stairs. Crusoe hesitated, wondering what to do. There were two stairways—mirror images of each other—that led up from the ground floor of the fort to the next floor. If Lord Sebastos chose the stairway that Crusoe was standing on, then Crusoe would have to quickly run up to the next floor without making any sound and find a place to hide. If instead he took the other stairway, then when he reached the landing halfway and turned around, he would see Crusoe on the stairs across the other side of the balcony area.

Crusoe was trapped.

⸺◦⃝◦⃝◦⸺

Three Years and Six Months
Since the Shipwreck

This was the third cave they had lived in since they had met. It was also the smallest and the worst positioned, but they hadn't had much choice. Red Tiberius's crew of savage pirates had found the other two, and they had gradually worked out which places Crusoe and

Friday preferred to go for fish, for lobsters and crabs, for wildfowl, for fruit, and for snails. Now there was likely to be a hunter in hiding, and traps set, in all of the places they usually went.

Huddled together and pressed against the cold, wet stone, they talked in low voices about their options.

"I thought your father would have given up by now," Crusoe murmured.

"My father never gives up on anything," she whispered back. Her breath was warm against his cheek. She shifted slightly, into a more comfortable position, and Crusoe realized that he could feel the beating of her heart against his arm. "That's what makes him such a good pirate, and such a good captain."

"And I suppose the fact that his first mate wants you for his wife doesn't help anyone forget about you."

Her heartbeat suddenly sped up. "Probably not," she murmured calmly, but Crusoe could hear the undercurrents of hatred and fear in her tone of voice.

"We'll keep on moving ahead of them," he said, trying to sound reassuring even though he didn't feel reassured. "We can always find somewhere to go that they don't know about."

"They found us several times already," she pointed out, "and the island isn't that big. There isn't much ground left that we haven't explored."

"There's the south area."

"Difficult to get to because of the sharp crags and the broken ground." He could feel her head shaking. "And there's precious little vegetation over there. We'd never survive—that's why we've never gone there in the past two years."

"I'll keep you safe," he whispered.

"I know," she said, and moved closer to him.

He thought she fell asleep for a while, because her breathing became shallower and her muscles relaxed against him, but after a long time she suddenly said, "I think we need to make them think we're dead, or we've left the island. It's the only solution."

"All right." He thought for a minute. "If they think we're dead or gone, then they'll stop looking for us, but I don't know how . . ." His voice trailed off as his thoughts raced ahead. "Yes—I think I know how we can do it."

She shifted, her face upturned toward his in the darkness. "How?"

"It's going to be risky. We'll need to go hunting without them seeing us, and then we'll need to deliberately attract their attention and get them to chase us."

"Hunting?" she questioned. "Hunting what?"

He grimaced, knowing that she couldn't see his expression. In a plan that was going to be pretty difficult to execute, this was going to be the trickiest part. "Wild pigs," he said.

"The ones with tusks and sharp teeth? The ones that nearly killed you the first time you tried to catch them for food? The ones you've avoided ever since?"

"Yes," he said. "Those ones."

They waited until after sunset to leave the cave. In that time they slept for a while, and then Crusoe explained his plan in more detail. By the time the moon was casting its sterile, silvery light across the forest, they knew they should move.

In the darkness, they crept silently through the forest, toward the area where they knew the wild pigs congregated to sleep at night. It wasn't an area they usually went, so there were unlikely to be any pirates there hunting for them. There were several trails leading away from the area of crushed bracken and mud where the wild pigs slept, and quietly they set up vines, looped and secured with slipknots, across two of the trails downwind of the pigs. The loops were held open with forked branches rammed into the soft earth.

All the time they worked, Crusoe could hear the snorting sounds of sleeping pigs coming from a short distance away. The two of them *were about as close as they could get—the pigs had good senses and would smell them if the wind changed, and there were bound to be one or two awake as guards. The good thing was that there weren't liable to be any pirates around—they also knew the dangerous and unpredictable nature of the creatures.*

Once the traps were set, the two of them got together again in the shadow of a large bush.

"You know what to do?" Crusoe asked.

"You go upwind of them and make a lot of noise. They start running. Hopefully two of them will get their necks caught in the traps. Once the rest of them have gone, I kill the pigs with a heavy stone." She put a hand on his arm and squeezed. "You know that the pack leaders will head for you, rather away from you? These pigs are vicious, and they don't fear anything."

"I know." He felt a tremor within his chest, but he tried not to show it. "I'll be careful."

"You'd better be. I wouldn't want to have to survive on this island by myself." She punched him in the chest, then slipped away into the shadows.

Taking a deep breath, only part of which was to prepare for the forthcoming ordeal, Crusoe began to circle around the area of forest that the pigs had decided to call their own. He moved as quietly as he could, but he was painfully aware of each twig that cracked beneath his feet and each bush whose leaves whispered together as he brushed past it.

Eventually he was in position. He could feel the faint breeze on his ears, coming from behind him and blowing his scent toward the pigs. The snuffling sound they made while they were asleep was different now—quieter, and somehow more watchful.

He glanced around, checking his line of escape. There was a large tree with a sloping trunk a little distance away; he was pretty sure that he could scramble up it to safety before the pack leader got to him. Pretty sure.

He took a deep breath and braced himself.

He started running forward, toward the pigs, with his arms spread wide. Branches snapped as he ran, and dead wood cracked beneath his feet. He could feel his spread hands being scratched by sharp twigs.

Ahead of him there was a sudden uproar—snorting, high-pitched squeals and the sounds of many bodies suddenly in motion away from him. He knew what was going to happen next, and he didn't have much time. Stopping, he whirled around and ran in the opposite direction, toward the sloping tree.

Behind him, something large ran straight through the bushes toward him, shouldering the twigs and branches aside as if they were straw. He glanced over his shoulder as he ran, and saw a nightmare vision of hair, tusks, teeth, and small red eyes burst out of a clump of foliage as if it had been fired out of a cannon. He tried to speed up, but his foot caught in a tangle of roots and he fell forward. Visions of the wild pig catching up with him and tearing into his back with its sharp teeth filled his mind. He converted the fall to a clumsy roll and managed to use his momentum to bring himself back to an upright position, but the pig was closer now, snorting and grunting. He thought he could hear another one, off to his left.

The sloping tree was just ahead of him, its silvery bark highlighted in the moonlight. He ran for it as fast as he could, leaping the last few feet. Teeth grazed his heel but failed to get purchase, and he ran up the trunk of the tree to the point where it straightened up.

He looked down, just as the massive lead pig hit the tree without slowing down. The trunk shook as if an earthquake was happening, and he had to wrap his arms around it to stop himself from falling. The pig didn't waste its energy trying to climb after him—pigs weren't built for climbing—but instead opened its jaws wide and started biting chunks out of the tree trunk in an attempt to get it to fall. Its teeth were sharp enough and its jaws strong enough that within a few seconds, it had gotten a quarter of the way through, sending white chips of wood flying in all directions.

Crusoe had chosen his escape route carefully, however. He scrambled farther up the tree, using the branches as hand- and footholds. As the trunk grew thinner, it started to bend under his weight, and he used that weight to make it bend toward another, stronger tree nearby. When he was close enough, he jumped.

Below him the two pigs were both chomping away at the trunk. They didn't even notice that he had moved to a new tree.

As quietly as he could, Crusoe edged out along a solid-looking branch until he was close enough to a third tree that he could just step across the gap. In that manner he moved far enough away from the infuriated pigs, and sufficiently downwind of them, that he could cautiously scramble down to the ground and move away, toward where he knew Friday would be waiting.

She was, and she had two dead pigs with her. The looped vines were still around their necks, and there was blood on their heads where she had hit them and killed them. When she saw him, she said nothing, but her expression gave away her relief and happiness that he was safe.

"What now?" she whispered.

"Now," Crusoe answered tiredly, "we have to carry them away from here, and we have to shave them."

CHAPTER THIRTEEN

The footsteps seemed to be heading away from Crusoe. He kept his fingers crossed.

Suddenly he heard the sound of boots scuffing on stone steps coming from the stairwell across the other side of the balcony. Crusoe stared across, his head barely above the level of the stone. As soon as the sound of Lord Sebastos's boots changed, when he reached the halfway landing and began to turn, Crusoe quickly withdrew to his own landing and around the corner, to the lower flight of steps.

It worked. Sebastos kept heading upward. He hadn't seen anything.

Crusoe was torn. Part of him wanted to follow Sebastos upstairs to check that the guarded room he and Friday had found on the top floor actually held Isaac Newton, part of him wanted to make sure that Friday didn't accidentally run into Sebastos, and part of him knew that he might not get another chance to rescue the countess. For a long moment he froze, torn between heading up the stairs and heading down. In the end, he headed down. Rescuing the countess was the most important task right now. Friday could take care of herself.

He listened for a minute, but there was no noise from the hall apart from the crackling of logs in a fireplace and the whisper of the countess's satin dress shifting as she moved around. As far as Crusoe could tell, there were no guards.

He continued on to the bottom of the stairs and entered the large hall.

The Countess of Lichfield was sitting on a divan, staring into the flames of a roaring fire, and she was alone. He glanced around, orienting himself. The fireplace was off to the left. To the right was a massive door that must lead outside.

"Countess!" he called.

Her head snapped round. "Mr. Crusoe! But—" She glanced urgently toward the stairs that Lord Sebastos had gone up. "What are you *doing* here?" she asked in a shocked voice.

"Rescuing you," he said. "And Isaac Newton and his scrying orb as well. Segment W will be attacking soon—we need to get away."

The countess's porcelain-white and porcelain-smooth face clouded over, as if she was considering what to do. "But—what if we're discovered?"

Crusoe glanced toward the stairs. "We're all right for the moment. Most of the guards seem to be outside, or resting. As long as we're careful, we can evade anyone." When she still hesitated, he added urgently, "This might be our only chance—we have to go now!"

She nodded and stood up. She took a step toward the main doors.

"Not that way," Crusoe said. "There will certainly be guards outside. We need to go up."

"Up?" She looked around wildly. "But that makes no sense. If we go outside now, then we might manage to evade the guards."

He took a few steps forward and boldly took her arm. "My friend Friday is upstairs, along with Isaac Newton and his scrying orb. We need to fetch them as well."

Reluctantly she yielded to his gentle tug, and moved with him toward the stairs. Crusoe listened closely, trying to work out if Lord Sebastos or anyone else was coming down, but he couldn't hear anything. He pulled the countess up the stairs.

FRIDAY SLIPPED ALONG her corridor, away from the balcony. She couldn't hear Robin going down to the next level, but she could sense him. She could always sense him. She knew how he would be moving now—sideways, his back flat against the stone and his hands spread out, pressed against the stone as well, sensing vibrations as much as listening for sounds.

She had to put her worry for him out of her mind and concentrate on her own exploration. The corridors on this level were almost identical to the ones above, with the difference that there were tapestries hanging on the walls between the doors. They showed hunting scenes and battles. Some of the doors on the inner side of the corridor were fully or partially open as well, revealing rooms with chairs and tables or beds in them. She had to move carefully past the doorways, in case there was anyone inside the rooms, but she never saw anybody, and the furniture was covered in dust. The doors on the outer side of the corridor were closed, but she checked one of them and found the same thing as on the floor above: cannons, ready for action.

She moved silently along the corridor, pausing at the corners to check ahead for any guards. Unlike the floor above, this one seemed to be completely deserted. No guards, no guarded rooms.

She was passing one doorway when it struck her that this door was different from the others that she had seen. Unlike the rest of them, this one was studded with nail heads. Red velvet had been placed around the door jamb, maybe to stop any sound from getting in or out, Friday thought. It squeezed out from between the door and the frame like congealing blood.

She had to see what was in there—the door was so different from the others along that corridor.

Cautiously she pushed the door open and listened. There was no sound from within, so she entered the room.

It was dark, apart from the flickering light emitted by a single candle on the table. There were no windows through which sunlight or moonlight could enter. The walls were bare, marred only by the thick wooden door. In the center of the room was a table with a tablecloth hanging to the floor, a chair, a candle, and a shape on the table that was covered with a silken cloth. It looked strangely similar to the object that had been stolen from the *Great Equatorial*.

Friday reached forward and pulled the cloth away from the object on the table. She was not surprised to see beneath it a black orb about the size of a grapefruit on a silver base with feet carved into the shape of claws.

Either this was the orb that had been taken from the *Great Equatorial* or it was its twin.

She stared at it for a long moment, feeling a strange pull. Like before, it was hard to look away. The surface of the orb seemed to swirl, as if there was something inside the orb, moving. After a while—and she was shocked to realize she didn't know how long it had been—she thought she could see a faint red glow seep through the darkness. Eventually she had to turn around and face the door, just to break the spell of the thing . . .

. . . Just as the door opened and a guard in armor appeared. He was carrying an object made of wood and metal, like a crossbow but without the metal bow.

There was nowhere that Friday could go; she was as exposed as a moth on a white bedsheet. The guard saw Friday, and his face crumpled in shock and surprise. He opened his mouth wide, preparing to shout a warning.

Friday punched him in the face.

He fell back into the doorway. Friday grabbed his boots and pulled him into the room. The door swung closed as she dragged him away. Before he could reach for his sword, Friday jumped on top of him. He bucked, trying to shake her off, but she grabbed hold of his breastplate with one hand to stop herself from falling sideways, and with her other hand she grabbed the wood-and-metal object he was carrying and hit him with it until he stopped moving.

She could feel him breathing beneath her, and she could hear the rattling in his throat, but his eyes were closed and there was blood on his forehead. She stood up, breathing heavily.

The guard on the floor was still panting heavily. Quickly she tore the black silk cloth into strips and used them to bind his hands and feet. There was a fine web of blue lines on his right hand.

She heard a noise from outside. Someone was at the door.

She looked around desperately. There was nowhere to hide. The room was empty apart from the table and the chair.

Quickly, Friday grabbed the feet of the unconscious guard and dragged him beneath the table. She had to fold him up to fit beneath the tablecloth without any part of him sticking out. As the door opened, she ducked down and joined him, rearranging the cloth to hide both her and him.

As the cloth settled around her, she held her breath.

Feet approached the table.

The man sat on the chair with his back to the door. From where she was hidden beneath the table, Friday thought that he was staring in silence at the object above her. She looked out, past his feet; the flickering of the candle flame made it seem as if there were other living things there in the room with them, shifting around, but she knew that was an illusion. At least, she hoped it was.

Abruptly the door to the room opened. No noise of any approaching visitor had made it past the velvet-muffled doors, and it was only the squeak of the hinges that gave away the fact that someone had entered. That and the appearance of a pair of boots standing beside the chair.

"Do you have anything to tell me?" a deep and harsh voice said from somewhere in the room. The stone walls suppressed any echoes, and made the voice sound flat, emotionless.

Friday was desperate to see who was speaking. She leaned over until her face was against the floor and slid her head underneath the edge of the cloth until she could see upward. The man whose boots had appeared was wearing black hose, a black doublet, and a black cape. It was difficult to tell from the angle she was viewing at, but Friday was fairly sure that he was also wearing a grotesque mask made of black leather that had been folded into the semblance of a face and stiffened. Either that or his face was severely affected by some disease.

His hands were also covered with a pattern of blue mottling.

"I haven't started yet," the seated man said quietly. His voice was quiet and dry, like autumn leaves. He sounded old and tired, like a man who had outlived his proper time.

"Then start now."

"With you in the room? That might make things . . . difficult."

"Try anyway. And when I say 'try,' I mean, of course, 'succeed.'"

"Well?" The man in the mask was impatient.

"I see a boy." The old man concentrated harder. "He is young, but he is tall and strong. He has a medallion around his neck."

"What kind of medallion?" The voice was suddenly harsher than normal.

"It resembles what they call a wooden dissection—a piece that can be fitted together with other pieces to form a picture, except that this one is of metal. I cannot tell what it might be a picture of, when placed together with its brethren."

"Could it be a map?" the harsh voice asked.

"It could be any manner of things."

A pause, as if the man was frustrated, then: "What else can you see?"

"I see a girl. She is with the boy. They are close—not betrothed, but good friends who have been tested by the fire and by the elements and survived. They know each other's hearts."

Not betrothed? Friday thought. A sudden shiver ran through her at the thought of Robin—her friend for so long—being mistaken for a suitor.

"They are on an island?" the harsh voice demanded.

"They were on an island." Friday heard a hiss of breath taken in by the masked man. "They were also on a ship. It may have landed, or it may not. I cannot tell."

"Oh, they have landed," the harsh voice said. "They have been seen. They have . . . interfered."

"In what way?" the old man asked. His tone of voice indicated to Friday that he was pushing his luck, and he knew it.

"The boy knows something, and the girl, too, although they do not know that they know. It is possible that they may pose a threat to the Circle of Thirteen, and so they must be . . . dealt with." The masked man's voice grew louder, into what Friday suspected was a rant that ran through his mind on a perpetual basis. "No threat can be tolerated. The Circle of Thirteen's plans will come to fruition, and—"

The masked man stopped himself. It was the old man who finished the sentence.

"'No threat can be tolerated,'" he murmured, "'the Circle of Thirteen's plans will come to fruition . . . and the rest of the world will cower before us!' I am familiar with the rhetoric, Lord Sebastos."

The words resounded in the small room. From where she crouched, beneath the table, Friday felt a chill run through her.

"You go too far, old man."

The old man laughed. "At my age, there is precious little to fear, and death would be a welcome visitor. I am sure you will excuse my eccentricities, as I excuse yours." He paused. "Where is Isaac Newton?"

Friday suddenly stiffened alertly at the mention of Newton's name.

"Upstairs, under guard." He paused. "I would appreciate your instincts. Come up and tell me what you think."

A silence. Then: "Are you sure?"

"Your instincts, honed by the orb, are good. Meet with Newton, and give me your impressions. Does he know what he is talking about, or not? Does he understand the scrying orbs, or is he just playing with them?"

"Is he fit to replace me?" the old man said. "Or am I irreplaceable?"

"You will be the adviser to the Circle of Thirteen for as long as you live, Dr. Dee, and I expect you to live forever, just as I expect to live forever, once the List has been purged and the stars set right."

"You've never let me see the List," the old man said. "If I knew whose names were on it, and how their deaths would result in the Circle of Thirteen being able to take over the many countries of this world and rule them, putting the entire globe under its dominion, perhaps it might help me in my work."

"Only the Circle of Thirteen is allowed to see the List," Sebastos replied. "And it is not for anyone else to understand the intentions of those forces that provided it to us." His voice dropped until it was even deeper than before, and he sounded as if he was again reciting something that he had committed to memory. "The Circle will become all-powerful when the stars are made right. The stars will be made right when those who *are* the stars are removed, thus making the stars themselves go dark. Those who are the stars must die so that the Circle may be changed and encompass everything that is." His voice changed back to its previous tone. "That is all you need to know, old man. Now—come!"

The old man got up. Both sets of feet moved away from the table. A few seconds later, the door closed behind them.

Friday sat beneath the table, stunned. Dr. Dee? Dr. *John* Dee? If it really was the same man that Sir William had told her and Robin about, then he must have been at least 150 years old. Surely it couldn't have been him. It must have been his son, if he had a son and if he had named his son John as well. A son would have been old by now.

Friday waited for one hundred beats of her heart and then slipped out from underneath the table, leaving the unconscious guard behind.

The room was empty. Only the table, the candle, and the object on the table remained. Without looking at it, she picked up the orb and slipped it into a pocket of her jacket. It dragged the jacket down, and she could feel its weight against her ribs.

It was warm. Surely it should have been cold.

She went to the door and opened it a crack, looking out, wondering if she could leave without being seen.

———⟨⊙⟩———

Two Years Since the Shipwreck

The girl grabbed his hand and stared into his eyes. Her own eyes were a deep brown. She closed her eyes for a moment in frustration and shook her head. She looked at him again, pointed at his leg, and made a walking gesture with two of her fingers.

Could he walk?

That was a good question. He nodded mutely, but he wasn't sure. He could feel the pain as a sick throbbing through his leg. The blood was splattering from it now onto the sand.

The girl glanced at his hand, where he realized he was still holding the woven sea-grass sheet that he had used to protect his head from the sun. She took it from him and held it up in front of his face. He looked at the sheet, then at his leg, then at the sheet again. He couldn't quite work out what she was suggesting. Everything seemed to be pulling away from him, as if he were falling down a dark hole.

She slapped him. Hard. His head snapped to one side, and everything came back into crystal-clear focus.

In the momentary clarity that had come with the shock of being slapped, he realized what she wanted him to do. He quickly wound the sheet around his leg and knotted it. The bleeding slowed to a trickle, but he felt like the flesh was swelling up both above and below the sheet.

She grabbed his hand and pulled him along, uphill.

Every time he put his foot on the ground, a spike of pain lanced up through his leg. He felt sick, and the world seemed to be fading in and out around him.

Toward the top of the hill the various rills and fingers of rock intersected to form a jigsaw terrain of rocky columns twice as tall as Crusoe. The girl pulled him through the maze to the other side of the hill, where the ground smoothed out as it sloped gradually down toward the tree line. It was open ground, and the two of them were as obvious as insects crossing snow. The small part of Crusoe's mind that wasn't consumed by pain hoped that they could get to the trees before the pirates got to the top of the hill behind them and saw them. He kept twisting his head, looking over his shoulder in case anyone appeared behind them. Fortunately they got to the trees in time. His feet scuffed against fallen leaves and tiny roots as they ran, nearly tripping him.

The girl stopped and looked around. She seemed to be searching for something. She glanced back at Crusoe, checked out his leg, and grimaced. He followed her gaze. It wasn't pretty. The tear in the flesh was longer and wider than before, forced open by the pressure of the running, but at least the tied sheet had stopped most of the blood flow. The flesh above the makeshift tourniquet was red and bulging, while the flesh below it was white. He felt sick just looking at it.

She glanced around, then turned back to him. She helped him to a seated position under a tree whose large, flat leaves provided shade.

Crusoe must have blacked out for a while, because it seemed like a moment later that he was alone, and he hadn't seen her go. He sat there in the shade of the tree, listening to the leaves rustling, the animals moving, and the birds calling all around him. Every second he expected the bushes to be pushed apart, and a pirate to emerge, sword in hand. He felt hot, and he felt thirsty. He leaned his head back against the bark of the tree and closed his eyes. If the pirates were going to appear, he wasn't sure that he wanted to know about it. There was certainly nothing he could do if they did. Maybe they'd be kind and just kill him while his eyes were closed.

After a while, drifting in a state that wasn't quite awake and wasn't quite asleep, he began to wonder if there had been a girl at all. Maybe he had imagined her. What about the pirates? Had he imagined them as well? Had he just injured his leg and fallen into a nightmare due to the pain and the shock? What was real and what wasn't?

A rustling in the bushes caught his attention. Despite what he'd decided about opening his eyes, his curiosity got the better of him. He lifted his head away from the tree—it felt twice the size that it should have—and looked.

It was the girl. She was holding a bunch of leaves.

Without any warning, she took the knife from Crusoe's belt and cut through the knot in the sheet that he had tied around his leg. The pressure from the blood above the wound caused the makeshift tourniquet to spring away rather than fall. Pain suddenly exploded inside his head as if he'd been struck by lightning. He had to put the back of his hand across his mouth to stop from screaming and giving away their position.

When the pain receded enough for him to be able to see what was going on around him, the girl had crushed the leaves and smeared the resulting liquid into the wound on his leg. It seemed to be having an effect; the bleeding had slowed down, and his leg felt . . . distant and fuzzy.

She took his hand and moved his fingers so that they were pinching the wound closed from either side. She looked into his eyes and nodded. He pressed hard. The resulting wave of pain almost made him black out again, but he managed to hold on.

She vanished for a few moments, then returned holding something small between her fingers. It was moving, and it took Crusoe a moment to realize that it was an ant—a red ant, about the size of the last joint on his little finger. Its jaws were disproportionately huge, taking up most of its head.

"What . . . ," he said through a dry throat and cracked lips, "what exactly do we need an ant for?"

He had a horrible feeling that he already knew.

She didn't say anything. With an apologetic shrug, she reached down and put the ant's head against the wound that he was holding closed.

It bit—jaws snapping shut on either side of the wound. Maybe it was the green leaf sap, or maybe it was the shock, but Crusoe couldn't feel anything.

The girl twisted the ant's body. The head stayed where it was, jaws clamped on Crusoe's wound, and she threw the body away.

The girl disappeared, then reappeared again with another ant. She put it next to the first and repeated the process—bite, twist, throw.

She vanished again. Crusoe stared down at the two ant heads that were clamped on the wound. He could see what she was doing, and he started laughing. What a clever solution.

It took twelve ants in total to cover the length of the cut. Eventually Crusoe let go. The line of ants' jaws held the flesh closed. It looked ugly, but it worked.

"What's your name?" Crusoe asked.

She stared at him. "Name?" she repeated.

He touched his chest, above his heart. "My name is Robinson Crusoe," he said. "We can talk about everything else later, but yes—I do want to know your name. My father always said that introductions are important." He knew he was babbling, but he couldn't help himself. He felt so light-headed, he might just float away.

She laughed suddenly: a bright, clear, bubbly sound. "Vijaya Dinajara," she said, touching her own chest.

Crusoe was about to tell her that it was a lovely name, but he passed out before he could say anything.

CRUSOE AND THE countess reached the top of the stairs at the same time that Friday emerged from the corridor onto the balcony. She was carrying something, but he couldn't see properly what it was. The countess was leaning heavily on Crusoe, her arm around his neck and her weight dragging his head close to hers. His arm was around her waist, holding her up.

When Friday saw how close the two of them were, she frowned. Her gaze met Crusoe's, and there was a question in her eyes. She looked disappointed in him, almost betrayed. He felt a sudden need to explain to her that the countess was exhausted by her ordeal, and needed his help climbing the stairs, but before he could say anything, Friday shrugged slightly and looked away.

"You got her," she said without any obvious relief in her voice. "Good."

Crusoe wanted desperately to say something to explain the fact that he appeared to be actually cuddling the countess, but the countess had turned her head and was looking up at him, wide-eyed. He could feel her breath on his neck. This wasn't the best time to have this discussion. "Newton?" he asked instead in a whisper.

"Upstairs, where we thought he was. A man with a gruff voice went up there to see him. He took another man with him—I think it was that Dr. Dee we were told about."

Crusoe frowned but decided not to say anything. This wasn't the time to talk about men who would have to be well over a hundred years old. "I heard the man with the gruff voice talking about going to see Newton," he said. "His name is Lord Sebastos, apparently." He looked at the countess, carefully releasing her waist and disengaging her arm from his neck. "Who is he? Do you know what he wants?"

The countess pouted and shook her head. "He said so many strange things, I didn't know what to think. But he did treat me with civility."

"Is he a real lord?" Crusoe pressed. "From the king's court?"

"I have never seen him before," the countess said.

Crusoe nodded, satisfied that the countess didn't know much more than he did, but when he looked over at Friday, she was still frowning, but now it was as if she was worried about something she had heard or seen.

"What about the orb?" he asked, suddenly remembering the third part of their mission—and, as far as Sir William Lambert was concerned, the most important one.

She patted her pocket.

"Right," he went on. "In that case, we need to get Newton and get out of here."

Friday nodded. "How exactly are we going to get out of here?"

"I'm still working on that."

"The trouble is," she continued, "we need to go up to get Newton, but the main way out is down."

"And there's half a ton of guards right outside the door."

"But be fair," he countered. "They'll be facing the other way."

Friday smiled. Crusoe knew, like she did, that in the end, they would find a way to safety. That was what they did.

Friday headed up the stairs, toward the next floor. Crusoe followed, pulling the silent countess with him. She seemed . . . not exactly shocked by the way events were going, but she had an expression on her face that indicated things weren't going quite the way she had expected, and she was having to adjust her mental frame of reference.

Now that he was behind Friday, he could see that the thing she was carrying was one of the strange weapons that the guards outside the room where Newton was being kept had been holding. One of the things that looked like half a crossbow. She must have picked it up somewhere along the way.

"Our best bet," Crusoe whispered, "might be to find a place for us to hide, and then wait until John Caiaphas's men overrun the fort."

"*If* they overrun the fort," Friday whispered back. "But I agree—hiding is our best option, for now."

They got to the top of the stairs and peered out into the corridor. It was empty in both directions.

"The room where we think Newton is being held is on the other side of the fort," Friday pointed out.

"But the room is only a third of the way down from one end," Crusoe said.

They both looked at each other with the same thing going through their minds.

The countess looked from one to the other. "Do you two never actually finish a thought?" she asked.

Crusoe glanced at her. "One of us approaches them from the long side of the corridor—calmly and without any obvious weapons," he said. "They will both turn to see who is coming. When it's clear that they don't know who the approaching person is, they will start to tense up and concentrate on the possible threat."

"At which point," Friday went on, "the other one of us runs at them down the shorter side of the corridor and knocks them down."

"Following which there is a fight, which we win." Crusoe smiled. "It's the obvious tactic."

"To you, perhaps." The countess sighed, shaking her head.

"If what I heard is true," Friday pointed out, "then Lord Sebastos and his adviser are both in the room with Newton."

"We need to wait until they come out before we make our move," Crusoe said. "Whichever one of us they are heading toward needs to hide in one of the rooms with the cannons."

Crusoe gazed into Friday's eyes. She gazed into his. Then, without another word being said, she turned and headed off down one branch of the corridor.

"Come on," Crusoe said, and pulled the countess in the other direction.

They turned a corner—after checking that the corridor beyond was deserted—and ran to the next corner. Crusoe crouched and looked around the edge. Two-thirds of the way along the corridor, the two armed and armored guards were still standing outside the room where Crusoe thought Newton was being kept.

"What now?" the countess hissed from behind him.

"We wait for Lord Sebastos and his friend to leave," Crusoe repeated.

They waited there for several minutes. Crusoe slipped into a kind of waiting meditation that Friday had taught him back on the island—a way of passing the time without getting bored or getting edgy. He could sense, however, the countess behind him, taking small steps back and forth. She was obviously worried.

His calm state of mind was abruptly shattered by a trumpet blaring a loud fanfare from somewhere downstairs.

It was an alarm—a call to arms. John Caiaphas's attack had started.

CHAPTER FOURTEEN

Without making any conscious decision, Crusoe found himself leaping to his feet and dragging the countess around the corner and into the final stretch of corridor. It was only after five long paces that his mind caught up with his muscles, and he realized what Friday would also have realized: within a few minutes, the corridor would be swarming with soldiers heading for the cannons, ready to repel the invading force. It didn't matter that Lord Sebastos and his adviser were in the room with Newton; if Crusoe and Friday didn't act now, they would be caught.

The two guards had snapped to attention, aware from the sound of the trumpet that something important was happening.

Crusoe and the countess had halved the distance between them when the guards caught sight of something moving. They both turned and raised their strange wood-and-metal weapons.

"Stop right there!" one of them shouted.

Behind the men, Friday ran full tilt around the corner and hurtled toward them on bare feet.

Crusoe raised his hands, still walking. "There's an emergency," he called out. "I've been told to come and check on the prisoner."

"I've never seen you before," the other guard snapped. "What's your name?"

Friday was halfway toward them now, and speeding up.

"I'm . . . Lord Sebastos's son!" Crusoe said, hands still held up. He moved so that he was standing between the guards and the countess, protecting her if they fired their weapons. "Look, I know he's in there. I need to see him!"

"Stop or we—" the first guard started to say, but then Friday leaped into the air, somehow turning so that she was flat and parallel to the floor, rolling over and over in midair, and hitting them both—*smack*—in the backs of their heads. They fell forward, and so did she, still rolling.

Crusoe sprang forward and tackled the guard on his left, anticipating that Friday would know to take the other one. The guard was trying to get up. Crusoe grabbed the weapon, which he had dropped when he fell, and swung it around. The end of the weapon caught the guard beneath his jaw. He fell backward, hitting the stone floor hard.

Friday meanwhile had converted her roll into a handspring. Now on her feet, she rushed at the other guard. He had gotten to his knees and was aiming his weapon. Something went *zing*, and Crusoe saw a flash of light. Friday ducked to one side, and something metallic flashed past her and struck the ceiling, leaving a bright gash in the stonework. That gave the guard enough time to get to his feet. He pulled back a lever that ran the length of his weapon, hinged at the back. Crusoe heard a sound like a giant clock spring being wound up. The lever sprang back to its original position, and the guard took aim again. Before he could fire, Friday was standing in front of him. Her foot flashed up and forward as she pivoted, catching the guard in the side of the head. He fell into the wall, dropping his weapon.

The whole fight had taken about ten heartbeats.

Somewhere back toward the stairs, Crusoe could hear the *clink, clink, clink* of metal-shod feet hitting stone. The soldiers were coming up the stairs.

He moved toward the doorway, gesturing to the countess to follow him as he did so, but he suddenly realized that Friday was heading down the corridor. He was about to ask what she was doing, but she bent down, picked something up, and then started back toward him. She held it up—a metal disk with sharp, serrated edges that glowed in the light from the lanterns.

Crusoe glanced at the weapon in his hands. Somehow it was designed to launch these metal disks spinning through the air until they sliced through whatever they hit—flesh, wood, or cloth. This weapon was incredible. It had the power of a crossbow, but it could obviously be reloaded much faster.

He moved to the door. There were bolts attached to the door, top and bottom, which could slide into fixtures on the doorframe, but they were both slid back now. Crusoe threw the door open as Friday moved to his side.

The room inside was small, with a bed, a chair, and a table. Isaac Newton was standing over by a barred window, looking even more disheveled than the last time Crusoe had seen him. The walls of the room were covered with mathematical equations and odd words that had been scratched into the stone with something hard and sharp, maybe Newton's belt buckle, or the edge of a metal button. Wherever he was, it seemed that he couldn't stop writing.

Sitting in the only chair was a large man. He was dressed completely in black, and he was wearing a black leather mask that had been twisted into the shape of a bird's beaked face. The starkness of his clothes only served to highlight the fine series of blue lines that crossed his hands, making him look as if he were wearing gloves made of sky-blue lace. But these lines were part of him, part of his skin.

His gaze, even through the eyeholes in the mask, seemed to strike Crusoe like a physical blow as the man glanced toward the door, and the interruption.

Lord Sebastos.

Behind him stood an elderly man. A very elderly man. The lines on his face were wrinkles, etched into the skin by the hand of time. His face looked like an apple that had been left to dry out in the sun.

Crusoe took several steps into the room, leaving a space behind him. He knew that Friday was going to want to drag the unconscious guards inside.

Lord Sebastos stood up. He was taller and bulkier than Crusoe anticipated. His head almost touched the ceiling of the room.

Behind him, Crusoe could hear whispered comments as Friday tried angrily to persuade the countess to help her move the unconscious guards. The countess seemed to believe that the nobility didn't do that kind of thing, even if they had just been rescued from imprisonment.

"Crusoe?" Newton said disbelievingly. "And . . . and Miss Friday?"

"Your rescue party has arrived," Lord Sebastos said in a harsh, dark voice. "A shame their mission is doomed to failure." He glanced past Crusoe and Friday into the corridor, where the sound of the trumpet alarm could still be heard blaring. "This corridor will be filled with armed guards at any minute."

"And the fort will be filled with our soldiers in a few minutes more," Crusoe said. He could hear dragging sounds from the doorway, but he didn't look around.

"We have cannons. They have, what? Small wooden boats? The contest is hardly equitable." Lord Sebastos smiled. "Which is just the way I prefer my battles."

"We're taking Isaac Newton," Friday said, joining Crusoe.

Sebastos's hands clenched in a sign of his anger. "Do not dare to tell me what you are going to do, child," he snarled.

Friday, standing in the doorway, brought the weapon she was holding up and pointed it at Lord Sebastos. A sudden *zing* filled the room. This time, Crusoe saw the sharp-edged metal disk as it flashed through the air, slicing through a lock of Sebastos's hair before embedding itself deeply in the wooden window frame.

"Oh," she said with fake surprise, "that's how it works!"

Sebastos reached up and brushed the severed lock of hair from his collar. His face was still contorted in anger, but his gaze was caught by something in the doorway behind Crusoe and Friday. "Countess—" he started to say.

"Lord Sebastos, I fear I must take my leave of you," the countess interrupted in a calm voice. "Fun though this . . . captivity . . . has been, I have other appointments to keep."

Sebastos stared at her for a long moment, then looked at Crusoe and Friday. "This is not over," he said quietly. "Be assured of that."

Crusoe gestured to Newton to join them. "Quickly—over here. We need to find a way out."

Newton moved toward the doorway, detouring around Lord Sebastos and the old man standing quietly behind him. He glanced regretfully at the etched calculations on the walls, as if desperately trying to memorize as much as he could before he left.

Newton passed between Crusoe and Friday, and then stepped over the two guards. Friday took his arm and helped him out.

The old man standing behind Lord Sebastos smiled at Crusoe and nodded.

Crusoe glanced at Lord Sebastos for one last time before stepping backward, pulling the door shut and quickly sliding the bolts across to secure it.

He glanced left and right down the corridor. Nobody in sight, but lots of noise of people moving.

He was about to tell the countess to follow him and Friday to safety when a massive *boom* shook the fort. Dust filtered down from the cracks between the stone blocks in the ceiling. It was as if a sudden mist had appeared everywhere.

Another shocking *boom*. Any dust that had settled on the stone floor suddenly leaped up into the air again. Crusoe felt as if someone had slapped his hands hard against his ears. He looked at Friday and the countess. Friday had a pained expression on her face, but the countess had her fingers in her ears, and her eyes screwed tightly shut.

Crusoe took three steps down the corridor, but from out of the stone-dust mist emerged the figures of three—no, four—of the Circle of Thirteen's soldiers. They had their weapons already raised, and they must have known about the intruders, because they opened fire immediately. Sharp-edged metal disks zipped past Crusoe like vicious wasps. One caught the side of his head, and he felt like a line of fire had been drawn across the skin. Blood immediately started to trickle down his face. Another disk plucked at his sleeve, leaving a gash in the material. Behind him, he heard a gasp. In front of him, he heard a series of clockwork *whirr*ings as the soldiers all pulled back the sprung levers on their weapons, ready to fire again.

Crusoe brought the weapon he was carrying up and fired back. The spinning disk caught the first man in the shoulder. He staggered, discharging his weapon straight up into the ceiling. The spinning metal, hitting the ceiling, caused a burst of sparks like a flint struck against rock. Friday fired as well, over Crusoe's shoulder. Her disk ricocheted from the stone wall to Crusoe's left. For a moment he thought she had misfired, but the disk zipped sideways, cutting a second soldier across the chest and a third one across his cheek before hitting the opposite wall, leaving more sparks behind.

The fourth guard pointed his weapon directly at Crusoe's face. Beneath his helmet, he was smiling grimly as his finger curled on the metal trigger.

⟞⟝⟞⟝⟞

Two Weeks Since the Shipwreck

Looking down from the bank of the river, Crusoe could see motionless fish swimming in the water.

They were motionless because as fast as the current carried them toward the ocean, they were swimming equally fast upstream. It looked like they were just hovering above the reeds in the riverbed.

He was starving. It had been two weeks since the shipwreck, and his stranding on the shores of this place. He didn't know anything about it, except that the fruit hanging so temptingly from the trees gave him crippling pains in his stomach, and the small pigs and other animals ran too fast for him to catch. If he didn't get some food soon, he was going to die.

He had gone through a whole spectrum of emotions since the shipwreck. Relief had been the first reaction when he awoke on the beach with the sun shining in his eyes—that, and gratitude. He had wandered the beach for a while, not quite believing the fact that he was still alive, but the sight of wreckage on the sand, and the personal possessions of the crew, curdled the relief and gratitude until it turned into despair. He had stopped walking, fallen to his knees, curled into a ball, and sobbed until he passed out.

When he woke, it was with a sense of disbelief. The shipwreck hadn't happened, and he was still lying in his hammock, swinging from the hooks in the bulkhead. He'd had a terrible nightmare, and now he was safe. The only reason he couldn't hear the voices of the crew was that it was a Sunday, and they were crammed into the ship's chapel with the captain, singing hymns and praying for calm seas.

Part of him knew that it hadn't been a dream, that the shipwreck had actually happened, and that he was stranded on a desert island somewhere, miles from civilization. He tried to quell that little voice inside him, but eventually he had to admit that it was sand beneath him, not canvas, that the warmth on his face was the sun, not a lamp, and that the crying of the gulls was too close to be on the other side of a thick wooden bulkhead. And when he opened his eyes, of course, there was blue sky above him, not a wooden deck.

A fierce wave of childish anger swept over him as he lay there, and he clenched his fists furiously. How was it that he was still alive, with nobody to look after him, when everyone else was dead? It wasn't fair. God shouldn't organize the universe that way—would it have been so terrible if one other sailor had survived to help him? Would it have been so terrible if his father had survived? And what about the captain? Wasn't it all his fault that the Rigel had been wrecked? He should have been paying more attention to his maps.

After several hours cursing God, the universe, and the captain, the anger drained away, leaving behind it a desperate desire to talk to God, to somehow offer a bargain that would cancel everything that had happened in the past twelve hours. Maybe if he promised God that he would live a better life—no, promised God that he would build a church with his own hands when he grew up and dedicate his life to good works—then maybe God would put him back in his hammock on the ship. Or give him a few other survivors to help him. Or save his father from death.

None of that happened. The anger bubbled within him, going no-where. Eventually it seemed to fade away, leaving him drained. He lay there, staring at the sky, knowing that he had been shipwrecked, that everyone else was likely to be dead, and that if he didn't get up and look for food and shelter, then he would just lie there and die of exposure, or starvation, or both.

So he just kept lying there, drifting in and out of sleep, until a gull landed by his face and tried to peck his cheek to see if he was edible. He rolled sideways, shouting and waving his arms, and the gull took off in a panic, but with a look in its eyes that suggested it knew that now he was alive and moving, but later on he wouldn't be, and the gull would still be there, waiting.

Over the next few days, he had gone through the same cycle of extreme emotions—relief, despair, anger, bargaining, and acceptance—again and again, but he kept himself moving. He collected wreckage from the ship, and thick branches and large leaves that he could use to make a shelter. He found fruit hanging from trees near the water. He tried catching some of the animals that wandered near him, but they were too fast. He would have to build some kind of trap, although he had no idea how. And then he discovered the fish.

He stepped carefully into the water. It was cold against his skin, snatching the warmth from him. The fish shifted slightly, but stayed where they were. He stood above them, hands poised, waiting for the right moment to grab one. The sun was shining in his eyes, and he could feel its rays burning his forehead and his shoulders, but he ignored all that. He concentrated on one fish in particular—the largest one, dappled with brown on its upper skin and with silver scales below. He bent closer to it, tensing. Suddenly he bent and reached forward, his hands plunging into the cold water. For a second he could feel its slippery skin beneath his fingers, but then it thrashed its muscular tail and slid from his grip.

Cursing, he glanced around. All the fish had reacted to his attack. They had swum away, some upstream and some downstream. Now they had come to a rest again, hanging there in the water as if taunting him to try again.

Despair welled up again within him, and he began to sob.

THE FORT SHOOK to its foundations. The solder's aim was knocked off, and his disk spun harmlessly away through the dust-filled air, leaving a trail behind it like the wake of a boat in water.

Crusoe backed rapidly away, turned, and ran. Ahead of him, he saw Friday pushing the countess in front of her. Newton was following, his head moving back and forth as he tried to keep track of what was going on. Crusoe knew that they had to find somewhere to hide soon, or they would be trapped.

Five spinning metal disks flashed toward them from out of the dust cloud, followed by five shadowy shapes. Friday pushed the countess sideways, against the wall, and used the momentum to push herself toward the opposite wall. Newton dived for the ground, leaving Crusoe facing the oncoming swarm of deadly metal shards. He quickly raised his own weapon and held it in front of him, tilted at an angle. As soon as he felt the impact of the first two disks embedding themselves in the wooden stock, he whirled the weapon around. One more disk thudded into the wood, while the last two *twanged* off the weapon's metal parts and hit the wall and the ceiling.

Friday and the countess were backing away from the oncoming soldiers. Crusoe grabbed Newton's collar and hauled him up. He turned to face the soldiers heading toward them from the other direction.

Crusoe's mind suddenly caught up with something that had happened less than a second ago. One of the spinning metal disks that had bounced off the metal of his weapon had hit the ceiling, while the other one had hit the wall, but the sounds had been different. The one hitting the ceiling had made a sharp, almost musical noise, while the one that had hit the wall had made a dull thud.

It hadn't hit a wall; it had hit a door.

Crusoe fired his weapon at the oncoming soldiers, seeing the disk carving a path through the thick mist. *Boom* went another cannon, raising more stone dust, and the disk seemed to jerk sideways before continuing on. Behind him, Friday fired in the opposite direction. Crusoe moved to the wall and felt rather than looked for the door. Finding it, he threw it open and pulled Newton inside the room. Moments later, Friday was pushing the countess inside.

As he pushed the door shut, Crusoe saw sharp metal disks spinning from both directions along the corridor. The soldiers, not realizing in the confusion and the clouds of dust that their quarry had found a hiding place, were still firing, but at one another.

He shut the door and let them get on with it. They would realize their mistake eventually.

There was a leather strap on the weapon, he noticed, and he slung it across his shoulder while he looked around. There was less dust in this room, which was on the inside of the fort. It appeared to be another storeroom. Seeing a pile of wooden boxes over by a wall, Crusoe quickly started pulling them apart. Friday, realizing what he was doing, joined in. Once they had sufficient splintered wood, they started jamming it beneath the door, kicking it to force it in place even more firmly. With the wood stuck there, it would be almost impossible to push it open from outside.

Which meant they were trapped there, but that was a problem for later.

One thing at a time, he told himself.

As Friday checked that the countess and Newton were all right, Crusoe crossed to the window and glanced out into the central open area of the fort. It was chaos out there: soldiers running in all directions, and the things that Friday had described earlier as being big black tents were still there.

He glanced left and right outside the window. No ledges they could use to get out that way. Even if they did, the chances of them being seen from below, or even of the countess or Isaac Newton falling, were too high.

He turned to stare around the room, looking for some kind of inspiration, some means of escape . . .

He saw the wooden trapdoor in the ceiling. It must let out onto the roof—similar to the one that he and Friday had used to get into the fort earlier.

Friday saw it at the same time as him. She glanced at him and nodded.

He started pushing the boxes that they hadn't pulled apart earlier into a rough staircase leading up to the ceiling. Once Newton saw what they were doing, he joined in enthusiastically. The countess watched, expressionless, from the side.

Within less than a minute, the rickety construction was complete. Friday, being the lightest, scrambled up and pushed the trapdoor open. A rush of cold air disturbed the stone dust hanging in the air, making it swirl like miniature tornadoes. She stuck her head outside and looked around, then crouched back inside.

"Empty," she said breathlessly, "but I don't know for how long. There are cannons up there as well as inside the fort. They'll get soldiers up there to fire them soon enough."

Someone outside started to bang on the door. The wood that was jammed into the crack between the door and the stone floor began to shift.

That decided it.

"We go up," Crusoe ordered.

Friday climbed out, then held a hand down for the countess. She stared up. "I am not going up there!" she announced.

"If you stay here, you'll die," Crusoe pointed out.

"Perhaps," she said, "but at least I'll die with dignity, not scrambling around like . . . like a milkmaid!"

Crusoe opened his mouth to argue, but Isaac Newton grabbed her around the waist, picked her up, and held her upward, struggling. Friday reached down, grabbed her arms, and pulled her up through the trapdoor.

"That was . . . bold," Crusoe said, smiling at Newton.

"Always wanted to grab a countess," Newton announced. "Never had the courage until now." He nodded at Crusoe and scrambled up the pile of crates and out the trapdoor.

Crusoe looked around, then went the same way. At the top he kicked out, knocking the pile of crates over, and then slammed the trapdoor shut behind him. That might buy them a few extra minutes of confusion.

It was dark outside, and a cold wind was whipping across the roof. Crusoe could see, by the light of the stars, a whole flotilla of ships and boats out on the Thames Estuary. *Those must be the Segment W forces*, he thought. Presumably there were other boats trying to dock at the quays at the front of the fort, and being repulsed.

Several more *bang*s echoed through the night air, as cannons fired. Their flames momentarily lit up the seascape. Out on the waters of the estuary, Crusoe saw several pillars of water leap up as the cannonballs impacted the sea. He also saw a boat hit by a cannonball explode into shards and splinters of wood. Its sail flapped away on the wind like a ghost.

He realized that Friday was standing by his side. "What now?" she asked.

"I don't know," he said. He looked around. "How many of these trapdoors are there up here? Can we block them all before any of the soldiers start coming up to man the cannons and find us?"

Friday grimaced and pointed across the stone roof toward one of the towers. "Actually," she said, "we missed something. There are doors in those towers."

Crusoe followed her pointing finger. There was a door leading from the tower onto the roof. It had been hidden by the stonework, but it was opening now as he watched, and soldiers were running out. They were looking for cannons, but they were going to find the four escapees pretty quickly.

Crusoe cursed under his breath. It looked as if they were out of options and out of luck.

A familiar shouting voice attracted his attention. It was coming from the open area in the center of the fort. He crossed to the edge and glanced over.

Down in the center of the area, the masked figure of Lord Sebastos was striding around, giving orders. He had obviously been rescued from the room where Crusoe had locked him. As Crusoe watched, he backhanded a soldier who had dared to question one of his orders, sending the man flying through the air to hit the ground with an audible *crash* of armor.

"Launch the balloons!" Lord Sebastos shouted, his voice echoing between the interior stone walls of the enclosure. "I need observers up there reporting on the positions of the enemy ships so that the cannons can fire accurately!"

Someone had obviously been waiting for the order, because with a flare of firelight, the black objects that Friday had thought were tents began to swell and rise. They were similar to the floating thing that had been used to kidnap the countess from her manor house, and they were floating closer and closer to where Crusoe stood watching, like the poisonous jellyfish that floated through the crystal-clear seas around the island.

He turned to catch Friday's eye, then glanced down at the balloons. She nodded in understanding.

He glanced at the soldiers who were spilling out of the tower doorway now. Most of them were preparing the cannons, loading them and using the long metal ramrods to tamp them down, but several of the soldiers had seen the four escapees and were coming across the roof toward them. Doors in the other towers were beginning to open as well.

Even if they did escape, there was enough firepower and manpower in the fort to wipe out the Segment W forces. Crusoe clenched his fists in frustration. What should they do? What *could* they do?

The nearest balloon was rising past the edge of the roof now. Crusoe moved as near as he could. Friday did the same by his shoulder. Behind them he could sense, rather than see, Isaac Newton putting his arm protectively around the shoulders of the Countess of Lichfield.

The balloon rose higher, and Crusoe could see the basket that hung beneath it. There was a single man in it, manipulating a bucket filled with fire so that hot air would feed up into the balloon's swollen shape, keeping it aloft. The other balloons were rising parallel with it.

And beneath the basket of this balloon, several ropes hanging down that had been used to secure it to the ground.

He backed up three paces, then ran toward the edge. Launching himself into empty space, he flew across the gap between the roof and the hanging rope. Beneath him he could see, far below, the green grass growing on the enclosed area in the middle of the fort. He swore he could even see Lord Sebastos gazing up at him furiously.

His hands caught the rope and clutched at it desperately. He swung, like the clapper on a church bell, away from the edge of the roof. The weapon that was still slung over his back by its leather strap bounced painfully against his shoulder blades. The balloon was still rising—slower now with him hanging off it—but the rope was long enough to touch the roof as he swung back again. He was aware of Friday grabbing at it and pulling—tying its end around the nearest cannon. The balloon stopped rising with a jerk.

Crusoe swarmed up the rope to the basket. The man inside had seen what was happening and was leaning over, jabbing at Crusoe with a sword. Crusoe waited until the sword had passed by his head, then grabbed the man's arm with his free hand and pulled. Unbalanced, he fell out of the basket, heading past the edge of the roof with a cry of terror and falling toward the ground. Crusoe grabbed the falling sword and shoved it under his arm to keep it safe as he slid back down the rope.

On the roof, Friday had tied ropes around Newton's chest and the countess's waist and shoulders. She grabbed hold of a third rope and wound it around her own waist, knotting it roughly. Each of them was hanging from a corner of the balloon.

Crusoe, aware of the soldiers now running across the roof toward them, slashed at the rope tied to the cannon. The rope parted, and the balloon started to rise again. Crusoe grabbed for the end of the rope at the fourth corner and began to haul himself up again, muscles burning and sinews stretching agonizingly.

His feet swung just over the heads of the soldiers as the wind caught the balloon, sending it away from the sea.

Crusoe looked down. They were over the space in the middle of the fort now. Soldiers scurried far beneath him like ants, and then they were gone, as the balloon drifted over the other side of the square fort. The trouble was that the combined weight of the four of them was causing the balloon to sink rather than rise. As they got to the far side of the fort, the side farthest away from the sea, Crusoe's feet just brushed the stonework before he could see the ground far below.

The balloon was sinking faster now. The stone walls of the fort were off to his side, with the cannons pointing out of the windows. Crusoe found himself staring directly down one of the cannons. He swore he could see the cannonball at the far end, the pink blotches of the faces of the soldiers behind it, and the flame they were holding against the fuse.

The wind caught the balloon again and pushed it sideways as the cannon fired.

The explosion was deafening, and the sudden blast of heat blistered Crusoe's face, but the cannonball *swished* past him and out toward where Segment W's forces were approaching from the land side.

Crusoe looked around. The countess, hanging from her rope, appeared to have passed out. Newton was glancing around with amazement and interest. Friday was looking at Crusoe. He knew exactly what she was thinking. The balloon was sinking too fast under their weight. They weren't even going to get off the island before they hit the ground—right in the middle of the fight.

He looked down. Fifteen feet to go.

He looked up, into Friday's eyes. She stared down at him. Her lips opened as if she was going to say something. She began to shake her head. For a moment he couldn't let go of the rope—he wanted to stay there, with her, to hear what she had to say to him—but the small part of his heart that wasn't devoted to her told him that he had a task to complete, and if he didn't complete it, people would die. More importantly, *she* might die.

He sliced through the rope above him and fell toward the earth.

CHAPTER FIFTEEN

Crusoe hit the earth with a bone-jarring *thump*. His legs immediately crumpled beneath him, and he rolled over several times before coming to a halt in some bushes.

He looked up. The balloon was drifting away, gaining more height now that he wasn't pulling it down. He could see the countess, Newton, and Friday all tied to their ropes. Friday was staring down at Crusoe. He couldn't see the expression on her face, but he could imagine what it was.

She was pulling at the knot fastened around her waist. For a moment he thought she was going to release herself and fall, in some desperate attempt to come and help him, but she started to climb the rope toward the balloon's basket. It was up to her now to bank the fire so that the hot air would gradually cool down, and the balloon would slowly come to earth somewhere safe.

They were going to be all right. He had to worry about himself now.

And he had to worry about John Caiaphas's attacking forces, which were being mowed down mercilessly by cannon fire.

He glanced around, getting his bearings. The fort was behind him: a hulking black presence in the night, lit up every few seconds by the firing of its cannons. He was on the sloping ground that ran down the island from where the fort stood at the far end, over-looking the sea, to the quays and the stretch of the Thames that separated it from the mainland. John Caiaphas's forces were still across on the mainland, vainly trying to cross the river. The can-nonballs, whistling above Crusoe's head, were holding them back.

He knew what he had to do.

He turned back and headed toward the fort, crouching down to avoid being seen by the soldiers inside and being hit by any low-flying cannonballs.

He was heading uphill. His muscles were complaining, and the cut on the side of his head was burning. He desperately wanted to rest, but he knew that he couldn't, not yet. He still had a job to do.

That was something he had learned from the island. If some-thing needed to be done now, you did it. You didn't put it off, you didn't wait for someone else to do it, because if it didn't get done now, then there would be consequences—hunger, injury, dis-covery. You had to do it, whatever it took, whatever the cost in pain, injury, and exhaustion.

But it didn't mean he had to like it.

He got to the wall of the fort, about halfway between the main archway that led inside and one of the towers at the corners. The cannons in the openings above his head were firing—each one taking a minute or so to reload, but so many of them that there was always at least one or maybe two firing at any one time. It was like a constant roll of thunder, so loud and so close that he could feel the impact of the sound on his skin and in his chest.

He slipped along the wall, keeping one hand against it for guid-ance. The stones vibrated every time a cannon fired, and that ob-servation caused a small seed of an idea in the back of his mind to grow into a plan.

When he got to the arch, he glanced around the edge. There was a pair of large wooden doors studded with nails inside, but they were open. Maybe some of Lord Sebastos's men were still down at the piers, fighting off John Caiaphas's men, and he was giving them a line of retreat. Or, more likely, he was leaving an opening for reinforcements to exit the fort and come to the aid of the defenders at the piers. Whatever the reason, it meant Crusoe could slip inside.

He had seen the interior square from above, several times, but this was the first time he had seen it from ground level. The balloons had left now, but soldiers were still crisscrossing it, carrying barrels of gunpowder and cannonballs from some location inside the fort or going to fetch more.

Several bits of armor had been left lying around on the ground. He scooped them up and strapped them on, pulling a helmet over his head. He still had the strange Circle of Thirteen weapon strapped over his shoulder, and he walked across the open area, toward where the soldiers were fetching the barrels of gunpowder and the cannonballs, as if he had every right to be there.

As he got to a doorway, Lord Sebastos came out. He was shouting at one of his senior officers and didn't look at Crusoe. For his part, Crusoe turned his head away and quickly moved past them.

Inside he followed where the soldiers were going to get the gunpowder and the cannonballs. They were heading down a long stairway that twisted back on itself several times before it opened out into a dungeon area beneath the fort. Crusoe went with them. The walls were damp, with fungus growing on them. There was a pervasive smell of something rotten down there, and an airless, leaden feeling.

Through an arch at the end of a long corridor, Crusoe found the main supply area: a vast underground hall stacked up with barrels of gunpowder on one side, boxes of cannonballs on another, piles of armor and uniforms on a third, and racks of those strange new weapons on a fourth. There were soldiers everywhere, some approaching the various piles empty-handed, and some walking away carrying things—either individually or in twos and threes for the barrels of gunpowder. Oil lanterns hung from walls and pillars, casting illumination in various directions but sending black patches of shadow in others. The roof was vaulted, almost church-like. Crusoe wanted to stop and get his bearings, work out what he had to do next, but he knew that he had to look and act like everyone else. He couldn't just stand there gazing around, otherwise he would get caught. So he had to do his observations on the move.

The cannon fire from the fort above was shaking the very foundations of the building. Dirt and dust was raining down on them from above.

Crusoe walked toward the rows of barrels, but instead of taking the first one he came to, as everyone else was doing, he kept on walking. When he got to the fifth barrel back, he moved behind it, so that he wouldn't be seen. Taking his knife out of his pocket, he bent down and started chipping away at the bottom of one of the staves, trying to carve out a small hole. He looked up every few seconds, checking on how many barrels had been taken away. By the time three of the four shielding him from view had been taken, he was still hacking away at the wood. Just as the soldiers took the fourth and nearest barrel, he felt the wood give way and something powdery spill out. He quickly moved backward, into the shadows.

As two soldiers arrived to take his barrel, he joined them, keeping his face hidden but helping carry it away, toward the distant arch. He had managed to position himself so that he was closest to the hole. Only he could see the gunpowder spilling out and leaving a trail along the ground.

When he was nearly at the arch, he heard someone behind him call out.

"Hey! There's a spill! You've got gunpowder comin' out of that barrel! Hey—you by the arch!"

The men who were carrying his barrel stopped and put it down. They looked back. When they saw the line of gunpowder leading back to the remaining pile of barrels, they started swearing.

Crusoe moved away from them, off to one side.

He unstrapped the weapon from his back and swung it around, pointing it back the way he had come.

"Oy—what you doin'?" someone called.

Soldiers turned to look. Some of them were looking at him.

It had to be now.

He fired the weapon. A metal disk zipped out of the front, glittering in the light of the oil lanterns. It flashed across the open space and hit the stone floor just beside the line of gunpowder, leaving a bright gash of fresh stone behind as it bounced off into the distance.

Soldiers were shouting now. He ignored them, hauling back on the arming lever and feeling the clockwork and springs inside tensing as he pulled.

Somewhere inside the weapon, another metal disk clicked into position.

He pulled the trigger again. Another disk fired. This one went too high—spinning over the top of the gunpowder and vanishing off into the darkness.

A hand grabbed him from behind. He lashed back with his elbow, feeling it hit someone's face. The soldier fell back with an inarticulate yell, and Crusoe hauled on the arming lever again, nearly trapping his finger between it and the stock of the weapon. Again, the clicking and ticking of the springs inside sent little tremors through the weapon. He could sense the tension in the spring as it wound tighter and tighter.

He squeezed his finger on the trigger. Someone crashed into him, making him stagger, but somehow he kept his aim straight as the weapon fired.

The spinning button of lethal metal cut its way through the air. It hit the stone just next to the trail of gunpowder.

And this time, the serrated metal edge grinding against the stone caused a flash of sparks.

The gunpowder lit. A line of spitting sparks ran in both directions—toward Crusoe in the arch, and toward the pile of barrels.

There was sudden and complete pandemonium in the underground hall. Within a few seconds, every soldier who had seen what was happening was running for the arch, knocking over or pushing out of the way those soldiers who hadn't seen, or had seen but hadn't worked out what was going to happen.

Crusoe turned and ran through the arch, feeling himself being carried along by the stream of desperate humanity. People were shouting and screaming—warnings, curses, threats, and prayers, a cacophony of babble.

They were pounding up the stairs now, pressed from behind by a desperate crowd. Men fell and were trampled underfoot. Others were pushed into the rough stone walls and were scraped along by the press of people behind them, their flesh tearing on the rough stonework. Screams joined the rest of the noises.

The worst points were the places where the stairs twisted back on themselves. There the soldiers had to slow and reverse direction suddenly. There was pushing, shoving, and fights breaking out, causing knots of confusion where no movement could occur. Soldiers were climbing over other soldiers in a desperate attempt to get clear.

Crusoe found that his best option was to go low. He was smaller than most of the soldiers anyway, and he could slip past them and sometimes even between their legs before they knew he was there.

The air was getting fetid now, thick with the reek of fear. Crusoe started to use his elbows to force his way through the throng. All the time, every single second of his flight, he knew that the lit gun-powder was getting closer and closer to the pile of barrels.

At least, he hoped it was. If someone had brushed it with their feet in the rush, then maybe they had scattered the line of powder or stamped out the fire. This hellish flight might be for nothing.

It seemed like an eternity of climbing up the stairs, but it must have only been a minute or two before he reached the open air. He spilled out into the space in the middle of the fort with a waterfall of desperate humanity, all seeking safety. Some of the soldiers were shouting warnings to their companions outside to evacuate, but some were just running, leading by example.

Crusoe was ten feet away from the arch when the lit gunpowder finally reached the barrels.

The entire earth seemed to rise up beneath him. He sprawled to the ground, twisting so that his back hit first, taking the impact. His sword and the strange weapon flew away from him. He could see people apparently flying through the air, pushed by the ex-panding gases, their arms and legs waving wildly. Big square stones from the walls, the ceiling, and the floors were flying alongside them as if they were children's toys. And underneath it all, like some vision of hell emerging into the world, there was a sullen red glow, a fireball tinged all around with black smoke, incinerating everything that it touched like a satanic apparition rising to meet the apocalypse.

The world went mad. Crusoe didn't know how he got out, only that the next thing he knew, he was several hundred feet away from the fort, tripping and falling, rolling, and looking backward to where the Circle of Thirteen's base, its foundations blown to smithereens, was slowly slipping away, sliding down the far chalk cliff face and into the sea, taking its cannons, its army, and hope-fully Lord Sebastos with it.

—⟨⟨⟩⟩—

Three Years and Six Months
Since the Shipwreck

Crusoe could tell where the pirate was because he could smell the man: a rancid odor of sweat, bad feet, and worse teeth. Did all the pirates smell this way, he wondered, or was this one particularly bad at washing and looking after himself? Could he even smell himself, or was he oblivious to the stench? Crusoe couldn't help but wonder, as he crouched less than twenty feet away from where the man was perched on a low tree branch, hidden by the foliage, if his time on the island had improved his ability to track things by smell and by sound, as well as by sight. He certainly felt more alive now than he ever had before. He felt as if his senses and his reflexes were finely honed by time and experience.

Friday would be near the cliffs, off to the east. They had chosen this spot carefully, knowing that one of Red Tiberius's less able pirates often set watch there, but knowing also that there were cliffs nearby, falling sharply to the sea, and that the forest went up almost to the edge of the cliff.

Time to go.

Crusoe stood up and started to move—not toward the pirate, but on a path that would take him past the man. The stench of sweat, tooth decay, and foot rot grew worse as he got nearer. How could anybody bear to be on a ship with him?

He heard the man suddenly stiffen as he first heard and then caught sight of Crusoe. The pirate tensed, ready to leap. Crusoe imagined him there, one hand steadying himself on the tree trunk and the other holding a knife, thanking his lucky stars that fate had sent the boy his way so that he could impress his captain with a quick and bloody kill.

Crusoe braced himself. Instinctively he wanted to run, but this had to be done properly for it to work.

He sensed rather than heard the pirate prepare to leap. At the last possible moment, Crusoe stopped, as if he had heard something, and stepped to one side. The pirate came crashing down through the foliage, robbed of his easy prey. He landed awkwardly, but whirled around fast and lunged, knife held out in front of him.

Crusoe tried to look surprised, even shocked. He turned and ran.

"He's seen us!" Crusoe called. He knew that Friday couldn't hear him, but that wasn't the point. He wanted the pirate to believe that he and Friday were together.

The chase took them along one of the minor game trails that Crusoe and Friday both knew about—a narrow and winding path through the bushes that was used by wild pigs and by small deer-like creatures. Crusoe realized within a few moments that the pirate was faster than he had expected—he had thought he would have to keep slowing down to allow the man to keep near to him, but that wasn't the case. This man was athletic, and Crusoe could hear his breathing just a few feet behind him as they sprinted through the forest. Once or twice his clutching fingers even managed to brush against Crusoe's back, and Crusoe had to summon up reserves of energy that he didn't even know he had to keep ahead.

He hardly had enough breath to run, but he managed to croak out, "Keep going! He's closing on us!"

The plan depended on Crusoe getting out of sight of the pirate for a moment, but the man was too quick for that. No matter how quickly Crusoe ran, the pirate was immediately behind him. Fortunately the game trail twisted to run parallel to the cliff when it got near the edge of the forest. When Crusoe got to the turn, he switched direction to follow the trail, and then, before the man could shift his direction to follow, he diverted off the trail and into the bushes. He heard the pirate stumble as he came around the turn and realized that his prey had vanished. Crusoe ran a few steps in silence, then yelled, "Careful—I think the cliffs are nearby." Hearing the shout, the pirate turned to follow.

Just as he saw the edge of the forest and the sheer drop of the cliffs a few feet beyond, Crusoe dived to one side, into the shelter of a large bush. As the pirate ran past, he parted the leaves and stared out.

Seconds before the pirate burst out of the forest and onto the few feet of clear ground before the cliffs, Friday—hidden to one side— used a bent branch to launch the two pig carcasses that she and Crusoe had caught the day before out and over the cliff. Crusoe saw them arc over the edge through the foliage. They had been shaved, so their dark skin showed through better, and dressed in some old rags that used to be Crusoe's and Friday's clothes. By the time the pirate emerged from the forest, the pig carcasses were falling away, toward the distant sea. It would look, hopefully, like Crusoe and Friday had run off the edge of the cliff by accident.

For a horrible moment, Crusoe thought the pirate was going to accidentally run off the edge of the cliff himself. Under other circum-stances, that might have been a good outcome, but not now. Now Crusoe and Friday wanted him to go back and report that the two of them had perished, fallen to their deaths.

The man stopped just in time. Crusoe heard his intake of breath as he saw the bodies falling. Breathing heavily after his run, he still managed to let loose a string of profanities as he realized that his prey was forever out of reach.

Crusoe stayed there until the frustrated pirate walked back toward the game trail. He gave the man plenty of time to leave, then he walked out onto the cliff edge. Seabirds were circling in a blue sky, and far below, the sun glittered blindingly off the waves.

Friday emerged from the bushes at the same time. She joined Crusoe on the edge. His arm went around her shoulders, and her arm went around his waist. They stood there silently for the longest time, knowing in their hearts that they were free from the threat of Red Tiberius and his crew.

Now, Crusoe thought, all they had to do was get off the island.

The trouble was that, looking sideways at Friday's perfect profile, he wasn't sure that he wanted to.

"I TAKE IT this is your doing?"

Crusoe turned around slowly. His vision was blurry, and every single muscle in his body ached—including several that he hadn't even realized were there. He just wanted to sleep.

That pleasure was going to be denied him.

Lord Sebastos was standing behind him. Smoke was coming off his clothes as if he were about to spontaneously combust. His scowling face gave a similar impression. He held a sword in his hands: a strange weapon that had a long hilt—long enough that it could be held with both hands—and a short blade that curved and grew wider as it got farther away from the hilt, then ended in a wickedly sharp backswept edge. The metal was black rather than silvery. It looked foreign—possibly Chinese. Crusoe thought tiredly that it would make sense—the balloons were probably Chinese in origin, if Friday was correct. Maybe the Circle of Thirteen had roots in the Far East.

He didn't think he would get the chance to inform Segment W of that fact.

He smiled—as far as he could—at the glowering Lord Sebastos. "Glad to be of service," he said.

Sebastos put his head to one side. "You are the boy—Crusoe. Is that right?"

"Robinson Crusoe, at your service."

"I was warned that you were coming to London. I should have taken action then, rather than wait and see whether you could be turned to our purposes." He shook his head. "There were others in the Circle who said you should have been killed on the island to stop you from telling anyone what you had seen there—you and the girl. I argued that you should be encouraged to join us, but that fool captain on the *Stars' End* failed to follow his instructions and keep you on board until we could get there. By the time we were ready, you had already been approached by Segment W, and it was too late."

The island? Crusoe felt a shiver run through him at the mention of the island. How did Lord Sebastos know about it? Had the Circle of Thirteen known about Crusoe and Friday all along? What could they have seen there that would be of any interest to the Circle?

Before he could think through Lord Sebastos's implications, Crusoe was distracted by the black-dressed man hefting the strange sword, swirling it in the air in front of him as if it weighed nothing. "Strange that a mere boy could have such a destructive effect on our plans."

Crusoe looked around him. There was rubble and chunks of burning wood, but nothing that he could use as a weapon.

Except . . .

A few feet away from him lay a ramrod belonging to one of the fort's cannons that had been thrown all that way by the force of the explosion. Both ends were blunt, but it was the only thing Crusoe could see that could possibly work.

He wearily bent down to pick it up. The ramrod was solid and heavy, and he had trouble moving it upright into a guard position.

Sebastos gazed at the ramrod, then at his own viciously edged sword. "Hardly a fair fight," he growled.

"You can call for help if you want," Crusoe said.

Sebastos snarled. "Your wit isn't going to save you, boy, and neither is that metal stick."

He suddenly stepped forward, bringing his sword above his head in a two-handed grip and sweeping it downward so fast that it was just a blur. Crusoe heard the *swish* as it sliced the very air apart. He brought his weapon up clumsily, just managing to get it above his own head before the sword impacted on it. The vibration jarred his shoulders, forcing him down to his knees. Fragments of iron and sparks flew into the air.

Sebastos took a step back. The vibration of the sword striking the iron ramrod appeared to have had numbed his arms as well. He brought the sword around and swung it horizontally, aiming for Crusoe's neck.

Crusoe flung himself to the ground. The sword swept through the air above him, slicing through several locks of his hair and sending them floating away. He rolled over onto his back and whirled the ramrod around, using the weight of the heavier end to help him. It caught Lord Sebastos at the knee. Crusoe heard a *crack*. Sebastos cried out and limped backward, holding the sword out in front of him.

Crusoe climbed to his feet again, using the ramrod as support. He leaned his weight on it, staring levelly at Sebastos.

A sound behind him made him turn reflexively. The fort had now completely vanished, having slid down the cliff and into the water, but the cliff itself was starting to crumble. The edge was twenty feet closer to him than it had been a few moments before. Chalk dust was billowing up, along with the smoke from the explosion.

He turned back—just in time to see Sebastos lunging at him silently, cutting through the air in a diagonal line that would sep-arate Crusoe's head and left arm from the rest of his body. Crusoe stumbled back. The sword ripped through his shirt, leaving a line of burning pain across his chest. He could feel blood trickling down his stomach, but he didn't dare look at the wound. Sebastos's sword had hit the ground, biting deeply into it, and Crusoe sensed that he had just a moment to seize the advantage. Using the ramrod planted into the ground as support, he brought his knee up into Sebastos's face. The man flew backward, leaving his sword stuck in the ground.

Crusoe's mind raced, flickering between two alternative courses of action. On the one hand, he knew he should grab the sword, pull it from the ground, and use it as a weapon. On the other hand, the roar of the crumbling cliff was getting closer behind him. He needed to get out of the way.

He ran toward Sebastos as the man was trying to get to his feet. He held the ramrod horizontally, with the club-like end aimed at Sebastos's chest. The ramrod hit the man directly over his heart, knocking him back to the ground. Crusoe let the heavier end of the ramrod drop, following Sebastos's body down and pinning it to the ground as Crusoe vaulted over his prone body. He caught a glimpse of the man's face, twisted in rage, as he sailed through the air, holding on to the lighter end of the ramrod.

He hit the ground and rolled, leaving the ramrod lying behind him. He came out of the roll running. Behind him he heard a roar of anger and frustration that turned into a cry of surprise. He turned his head just in time to see Sebastos climbing to his feet, one arm held protectively across his chest as the ground crumbled beneath him. He vanished, falling into a cloud of white chalk dust and gray smoke. Crusoe thought he might have shouted something as he fell, but the words were lost in the noise of shifting rocks and earth.

A root caught Crusoe's foot as he ran. He stumbled, falling to his knees and skinning his hands on the rough ground. Desperately he turned over, trying to roll away from the crumbling edge. His hands and his knees burned, but he kept rolling.

Eventually he hit a block of stone that had been thrown out of the fort when it blew up. There was nowhere else to go, and he watched in horror as the ground in front of him fell away to reveal the still-burning wreckage of the fort far below.

Everything that was holding him up gave way, and he fell. His last thought, before he plunged into fire and darkness, was of Friday's beautiful face, and the way she had stared at him, horrified, as he had dropped away from the balloon. He wished he could have told her that he . . .

The darkness took him, and there was no more.

CHAPTER SIXTEEN

F riday braced herself against the side of the small boat. The wind was whipping the waves into foam, and she could taste salt on her lips. Red and yellow flames from the burning fort illuminated the scene with hellish intensity. The bucking of the waves caused the scrying orb in her pocket to bang painfully against her hip, but that was the least of her worries.

"Can you see him?" John Caiaphas shouted from the rear of the boat. Beside him, the countess had huddled herself down, arms wrapped around her knees, hands clutching at her shoulders as if she were trying to block out the world. Isaac Newton was beside her, unsure whether to put his arm around her in reassurance or avidly watch the destruction around them.

Friday desperately scanned the water for what felt like the millionth time. Off to one side, she saw a patch of blackness on the water that could only be the waxed silk of the balloon, deflated now and looking like a stygian gateway to hell surrounded by reflections of the nearby inferno. The three of them had hit the water of the Wantsum Channel close enough to Segment W's forces that they were picked up within minutes, but there was no sign of Robin. Part of her wanted to believe that he was still alive because she would have felt a wrenching within her heart if he had died, but another part of her said that was romantic rubbish, and that people died all the time without anybody else knowing. Not even the people who cared for them the most.

Besides, she thought, Robin *couldn't* die. Not yet. Seeing him with the countess draped over his shoulders, back in the fort, she had suddenly realized not only how grown-up he had become but also how strongly she felt for him. Her heart had actually started to beat faster when she saw him again, and seeing him with the countess had torn at her emotions in an unexpected way. The two of them had spent so long together as children that being apart from him made her feel . . . incomplete. Some of that was the familiarity of childhood friends, but she knew now that there was more. She had strong feelings for him that had nothing to do with childhood or friendship.

But she might have realized it too late.

"I can't see him," she called. "Can you go in closer?"

"Not without risking the countess and the orb," John Caiaphas yelled back. "The way that fort is sliding into the channel, it's likely to set up all kinds of whirlpools and eddies. We'll get sucked under if we're not careful."

"But we have to find him!"

He nodded, eyes screwed up against the glare of the flames and the salt spume of the channel. The light made his face look like a demonic mask. "We never leave anyone behind unless we absolutely have to," he yelled, "but it's getting to the point that we might have to, otherwise we'd be snatching defeat from the jaws of victory." He smiled savagely. "I have to say, I admire his style. I'd love to know how he accomplished all this."

"When we get him back, you can ask him yourself!" She turned back to the roiling waters, trying to make out the shape of a head or a body. There were people in the water, some desperately swimming away from the carnage behind them, and some floating, face up or face down, but none of them were Robin.

The burning fort had slumped down the cliff and into the channel now, just a pile of stone that resembled a small hill rather than a place of defense. Steam and smoke rose from gaps between the stones and floated like mist across the water. Whatever Robin had done, it was impressive. But then, she thought, whatever he did was impressive in some way. She had never known anybody like him.

And she had never had the chance to tell him how she felt . . .

Something made her turn her head, as if it were one of Isaac Newton's lodestones attracted by some invisible force. Her gaze was drawn to a patch of water that was covered with shards of floating wood and fragments of barrels. There, in the center, holding on to a handful of wooden staves, was a dark shape.

Her heart jumped. It was Robin. She knew it was Robin.

"Over there!" she called, pointing.

"Are you sure?" Caiaphas was squinting, trying to make out what she had seen, but he was shaking his head. "It's just one of the guards from the fort," he said dismissively. "He's wearing a breast-plate and a helmet."

"It's him!" she insisted, trying to put as much conviction into her voice as possible. Her father had told her once that there was a tone of voice that commanders, leaders, and captains used to give orders—a sharp, loud, and absolutely confident tone that could cut through any confusion and had people leaping to obey before they knew what they were doing. She used that tone now, saying, "Steer to port and get ready to pull him in."

"Mr. Newton—take the tiller!" Caiaphas snapped. "Countess, with me!" He grabbed her arm and pulled her out of her comatose state, heading forward to join Friday in the bow of the boat. She didn't resist, moving more like a doll than a human being.

The boat's prow swung around, heading for the floating detritus. Caiaphas pushed the countess forward to a position beside Friday. He whipped off his belt, wrapped it around the mast, and quickly refastened it, then grabbed at the back of the countess's sodden and ripped dress with one hand and the waist of Friday's breeches with the other. "Forgive the impertinence," he yelled, "but I'm trying to stop you falling in as you lean over the edge."

The boat cut a curve through the water as Newton brought the tiller around. "Slow down!" Friday shouted, but the turn had positioned them so that the wind was blowing across it rather than from behind, and the sail began to slump. The boat slowed.

As they sliced through the detritus, Friday leaned over and grabbed for the body in the water, taking its arm. For a second, as she saw the breastplate and helmet that Caiaphas had described, she wondered whether she had made a mistake, but the countess grabbed for the other arm and pulled, and as the body rolled over, she saw with vertiginous relief that it was Robin. Together she and the countess pulled him into the boat, which lurched under the extra weight. Robin's eyes were half closed, but she could see that he was still breathing. She turned to the countess to thank her for the help. The countess was looking over at the fort. The flickering flames cast deep shadows across her face.

They also illuminated the rip in the shoulder of her dress, through which Friday could see her porcelain-pale skin.

And the fine tracery of blue lines, like a spiderweb, that covered it.

CHAPTER SEVENTEEN

They were sitting up in one of the "box" areas overlooking the central pit and the stage of the Globe Theater. Crusoe—bruised and battered but feeling much better after a night's sleep—glanced around the leather-topped table. Sir William Lambert was at the table's head, with Daniel Defoe on his left and John Caiaphas on his right. Farther down the table were Isaac Newton and Friday. Crusoe was at the far end, looking directly along its length at Sir William, who was examining some papers that Defoe had passed to him.

Crusoe glanced to his right. Down in the central pit area, Segment W personnel were walking in all directions, each on his or her own separate mission. All of these people were dedicated to preserving England and the king. It looked so calm, but he knew that this was just one end of the metaphorical stick he and Friday had been offered. The other end involved fire, explosions, and fights to the death.

Was this the kind of life he wanted to live? Was this the kind of life he wanted to expose Friday to? When he had brought them both back to England, he had imagined . . . what? Something more peaceful, certainly.

Maybe he had been naïve. Maybe he hadn't thought things through properly. The island had been an adventure for five years—first trying to survive, then trying to avoid being captured or killed by Friday's pirate father, and then later with . . . other problems. Had he really expected them to be able to settle down to a peaceful, danger-free existence for the rest of their lives?

What other options were open to them? Find another ship that would take them away, somewhere—a place where they could be alone together, like they had been on the island for so long?

He smiled to himself and glanced to his left, to where Friday was sitting. She was eating a peach, quite happily watching what was going on around the table. For a moment he didn't even recognize her. She was so different from the girl he had first met on the island. *That* Friday had been a girl. Now, looking at her, he realized that this Friday was a woman. A young woman, yes, but she had grown up.

She noticed that he was looking at her, and she smiled at him. He felt himself blushing under the warmth of her gaze.

"So," Sir William said finally, pushing his papers to one side, "where are we, now that the dust has settled?"

"The fort is now deserted," Caiaphas said. "Deserted and wrecked. We've tried to track back the ownership documents, but we got lost in a maze of well-made fakes. We may never know who bought it, although we know who was using it." He frowned, anger flashing in his eyes.

"Yes," Defoe said, "at least we know now that the Circle is real and not just a rumor. They have finally shown their face, and they appear to be more dangerous than we had thought."

"But why do they want more than one of these angelic scrying balls?" Newton asked. "We have no idea of their plans, apart from the nonsensical words that young Miss Friday here overheard about some kind of bizarre plan to get the world under their control by making the stars come right, and doing that by killing people who somehow embody or represent the stars."

Crusoe glanced across at Friday. He had shared with her Lord Sebastos's taunt about the island, but they had agreed between them not to mention that to Segment W. That was their own business.

"You are correct." Sir William sighed. "We have little idea who they are and how many other forts or castles they may be occupying in England. The man we have incarcerated here knows very little, according to John. He was just a hired mercenary. We know almost *nothing* about the Circle of Thirteen, but we need to find out more, and quickly."

"Well, we know that there are probably thirteen of them," Friday pointed out. "Not in total, because there were more than that number at the fort, but the ones in charge." She glanced at Crusoe and smiled again. "Maybe twelve, now."

"Not that I want to push away any credit," Crusoe said, "but we never found Lord Sebastos's body. He might have escaped."

"It was a long fall," Caiaphas said. "A long fall into waters that were churned up by the falling fort and the crumbling cliff. It would take an exceptional man to survive that."

"Robin survived it," Friday said softly, without looking at him.

"As I said, an *exceptional* man." Caiaphas stared at Crusoe and nodded his head in a gesture of . . . what? Respect? Acknowledgment? Acceptance? Crusoe wasn't sure. He just knew that it made him feel happier.

"We also know, or at least we suspect . . . that is to say, we have grounds to *believe*, that the Circle of Thirteen have some connection with the Far East, based on their use of balloons and the particular sword that young Mr. Crusoe here saw."

"A good point." Sir William nodded. "Defoe—make a note to follow that up with the diplomats at the king's court. Discreetly, of course."

"Of course," Defoe murmured.

"And," Newton added, "we know that they are collecting these scrying orbs. We thought that the one we had in our possession was the only one, but that is now obviously wrong. The question is, of course—why do they want them? What are these orbs *for?*"

"Foretelling the future, surely," Sir William pointed out.

Crusoe couldn't help but ask, "Then why would you need more than one of them? Once you've foretold the future, you've foretold it. One orb should be enough."

"Unless there is more than one possible future," Friday murmured.

Caiaphas slapped his hand on the table. "All this talk of fore-telling the future confuses me," he said. "I'm a simple man, a military man, and I like simple answers. One thing we've not mentioned is that we can identify anyone who belongs to or works for this Circle of Thirteen. I presume it is a tattoo that the people who work for the Circle use to tell who is with them and who isn't, but whatever its origin—"

"This discussion is interesting, but ultimately unhelpful." Sir William's voice cut through what was developing into an argument. "We cannot ask people suspected of working for the Circle of Thirteen to take their clothes off so we can examine their skin. It would cause outrage. Unless the markings are on their faces or hands, then we would never know about them—and even then, gloves would disguise markings on the hands and cosmetics would disguise them on the face."

There was a momentary silence, as if nobody wanted to raise the next obvious topic. Eventually Crusoe felt that he had to say something. "The Countess of Lichfield . . . ," he said hesitantly. "She had the same markings. Friday told you that she saw them."

"With the greatest respect," Sir William said carefully, "I think that Miss Friday may have been mistaken. After all, why would the Circle want to kidnap her if she was working for them, or with them?"

"You said it yourself when we were on the way to see the king." Crusoe gazed at Sir William, knowing that the head of Segment W didn't want to accept the truth but also knowing that he had to defend Friday's observation. "The kidnap was a ruse. The Circle knew that we would be pressured by the king to get the countess back, and that we would have to use the scrying orb in our possession to discover where she was. It was the orb they wanted, not her."

Friday looked over at him, catching his eye. We? she mouthed, and raised her eyebrows. He shrugged and smiled. It seemed that somewhere in his mind, a decision had already been reached. They were a part of Segment W now.

Sir William was nodding sadly. "You are right, of course. Much as I do not want to believe it, I *must* believe it. The countess is a part of the Circle of Thirteen—perhaps even *one* of the Thirteen."

"We should arrest her," Caiaphas said, striking the table again with his hand. "Question her."

Sir William was about to reply, but Defoe beat him to it. "We have no proof, apart from a mark on her skin. The king would never believe it."

"And," Friday pointed out, "we can use her. If she does not suspect that *we* suspect, then we can watch her, see where she goes and who she meets, and find out more about the Circle that way."

Sir William, Defoe, Newton, and Caiaphas nodded. Crusoe glanced over at Friday and mouthed *we?* She smiled and shrugged back at him.

It would seem that the decision had been made. They were staying.

"I think we have several paths ahead to follow now." Sir William looked around the table, catching everyone's eye. "We have the countess to watch, we have our prisoner to interrogate, we have the ruins of the fort to examine, and we have a possible link to the Far East to follow up. I think we will all be busy for a while, trying to establish the exact nature of the threat that the Circle of Thirteen poses to us, and to England."

"And possibly to the world," Crusoe added.

Sir William nodded. "Thank you all for attending. Directions will be issued shortly." He glanced around the table, meeting everyone's gaze. "I do not need to remind you that everything we have spoken of here, everything that has happened, is secret. There must be no discussion with anyone who is not a member of Segment W." His gaze lingered on Daniel Defoe. "And especially not any writing down of these events for later publication. What is secret now will be secret forever."

Defoe nodded. "Understood." He smiled at Friday. "Besides, I have other stories to hear, and to tell."

Crusoe promised himself that whenever Defoe tried to get Friday to talk about their time on the island, he would be there. Not to stop her from saying anything, but because he wasn't sure that he trusted Defoe's intentions. He sometimes looked at Friday in a way that made Crusoe feel . . . uncomfortable.

"Now," Sir William said, "go find some food and get some sleep."

As everyone started to rise from the table, Crusoe looked sideways at Friday and smiled. She met his gaze and smiled back.

"So we are staying, then," he said. "I'm sure we could find a ship heading back to the Caribbean if we wanted to. The island can't be that hard to find."

She shook her head. "No, we're staying. I think we're needed, and that wasn't true on the island. Our time there was"—she blushed and looked away from him—"wonderful for so many reasons, but I think this is where we need to be right now."

"You're right." He nodded. "But we're going back one day," he said softly. "I think we have to."

"Unfinished business," she murmured.

"Unfinished business," he agreed. He reached out and put his hand over hers. "Whatever we do, we do it together. I don't ever want to be apart from you again."

She turned to look at him once more, and he realized something he had unconsciously known all along—just how beautiful her brown eyes were.

"Together," she said.

He waited for her to say "forever," but she didn't. Maybe she was thinking it but couldn't say it. He hoped that was the case.

Time would tell.

EPILOGUE

In a room with thirteen walls, thirteen people were standing.

The walls of the room were made of opal: a precious stone that was usually used for rings and necklaces, but for this room had been mined in entire sheets. Each sheet of opal was a different color, ranging through white, gray, red, orange, yellow, green, blue, magenta, rose, pink, olive, and brown to the deepest black. Each of the sheets glittered with small specks of light that seemed to be deep inside them. The specks shifted as they were looked at, giving the impression that one was looking into infinity rather than staring at a sheet of precious stone.

The thirteen people were each standing against a wall. Their robes were made of material dyed the same color as the wall against which they were standing. Their faces were covered with leather that had been twisted and stiffened to form masks that resembled the pointed beaks of vicious birds. The masks were all colored to match the robes and the walls.

The room was illuminated by a pillar of sunlight penetrating into the room through a hole in the ceiling. The hole was closed off with a circular plug of transparent opal.

The person in the black robes and mask was a man, judging by his build. He glanced around at the others in the room, apparently looking for some sign of dissent.

"Are we agreed, then?" he demanded, his voice harsh. "The girl, Vijaya Dinajara, who now goes by the name of Friday, must be recruited by the Circle. It is for the sake of the plan. The orbs have told us so, and we may not disagree. I need the assent of everyone in the Circle before we proceed."

The person in the orange robes—a woman, probably—raised a hand. "If the orbs have spoken, then we must comply, of course, but this is . . . unusual. Unlike anybody else working for the Circle, the girl is not a stranger. She is related to one of us. I wish to ascertain, before we continue, that there will be no possibility of favoritism. If we recruit her and then order her to sacrifice her life for us, then she must be allowed to do so, and not saved from her fate." She turned to the person in the red robes and mask. "Are you with us, Red Tiberius? Do you accept the judgment of the orbs? Does the Circle remain unbroken?"

The man in the red robes and mask looked slowly around the room. His voice, when he spoke, was deep and tinged with a heavy accent.

"My daughter has rejected my authority," he said. His voice sounded like it was echoing from a deep and dark well. "I not only accept the judgment of the orbs, I welcome it." He paused, and when he continued, his voice had an undercurrent of fury in it, like a riptide beneath a calm sea. "If it is the will of the Circle that she betrays her friends in our service, then I smile. If it is the will of the Circle that she dies in our service, then I shall laugh."

"Then it is agreed," the man in black said. "So mote it be."

"So mote it be," the Circle of Thirteen said in unison.

ABOUT THE AUTHOR

Andrew Lane has written some thirty-odd books, ranging from fiction to nonfiction and from science-fiction novels based on popular TV series to adult crime novels. He has also written nearly thirty short stories that have been published in various magazines and anthologies. His best-known work to date is the highly successful Young Sherlock Holmes series of YA novels, of which eight have currently been published.